Donated by
Floyd Dickman

shrimp

Also by Rachel Cohn

Gingerbread
The Steps
Pop Princess

shrimp

RACHEL COHN

Simon & Schuster Books for Young Readers
New York   London   Toronto   Sydney

SIMON & SCHUSTER BOOKS FOR YOUNG READERS
An imprint of Simon & Schuster Children's Publishing Division
1230 Avenue of the Americas, New York, New York 10020

SIMON & SCHUSTER BOOKS FOR YOUNG READERS is a trademark of Simon & Schuster.
The text for this book is set in 11-point Caxton.
Manufactured in the United States of America
2 4 6 8 10 9 7 5 3 1

Library of Congress Cataloging-in-Publication Data
Cohn, Rachel.
Shrimp / Rachel Cohn.— 1st ed.
p. cm.
Sequel to: Gingerbread.
Summary: Back in San Francisco for her senior year in high school, seventeen-year-old Cyd attempts to reconcile with her boyfriend, Shrimp, making some girlfriends and beginning to feel more a part of her family in the process.
ISBN 0-689-86612-7 (hardcover)
[1. Interpersonal relations—Fiction.
2. Mothers and daughters—Fiction. 3. Stepfamilies—Fiction.
4. High schools—Fiction. 5. Schools—Fiction.] I. Title.
PZ7.C6665Sh 2005
[Fic]—dc22   2003023992

For Mom, Grandma, and Grandpa

Acknowledgments

Grateful thanks for their extraordinary support to David Gale, Alexandra Cooper, Beth Gamel, Xanthe Tabor, Virginia Barber, Jennifer Rudolph Walsh, Alicia Gordon, Amy Sherman-Palladino, Robert Lipsyte, and Ceridwen Morris. Hi to Joey Regan and Molly Regan, and thanks to The Writers Room in NYC for the awesome writing space. Most especially, big love and thanks to all the readers who wrote asking for a sequel.

shrimp

Chapter 1

My little sister Ashley officially took custody of my doll Gingerbread on my seventeenth birthday. You may say that seventeen is a little old to finally be relinquishing a childhood doll, but Gingerbread was no ordinary doll. She had been my lifelong soul sister number one, the cherished rag doll that was the one decent thing my bio-dad, Frank, had ever given me that wasn't a trust fund, genetic mutant tallness, or a summer in New York just spent with him that revealed he was a world-class dawg. And anyway if you did say *How old are you to still be carrying a doll?* I would just give you a blank look back like, *Why do you care?*

I was dead asleep b-day morning when I felt my new futon mattress shaking. My dreams told me to get out of bed and into the doorway: earthquake. The feel of flannel pjs rubbing my arms and the smell of hyper munchkins' Cocoa Puffs breath told my sleep otherwise. I opened my eyes to see the faces of my half-sibs, Ashley and Joshua.

"Happy Birthday, Cyd Charisse's Pieces!" Ash said in what sounded like basic yelling but was probably an attempt at a song. The futon frame creaked under her weight as she jumped on the bed. Ash is a second grader in age, but a fifth grader in weight percentile. The actual fifth grader, Josh, attempted to roll himself into the futon mattress, as if he wanted to mummify himself in it. Perhaps asking for the new futon as a birthday present to replace the old puke princess four-poster bed that used to be in my room—my mother's decorator's plot to curse my sleep—was not my smartest idea ever.

Ash said, "Guess what Mommy and Daddy got you for your birthday!"

"You're ruining it right now!" I groaned. I grabbed her and pulled her down onto the bed next to me. Ash and Josh were asleep when I'd returned the night before from New York, so this was the first time I'd seen them since getting home to San Francisco. I'd only been gone a few weeks that felt like an eternity, so I needed to see if Josh and Ash looked as different as I felt. They looked the same, maybe cuter: Josh, with his Buster Brown cut of light blond hair and baby blue eyes, got our mother's Scandinavian good looks. Ash, with her round cherub face and brown curls, takes after Sid-dad, who has a few brown hairs left on his mostly bald head but, like Ash, is always rosy-cheeked and happy to finish your dessert. After this past summer, I am well aware that I am a skinny, freakishly tall, black-haired clone of my bio-dad Frank, at least in looks. In personality I aspire elsewhere.

Ash rubbed her head of brown curls against my shoulder, then turned her eyes onto Gingerbread, lying on the pillow next to me.

"I think Gingerbread should effin come live with me," she whispered in my ear. Ash's summer camp must have had some kinda charm school effect to result in the successful downgrade of Ash's favorite F-word to *effin*. And, she'd had the decency to know not to speak such thoughts aloud in front of Gingerbread, although Gingerbread probably knew anyway. Wow, progress.

"No effin way," I whispered back. If I hadn't left Gingerbread behind in New York with Miss Loretta, her gingerbread-baking spiritual mother, why would I leave her with Ash, who is a holy terror? Although Gingerbread *was* getting cranky about my gallivanting around and had hinted that she might prefer a more laid-back lifestyle, like lying on someone's bed and watching over the other dolls.

Josh climbed on top of my stomach. "Mommy and Daddy got you something else besides this new bed. They got you a crappuccino machine." His mouth blubbered out a farting noise.

"It's CAPP-U-CCINO, not CRAPP-U-CCINO," I said. And ugh, I appreciated the *idea* behind Sid and Nancy's b-day prezzie, but not the reality of it. The whole point of my grand master plan to one day become the world's greatest café owner is to get out of the house, not stay in it. That's why one says, "I'm going *out* for a coffee," not, "Oh, let me whip up some decaf capps for the parentals and let's all watch a feel-good chick flick together." *Shudders.*

"Did you see the cupcakes last night?" Josh asked.

When I returned home from the airport, Ash and Josh had left a present on the dining room table for me: mini chocolate cupcakes with cream cheese frosting arranged on the table to spell out the words *HAPPY BIR* . . .

"Ash and Josh ran out of cupcakes after *bir,* Cupcake," Sid-dad had said when he found me in the dining room. He wrapped me in a bear hug, except I was the bear; he just comes up to my chin. My stepfather, but more than that cuz he's the only dad I've ever really known, was giving Ash and Josh credit for the cupcakes, but I knew the idea was his. When my mother and I first came to live with him, to his Pacific Heights house that when I was five seemed bigger than any castle I could have imagined in the Magic Kingdom, he took me by the hand to my new bedroom, where a tray of cupcakes were waiting for me on the dresser. The cupcakes spelled out, *WELCOME HOME CYD CHARISSE.* Nancy had tipped him off that I had a thing for cupcakes, which I have always considered infinitely superior to whole cakes. Cupcakes are their own little independent beings. That's why when Sid-dad isn't calling me Little Hellion, he uses his other pet name for me, Cupcake. If Frank, my bio-dad, ever had a nickname for me, it would probably be a Native American one, like Relieved When She's Gone.

I told Josh, "Yes, Hyper Boy, I saw the cupcakes, and thank you very much." I flipped down the bedcover on my other side and he plopped down next to me. I was trying to imagine ever lying down in bed with lisBETH and Danny, my half-sibs in New York. LisBETH and Danny are adults and there just wouldn't be room for all three of us in the bed anyway, but I still couldn't see the three of us close like I am with Ash and Josh. LisBETH, not Elisabeth, not Beth, *lisBETH,* is sort of like my mom—annoying, but there for you when you need her—but no way would I feel comfortable having a morning convo with lisBETH, eye-to-eye with bed head and teeth that hadn't been brushed yet. I barely know her. With Danny—maybe, someday.

Josh said, "If you were in New York this summer visiting your other sister and brother, how come they aren't our sister and brother too?"

Honestly I am all for being the cool big sister lying in her birthday futon in the middle of an Ash-Josh sandwich as they played with my hair on either side of me. But I do not think it is my responsibility to explain to them about how Nancy, our mom, was a twenty-year-old dancer-turned-model in New York who got pregnant by a married man, had me, dumped the married man, and later moved to San Fran to marry Sid-dad and procreate Josh and Ash with him, then waited almost seventeen years to send me back to New York to meet my bio-dad and his two grown kids. So I just told Josh, "Because the stepmonster fairy who lives in the attic decided I was the chosen one."

I was saved from further explanation by Nancy standing in the doorway to my bedroom. She was wearing a pale pink yoga outfit. With the pants cut low to show off her flat stomach and matching pert pink bra top, her blond hair pulled into a ponytail on top of her head, and a face of pink lip gloss and pink cheeks, she looked more like a teen queen than a close-to-forty mother of three. For a moment she looked happy to see the three of us lying together on my new bed, then her perfectly plucked eyebrows burrowed in and she frowned just a little, her classic joyless society wife pose, like she'd just bit into a lemon.

"I will never understand why you wanted that shoddy mattress and frame over the exquisite antique bed frame and premium mattress the decorator chose for your room. I guarantee you'll develop back problems within a week on that futon." She let out one of her vintage sighs, then, in what had to be a premenopausal mood swing, said, "Happy birthday, honey. Welcome home." She wandered away down the hallway.

I thought I felt Ash and Josh both flinch on either side of me when Nancy pronounced the words *welcome home* and *honey* at me. Before I left for New York, when I was grounded to my room owing to certain Little Hellion, not Cupcake, ways, Nancy and I were in a state of war. The pleasantries Ash and Josh last heard Nancy and I exchange mostly involved ear-curdling yelling followed by room-shaking door slamming. But since Nancy's unexpected NYC visit while I was staying with Frank bio-dad, since she really helped me there through my little meltdown incident there (note to self: Little Meltdown Incident would make excellent band name; must get musical talent), things are cooler between us. For now. Nancy has only recently upgraded Shrimp, the love of my life and one of the causes of the aforementioned grounding, from being referred to as *that boy* to calling him by his actual name (which really is Shrimp; I've seen his birth certificate). Who knows how long the new peace with Nancy will last once the new school year starts and fate undoes that cruel joke whereby Shrimp dumped me at the beginning of this past summer and returns him to his role as my one true love.

"What are you doing today?" Ash wanted to know.

"Wandering," I said. Wandering is like the biggest gift of all after the past lockdown sentence in my room. Now I am free to go where I please. And in New York I learned that wandering, with no specific destination and a bio-dad who can't be bothered to show you around, is the best way to feel the streets, even when the weather is sticky hot and the streets smell like baked garbage mixed with street vendor honey-roasted cashews.

I've never had a birthday to myself and I wasn't sure what I should do with it. I had no friends my own age with whom to celebrate, to go to the mall or to get fake IDs or what-ever it is normal seventeen-year-old girls with friends do on their birthdays. I hoped to hear from Shrimp, but I don't know if he even knew it was my birthday. For all that we were *muy* manifest destiny last spring, the fact is I never even told him about the things in my past that led to my little meltdown incident, I never saw pictures of or found out the names of his parents who were off in the Peace Corps. Plus, since we were technically broken up and all, I had no right to expect a present or even a phone call from him.

I told Ash, "I don't know where I am going today, but if Mom and Dad say okay, you can come along with Gingerbread and me. We're going to walk these city streets and just see what happens." I looked out my bedroom window high atop a hill in Pacific Heights to the view of the real Alcatraz island in the distance: This former prisoner would cherish this simple freedom.

Ash was dressed and out the door with me pronto. She was not going to mess with the simple freedom either, and did not complain once as we climbed Divisadero Street, a street so steep not even buses will navigate that section of it—and "Diviz" is a major city thoroughfare. We walked up, *wheeze,* up to the crest of Diviz at Broadway on top of Pacific Heights, then down, *deep breaths,* down toward California Street. Back when I was in boarding school in New England, I used to dread coming home to San Francisco even more than I hated stupid old New England. Now The City (as the natives call it) felt different. As Ash and I wandered past the Victorian houses I was seriously digging the cold Bay air whipping through my body, that oceany breeze mixed with the smell of eucalyptus and chimney smoke from all the houses with fireplaces. The feel and smell of the cold air made me warm all over, reminding me of Shrimp.

Ash took my hand as we crossed over to Fillmore, where I decided we should pick up the bus to the Castro, the queer cool capital of the world. My first order of business would be getting a decent cup of joe on Castro Street, then we could go to the Mission for burritos. You can get a decent cup of coffee in New York, at least at Danny's café, but there are no good burritos to be found in that city. Burritos are just an art form that should be left to the West Coast, I suspect. New York's got plenty of other things to brag about.

Of course, all the wandering time Ash spent on best behavior, attached to my hand and not complaining about the walking, turned out to be part of her scheme to butter me up. Later that afternoon, after we'd returned home, Ash invited me into her room. Gingerbread was lying on Ash's bed, obviously kidnapped during my shower. "She belongs here now," Ash pronounced. Then my little sister went in for the big kill.

Ash has a huge customized Barbie collection. Aside from Horror Movie Barbie (head lopped halfway off, torn and bloody clothes), Commando Barbie (camouflage bandana, pistol-whipping Ken with toy guns stolen from Josh), there is my personal favorite, Fat Barbie (dressed in a muumuu, sporting extra body girth and a double chin, thanks to the discreet placement of Silly Putty). I think Fat Barbie is genius but Nancy flipped out when she saw her. Our mother, whose statuesque blond Minnesouda beauty makes *her* look like a Barbie, is a size four on her bloated days. Nancy is so concerned about Ash's weight that she won't let Ash have the I Left My Heart in San Francisco Barbie, who wears a most excellent gold jacket with a long flared black skirt—very retro '50s—because the Barbie is made specially for See's Candy stores and Nancy was all worried about the subliminal message Ash might be getting. Maybe Nancy should take a step back and worry more about the not-so-subliminal message the smiley-faced, skinny, big-boobed Barbie female ideal gives a seven-year-old girl, but what do I know, as Nancy reminds me often.

But Nancy really would have lost it over Naughty Barbie, Ash's new creation that she outfitted while I was in the shower. Naughty Barbie, laid out on Ash's bed for me to inspect, was inspired by our time on Castro Street earlier that day. Shame on me for allowing my caffeine fixation to impair my judgment long enough to let Ash wander to the store next door while I was ordering a latte. Naughty Barbie, decked out in a form-fitting black leather bodysuit opened in a V-shape from her shoulders down to her navel, clutching a rubber whip in her hand, was inspired by the Barbie-sized leather outfits, whips, and chains that Ash bought without my knowledge at what turned out to be a Barbie fetish store next door to the café. My bad. I've only just been allowed to take the bus, and my birthday dinner was the point at which I intended to make my case for a driver's license. And Ash knew that I wasn't about to jeopardize my new freedom by admitting that I let my little sister wander into an adult store while I was feeding my coffee habit.

"What does *S&M* stand for?" Ashley asked, all angel-faced.

"Sugar and Mallomars," I told her. She shook her wide head, indicating she didn't believe my answer. I had no choice then. "What's your price, evil genius?" I asked.

Ash pointed at Gingerbread.

So I took up the issue with Gingerbread, who is somewhat of a telepath. I told her, *You know Ash only wants you because she wants everything that is mine, and you know she will get bored in like a week because you will not plot with her to destroy the universe that is her room, but the thing is, I am kind of stuck here. I am on a Shrimp mission, and I cannot let some S&M Barbie fetish accessories mess that up.* And Gingerbread was all, *These old rag bones are tired of traipsing around in your handbag every place you go now; gimme some rest and the remote control clicker already—yep, let's do it.* I said, *You are kind, Gingerbread. We know Ash will make every best effort to torture you, but I will let Ash know in no uncertain terms that she can trash her room, her dolls, and Mom's Christian Dior lingerie collection, but heads will roll if she tries that nonsense with you. Specifically, Barbie heads.*

And just like that, Gingerbread graciously accepted the new living arrangement.

I was sitting on Ash's bed handing over Gingerbread to my little sister, explaining the ground rules—Gingerbread is strictly a queen who shall reign from Ash's properly made bed and will not be found dangling upside down from Ash's dresser drawer handles, *ever*—when Nancy walked past Ash's room and then doubled back.

"I don't believe it," Nancy said, eyeing the exchange. She has been after me to ditch my doll almost since I took possession of Gingerbread, when I was five and my bio-dad Frank gave her to me the one time I met him before this past summer. "Did hell just freeze over?"

What else could I do?

The stakes are higher at home now with the new peace.

Chapter 2

I need to find Shrimp.

I went looking for him at Ocean Beach, at sunset on the last day in September before school started. I sat on the long concrete ledge separating the beach from the parking lot, layered in sweaters and tights and combat boots, but warm at the thought of reclaiming my lost love. And like clockwork, right after the big red sun dropped over the horizon, all the tourists hanging out to see the Pacific sunset ran to their cars cuz they were freezing their arses off in the San Fran chill. The tourist march was soon followed by an army of wet suited surfers emerging from the ocean, all hot bodied and scrumptious, toting their boards at their hips. The surfer dudes dispersed to stand at the back of their trucks, where they shivered as they changed from their wet suits into their regular clothes in the parking lot for all to see. Too bad for the tourists, who had all raced away in their rental cars and missed the truly great view that Cyd Charisse got to witness.

I searched for the tiny one among the battalion of surfers walking past the trucks and toward Great Highway, the locals who lived nearby and would walk home and hang their wet suits over their porches or balconies, but I saw no Shrimp, not even a Java. Not like I could have missed Shrimp anyway, the shortest dude with the spiked hair and platinum blond patch at the front. The two of us have some kind of cosmic connection, so even if I hadn't seen him, I would have sensed him. And no way would I have thought he would miss the last day of surfing before school started back up, especially with the extra high waves on account of a recent tsunami in Taiwan or wherever that had all the surfers at their trucks raving about the bitchin' curls.

This girl who was sitting on the ledge several feet away from me with a sketch pad on her lap yelled over at me. "You looking for Shrimp?"

I nodded, suspicious, thinking maybe this stranger girl was the famous Autumn who was a prime reason, I believe, for Shrimp deciding at the beginning of this past summer that he and I needed a relationship time-out. But Autumn was a hippie surfer chick, and the girl jumping off the ledge and walking toward me was a hefty Asian girl wearing army fatigue pants, black combat boots, and a white T-shirt with a picture of Elvis shaking President Nixon's hand, tucked in with a belt that had a Hello Kitty buckle. I admire big girls who wear hip-hugging pants with leather belts and tight shirts displaying Republicans; that is one rockin' look that no hippie girl burying her curves under faux Indian saris would ever dare. Also I could never imagine someone named Autumn having a crew cut of black hair with copper dye in the shape of a hand on top of her head.

"Do you know where Shrimp is?" I asked the girl. She had moved over to sit on the ledge next to me.

"Shouldn't you know?" she said. "I thought you two were inseparable."

I was about to say *Who are you to be knowing my business* when I recognized her—I knew her. She was in my history class last school year at the *École Des Spazzed-Out Enfants Terribles,* the "alternative" private school at which my mother enrolled me last year after I was kicked out of the fancy boarding school back East. The arty school for popularity-challenged freaks like me turned out to be not so bad, actually, even though I didn't show up at it as often (like, daily) as my mother thought (blame, Shrimp). The school is definitely better than any snooty New England prep school, though—but let's remember it's still a *school,* which in my opinion is a crap institution that is just a massive conspiracy hazing ritual. Those people who say "High school was the best time of my life" I am (a) very suspicious of and (b) convinced they are full of shit. Lucky for me, I've finally reached senior year, then freedom forever. Nine months to go and I can be set loose upon the world. Watch out, world.

Last year at school this girl had long black hair like mine that draped over the side of her desk when she fell asleep during class, a sleep that always ended up with her thumb in her mouth and drool falling onto her desk beside me. Her name was . . . I don't remember. Last semester was all about deep intoxication with Shrimp. I couldn't tell you about anything or anyone else that happened during that term.

"We broke up," I said. More like, he dumped me at the beginning of summer vacation because I was supposedly harshing his mellow when I accused him of fooling around with the Autumn chick while I was grounded to Alcatraz, formerly known as my room, for spending the night at Shrimp's. But true love is a force that cannot be denied, and I know that one way or another Shrimp and I will be together again.

And I am way more mellow now.

But where the hell is Shrimp? Call-by's to the house he shares with his bro have resulted only in answering machine pickups, and he hasn't come by to see our mutual bud Sugar Pie at the nursing home since the end of August and she doesn't know where he is.

"That hella sucks," the girl said. Helen! That was her name, just like my favorite famous dead person, Helen Keller. "You two were all over each other last year. I'm surprised I even recognized you, considering your face was always sucked into his every time I saw you at school. I heard Shrimp is off surfing in the South Pacific and he's, like, coming back to school when he gets around to it. Wanna go over to Java the Hut and find out for sure?"

"No," I said. The first time I see Shrimp again after our summer apart, I don't want our meeting to be in his brother's Ocean Beach café where Shrimp and I used to work together, that same spot where I developed this unquenchable side order PURELY PLATONIC crush on Shrimp's brother, Java, real name Wallace. Java is a taller, more filled out version of Shrimp who just so happens to also be a vision of physical perfection. He may be a coffee mogul, but Java's no Shrimp. Java's the guy you have sex fantasies about involving hot tubs and licking chocolate off body parts, the kind of fantasies you would probably go "Yuck" to if the actual opportunity ever presented itself. Shrimp's the guy you want to wake up spooned into for the rest of your life and not even worry about having a breath mint handy at first morning contact.

I glanced down at Helen's lap at the sketch pad, which

had a charcoal pencil drawing in the style of a comic book, picturing a short old geezer wearing a leather jacket, cowboy boots, and a bandana tied around his neck, and a long, salt-and-pepper, pointy beard hanging down from his chin. He was digging through a patch of trees, and the side view of his hunched-over body displayed the words BALL HUNTER on the back of his leather motorcycle jacket.

"What's that supposed to be?" I asked her. Ball Hunter man looked familiar.

"It's this comic book I am trying to develop. It's about this senior citizen superhero who hangs out at the golf course at Land's End hunting for golf balls that get lost in the trees. And, like, maybe solves mysteries and stuff."

"I've seen that guy!" At the top of the steep cliff that is Land's End, where the cliff overlooks the point at which the Pacific Ocean meets the Golden Gate (and where Shrimp and I first got together in his brother's hand-me-down Pinto, parked under the dripping trees at the crest of the windy road), there is a beautiful museum called the California Palace of the Legion of Honor. The museum is built in a neo-something or other design with a Rodin thinkin' dude sculpture in front. The Legion of Honor is also famous for being in some old Hitchcock movie starring some boss blond lady with freaked-out eyebrows who was *not* played by my namesake, that other Cyd Charisse, the fancy movie star–dancer with the long beautiful legs going on into forever. One time I sprang Sugar Pie from the home and we visited the museum together and she pointed out this gnomelike guy digging through the trees on the golf course outside. Sugar Pie said everyone in The

City knew the guy had some kind of supernatural power, and that's why he was never kicked off the course for hunting for the balls.

Helen was my new sorta idol. Aside from the fact that Shrimp is an artist and so I am naturally inclined to dig painting-'n'-drawing types, I truly admire people who can create life on a blank page where only white space existed before. I can barely draw a stick figure. My talents are more in the economics, customer service, and cute-guy-finding areas.

Helen said, "Well, the other thing I remember about you was that when your face wasn't attached to Shrimp's it was attached to a coffee cup. Wanna go grab a coffee in The Richmond, seeing as how you don't want to scope out Java the Hut for your boy?"

Helen got up from the ledge and headed off toward the cliff up to Land's End on the road leading into The Richmond District, clearly expecting me to just tag along.

I am a man's woman. I've spent seventeen years on this planet going from Sid-daddy's girl to ragdoll-toting tomboy to boarding school lacrosse captain's girlfriend to the one true love of the hottest pint-sized artist-surfer in San Francisco. Making female friends has never been a priority—for them or for me. The only real female friend I've ever had is Sugar Pie, who is old enough to tell tales about spiking the punch at USO dances during dubya-dubya-two and then taking advantage of a few good men. But this past summer, my newfound favorite (only) older brother, Danny, had told me Sugar Pie only counted for partial credit, that I needed to branch out.

So I got up from the ledge and followed Helen up the

cliff toward The Richmond, where the dumplings are better than the coffees, if you really want to know, but where apparently my first prospective friend who was a girl my own age was inviting me.

Chapter 3

Sad fact: Surfers aren't just beautiful; they can be stupid, too.

According to Helen.

Helen says that the art teachers at school think Shrimp has the potential to be a great artist, but he lacks ambition and drive. She says important gallery owners have come to school art exhibits because they're friends with the teachers, and they have expressed interest in Shrimp's work, but Shrimp blows them off. According to Helen, a "real" artist would kill for an opportunity like that. Helen says Shrimp could probably go to the best art schools in the world if he wanted, but he won't pursue opportunities from people who could help him push his talent to the next level. He'd rather be chasing waves than meeting other artists and studying in New York or Paris.

I don't know if I like that Helen knows things about Shrimp that I never knew. I knew he was talented, but I didn't know about the gallery owners; I never heard about teachers who want to help him get into famous schools far from home. So I had to tell Helen what she doesn't know about Shrimp, because she could never know him the way I know him. I said, "You're wrong. Shrimp wants to keep his art pure. He's not about selling out. He thinks great art is not about the canvas or the sculpture, but about the way the artist lives the life, well-rounded and, like, bonded to nature and whatnot."

"Bullshit," Helen said. "You believe that? That's just an excuse for him not to challenge himself to work harder, think bigger."

A waitress placed two cappuccinos on our table and walked away. The cappuccino foam was loose and watery; first sign of a bad barista. The foam should be dense and peaked like a snow-covered mountain. As I lifted the glass to my face, the coffee smell that should have awakened my nostrils to joy was instead weak and bitter. But I took the leap of faith, anyway, and downed a sip, but immediately had to spit the sip back into its cup. "The coffee here sucks," I told Helen.

"Wanna go somewhere else?" Helen said.

I nodded. Helen doesn't know diddly about my man or about proper caffeination. If we were to become friends, perhaps we needed to veer from any more paths leading to Shrimp discussion or consumption of bad coffee.

We left money on the table and wandered outside along Clement Street, my favorite street in The City, a long avenue of Chinese, Thai, and Vietnamese restaurants mixed in with Irish pubs, produce markets, coffee shops, and bookstores. My legs are many inches taller than Helen's, but I could barely keep up with her. Clement Street is like the way I imagine a street in Shanghai or Hong Kong: narrow and noisy from buses and delivery trucks, teeming with pedestrians and bicycles and grandmas pushing strollers with apple-cheeked Chinese babies so adorable that you just want to pick them up and smother them in kisses. Helen walked down this street like she owned it, barreling through the hordes of people and never bothering to wave back at the store owners who obviously knew her and were waving at her.

I was eyeballing the Sanrio store but Helen stopped her march to turn around, waited for me to catch up to her, then pointed to a Chinese restaurant across the street. "Mind if we go in there a sec so I can drop the sketch pad off? I don't feel like carrying this thing around."

I followed her inside the restaurant, which was dingy as could be—plastic tablecloths, fake plants standing in the corners, paper lanterns hanging from the ceiling—but was packed with diners, most of them Chinese. Sid-dad says San Francisco is full of great Chinese restaurants, but the great ones are not the tourist traps in Chinatown but the dingy ones out in "the avenues" in The Richmond and The Sunset, and the best way to figure out which are the best restaurants in either of those neighborhoods is just to walk into one that is filled with Chinese people.

I stayed behind Helen as she shoved through a line of people waiting to be seated, followed her as she marched through to the middle of the restaurant where tables were filled with bowls of noodles and dumplings and veggies swimming in soup, and seriously, the smell was so good I almost pulled up a chair at a stranger's table to join in. Helen stomped to the end of the dining room and back to the kitchen. I was following her up a back staircase when a scream that sounded like a banshee (at least the way I imagine a banshee would sound; I've never actually heard one) came from behind us. "AIIIYEEEEEEEEEEEEEEEEE! Helen . . . ," followed by an incomprehensible stream of Chinese words that I hope were curses because if so, then the yeller was doing a really excellent bawl out.

Helen stopped on the stair ledge and turned around to face the screaming woman standing at the bottom of the stair landing. The lady was wearing a pair of hot pink plastic dishwashing gloves on her hands and waving a bok choy like it was a murder weapon.

The lady ranted at Helen in Chinese for a good minute, gesturing to her head and banging the bok choy against it. When she finished, Helen snapped, "Get over it, Mom." Helen stomped up the stairs and I followed her. A door at the top of the apartment stairs opened to a huge San Francisco flat—a home taking up the whole floor of a building. I followed Helen into her bedroom, where she slammed the door so hard the floor shook.

Talk about a case of *déjà moi*. Just because I live in a Pacific Heights close-to-mansion doesn't mean a scene like Helen and her mom's, quadruple squared, hasn't played out Chez Cyd Charisse.

Helen's bedroom had clothes and belts and boots lying around all over, like a cyclone had passed through her dresser drawers and closet, depositing their contents randomly throughout the room. Her bed was unmade and surrounded by artwork on the walls everywhere, with random Warhol and Diane Arbus and Dalí prints mixed in with artwork that looked like Helen's Ball Hunter man style. The back of her bedroom door was plastered to every last inch with Wonder Woman pictures: old comic book covers, Lynda Carter *Wonder Woman* TV show shots, bubblegum cards, colored pencil drawings.

I didn't even have a chance to respond to the room—much less to ask *What just happened downstairs?*—when the Wonder Woman door flung back open. Helen's mom waved the bok choy at Helen again. She said, "You know the rules. Friend upstairs, door stays open." Then Helen's mom finished whatever she was saying in Chinese. Her mom was tiny, she seemed to drown under the smock she was wearing over her shirt, and she had long black hair like Helen's used to be, but with lots of gray at the roots and pulled back into a bun held together with two Chinese sticks.

Helen rolled her eyes. "Fine!" Helen said. "But I'm not getting rid of the shave cut. I don't care if Auntie is coming over." Helen's mother sighed—oh, it was just like my mother, just brilliant—and went back downstairs.

Helen sat on her rumpled bed. "Sorry about that," she said to me. "My mom is freaking over the new hair. I just got it done today on Haight Street, and she hadn't seen it yet. She can't do anything about the almost-bald shave, but my life is so over if I don't dye the copper hand out."

I had to commend Helen's mother's keen taste. Helen's buzz cut was cool, but the copper hand is just a fashion NO, a nice idea in theory but too much in reality.

I said, "How come she spoke a little in English to you, then the rest in Chinese?"

"Because the English part—about leaving the door open—was for you to hear and understand. The rest—about the hair and the shame if her sister sees her daughter looking like this—was just for me to understand."

"How come she wanted me to hear about the door being left open? What, does she think I'll have nightmares of Wonder Woman?"

"No, my mom doesn't want my friends upstairs since she walked in on me kissing another girl. It's amazing she even let you upstairs. Guy friends aren't allowed upstairs at all anymore. Give my mother a few more months and pretty soon *I* won't be allowed in my own room anymore."

Muy interesante. "Are you a lesbian?" I asked Helen. With her shaved head, combat boots, and buxom proportions of hips, stomach, and chest, Helen did have kind of a butch look.

"Way to stereotype, Cyd Charisse. God, that's a mouthful of a name. Can I just call you CC?"

I am all about new identities, plus that's what my brother Danny in New York calls me so I said, "Okay. But really, are you a lesbian?" I have known lots of gay men but never a girl who was gay.

"I'm tempted to say yes because being one would really piss off my mom. But I haven't decided either way."

"So what are you, one of those lesbians until graduation, until a guy comes around?"

"I would never be some hypocritical asshole like that. I like kissing girls and I like kissing boys. I just like *kissing*. Right now I'd say I'm bi, but I haven't experimented enough on either side yet to know for sure. Make sense?"

Totally. Being bisexual is probably like being bicoastal, like me. Like being part of two places—San Francisco and New York—and loving them both the same, happy to be in one yet always yearning for the other.

Helen tucked her sketch pad under her bed then glanced at her watch. She said, "All the hot Irish guys will be finishing their soccer league games over at Kezar Stadium about now and just hitting the pub. I've got at least two hours until the dinner rush downstairs is over and my mother starts getting on my case about school starting up tomorrow. Let's get outta here. The soccer guys have the sexiest Irish accents—I swear you can barely understand a word they say. And they wear these soccer shorts with these World Cup uniform shirts so tight, you'll wish you're like blind and you could read the guys' pecs in Braille. You think Shrimp is hot? Come with me early one Saturday morning when they show the satellite games live in the pub and all the Irish guys are sitting around, screaming at the TV over their Guinnesses. I might have convulsions just thinking about . . ."

Helen's suggestion had the makings of Cyd Charisse's former middle name, Trouble, written all over it. If Sid-dad were here, he'd be giving me the *This is how you get to be called Little Hellion* look. But Sid-dad was not here. And this time I had no problem keeping up with Helen as she zoomed from her room back down to Clement Street.

I like the way this Helen person thinks.

Chapter 4

The Little Hellion has been good for a very long time and was long overdue for a little hell-raising—at least for some *fun*. Count on my mom with her radioactive telepathy to call at exactly the moment trouble was about to accelerate.

Helen and I had gone into the pub and ordered Cokes. Helen and I look old enough to be in a pub; no one questioned us. We didn't push our luck by ordering alcohol. Why should we, when apparently there were plenty of over-twenty-one soccer guys, all sweaty from their games, who couldn't wait to bring us beers? What were we supposed to say—no? So when I was teasing the team captain, Eamon, with the fire-engine-red hair and green eyes, about was his name *A-men,* or *Eh, mon,* it's not like I actually expected that soon I would be outside the pub with him, pressed against the wall and forgetting about my true love—Shrimp, yeah, that's his name.

I guess it was a good thing I followed the hot Eamon guy outside, cuz there really would have been hell to pay if I had been inside the noisy pub and hadn't heard my new cell phone ringing in my jacket pocket, flashing the name *Nancy,* at the exact moment Eamon's pink lips were about to press into mine. Nancy thinks because we're not yelling at each other all the time now that we're gonna be like buddies, and that we should do girly things like go shopping and watch mother-daughter TV melodramas together, or, worst of all, chat on my loathed new cell phone. My parents have given me a new free leash to roam The City on my own, to take the bus and not be driven around by Fernando, Sid-dad's right-hand man, but the price of that new freedom is I had to agree to carry a cell phone so Nancy can check up on me at all times. I'm fairly sure the cell phone is my mother's form of a chastity belt for me.

Eamon stepped back from my mouth as I flipped open the phone. He lit a smoke, effectively killing any make-out occasion that might have been about to occur, as attaching my lips to a case of tar and nicotine breath is a big *You'd Better Be at Least an 8.6 on a Scale of Ten Hottie if Your Cigarette Mouth Wants to Suck Face with Me* situation. Eamon scored a probable 7.8.

My mother's timing never fails, I swear. "Yeah," I said into the phone.

"Where are you, Cyd Charisse? It's getting late. You're not still at the nursing home with Sugar Pie, are you?"

Give me a little credit. At least I hadn't told my mother I was at the library. Even she's too smart to buy that one.

I said, "No, I left there a while ago. I'm just wandering down Clement Street. I went into the bookstore for a while, now I'm just getting some school supplies." School supplies! Good one, Cyd Charisse. Even after two pints of Guinness, I could still come up with the parent-friendly lines. I hoped I hadn't slurred my words.

"It's after dark and I really don't like you wandering around strange neighborhoods on your own. Shall I send Fernando over to pick you up?"

"No!" I do not need the big broody Nicaraguan pulling up in a bling Mercedes with darkened windows and then sniffing my breath for alcohol. That could set the scene for a whole new round of Alcatraz incarceration.

"Well, get home soon, please. It's the first night before school and I don't want you out late. And I thought we could go through your new school clothes and see what goes with the new makeup I bought you, and we could try it on together." My mother maxed out the credit card on new clothes and makeup for me, and ya know what I will be wearing to school this year? The same thrift-store ensemble of short black skirts, black tights, ratty old flannel shirts, and combat boots I was wearing last year. I do like the Chanel lipstick, Vamp, dark and Goth against my fog-dweller pale face.

One superior feature I love about cell phones is when the signal breaks. "Home soonish, Mom," I said into the cell before the call dropped.

Helen stumbled outside, attached to the hand of Eamon's teammate. She grinned at me as we stood against the wall together. Eamon and his friend huddled at the street corner, smoking and probably discussing the hooking-up details—how do we get the girls to our place or at the very least to our cars, do you like the tall, flat-chested one or the Asian one with the crazy hair?

I am okay with scamming on hot guys, but tomorrow is the dawn of my senior year of high school, which will indeed be all about Shrimp, whenever I find him. My previous year of school was all about high drama—the trouble my ex Justin got me into, the getting expelled from boarding school, the returning home to San Francisco and fighting all the time with Nancy, the Alcatraz incarceration after the unauthorized Shrimp sleepover. Oh, then throw in the summer in New York meeting my bio-dad and his kids for the first time. So fer gawd's sake, didn't I deserve one wild night since I have been all about reformed-girl Cyd Charisse lately? I haven't touched a drink or even a joint in almost a year, since boarding school.

But still, no way was I going to hook up with any Irish pub guys, no matter how many pints of Guinness they brought me. An almost-kiss against the wall is one thing, but going past first base with an eye toward home base with a random guy is a whole other ball game. I'm not a skank like that, my prior batting average notwithstanding.

"So," I said to Helen. "Do you like the red-haired guy or the goalie guy? Because I need to get home."

"Please!" Helen said. "Neither. I like free beer. But it's a school night, CC, get real."

She grabbed my hand and dragged me back into the crowded pub before Eamon and his buddy even noticed we'd given them the slip.

One more beer, right? Damn, I didn't even know I liked beer before tonight, but those Guinnesses were tasty and filling. Who needs dinner? But soon I was sitting on top of a bar table, surrounded by a pack of guys eyeing my long legs dangling over the bar ledge and asking what songs I wanted them to fire up on the jukebox. Do guys really think any young female with any semblance of musical taste would actually *want* to listen to Jimmy Buffet? Let me just pause a moment to insert a finger down my throat.

I sent one guy off to cue up the Ramones on the box before the Jimmy Buffet guy could get there—please, S.O.S., *go*—while I tried to figure out if I could hit up any of these fine male specimens for a ride home without worrying about him hitting on me. The mathematics of that equation multiplied by the chemistry of how I would sneak inside my house without my mother noticing and get right into the shower to get rid of the smoke and beer smell and, yeah, possibly puke out all this beer while I was in the bathroom anyway, well, all this head work was literally making my head spin.

I looked down from the red EXIT sign I'd been staring at, wondering if I had enough cash for a taxi home, when I saw exactly the last person—besides maybe some evil dictator like Stalin or Pol Pot—that I could possibly want to have standing in front of me at the table ledge, glaring at me like I was busted, big time.

Alexei the Horrible said, "Well, if it isn't the Little Hellion. Let's see, if memory serves, last time I saw you was about two summers ago when you conned me into taking you to a movie and I didn't find out until later the only reason you wanted me to go was because the movie was rated R and your mother had forbidden you to see it. That would make you how old now?" Alexei wrote a fake equation in the air with his index finger. "Oh yeah, still not old enough to be in this pub."

Since Alexei the Horrible has been away at college or I was away at boarding school, it's been my privilege to erase the unfortunate fact of his existence in the long time since I've last seen him. He is Fernando's godson, practically Fernando's son because Alexei's dead father was Fernando's bestest friend in the history of the world, like a brother to him. My stepdad, Sid, about wishes Alexei were his godson too. He thinks Alexei is the most promising young man, fine upstanding blah blah blah Ivy League undergraduate since like the dawn of time. Sid-dad wrote Alexei's college recommendation letter, he helped Alexei get the big scholarships to finance the fancy education. Sid-dad is apparently not aware, as I have been since age eight when Alexei kicked me off my own new trampoline when no one was looking because he said I was a spoiled little princess and didn't even know how to use my own toys properly, that Alexei is, in fact, an overconfident overachiever uptight driven faux intellectual stuck-up suck-up (everything Shrimp is not).

But he also might be able to save my ass. "Alexei," I said. "Please, please, please, can you give me a ride home?"

It was funny to watch a guy as big as Alexei squirm. He was a state champion wrestler in high school and is one of those people who downs protein shakes like they actually taste good. Alexei said, "What's in it for me?" Luckily I didn't have to answer because Alexei added, "Actually I told Fernando I would stop by to help him move some furniture around. But still, helping the Little Hellion out, I don't know."

Fernando has moved into the apartment at the side of our house now that Leila, who used to be our housekeeper, moved back to Canada. Fernando's always been more like an uncle than a family employee, anyway, just one who knows the back streets to the freeway and makes kick-ass empanadas. Fernando has a long red scar running down the side of his leather face that he got during the civil war in Nicaragua, and I think that's why Sid-dad originally hired him, because Fernando is kind of scary-looking, until you find out Fernando's this close to being a Care Bear—that is, unless he's major pissed at you for having to retrieve you in the middle of the night from your boyfriend's. My stepfather is the CEO of a company with thousands of people working for him, but I think Fernando is the only employee Sid-dad actually trusts. I also think that while technically Fernando is the family driver, less technically but not officially, Fernando's status of driver is just a cover-up that saves Sid-dad from acknowledging that he has hired a security-type person for our family, while at the same time saving Sid-dad the trouble of having to find parking spaces.

I jumped off the bar table and stood eye to eye with Alexei, which had to be some sort of irritation to him because he likes little girly-girls, all petite and giggly and lip-glossed, who can't look him in his icy eyes like an equal. I knew I was supposed to be serious and busted and all that, but my insides were buzzed nice and my face couldn't help but break into a smile at Alexei. And for the first time possibly in the ten years in which it's been my unfortunate circumstance to be acquainted with him, Alexei smiled back at me. The smile was a strain on his Slavic face of red cheeks and high cheekbones and bushy eyebrows—really, he shouldn't smile, ever. "Alright, Cyd Charisse," he said. "I'll give you this one. But you owe me. Big time."

I said my good-bye to Helen and left with Alexei the Horrible. The price of the ride was this: lecture. What if a cop had been in the bar and asked to see ID? What was I thinking? Did I honestly expect that all the guys just wanted to buy beer for me, that they had nothing else on their minds? How could I be so naive? High school girls, even wild ones like me, should not be hanging out in places like that.

Oh, old man much? I had a nice little nod off going while Alexei told me about how he was taking a semester off from Fancy University and would be spending the time back home in San Fran working on some project that would look *great* on his resume. Snore.

Alexei the Horrible handed me one of those disgusting Listerine breath strips before we walked into my house. "You smell like Guinness and Marlboros," Alexei said. "Just go along with what I say."

My parents were in the study leading off from the main hall as we walked by. When he saw us standing at the study entrance Sid-dad said, "Alexei! What a surprise!"

Alexei said, "Look what I found at the bookstore on Clement Street. Very noble of her to want to take the bus, but I was on my way over to see Fernando, anyway."

Nancy looked up from the pile of invitations on her lap. She sniffed. "Who smells like smoke? And"—my mother scrunched her perfect little nose up—"do I smell beer?"

I was a little woozy but Alexei propped my back with his hand just as my legs were feeling like they needed a rest from this standing business. Alexei said, "Me. I was at the pub watching *Monday Night Football* with some buddies when I saw Cyd Charisse through the window, walking out from the bookstore across the street. Cyd was commenting on the smell the whole car ride over too. No, Cyd, I won't be mad if you hit the shower now instead of come help me unload boxes at Fernando's."

My parents really have blinders on when it comes to Alexei the Horrible, because football season hadn't even started yet and no way would Alexei care about watching a pre-season NFL game being played in, like, Japan. Sid-dad said, "Thank you, Alexei. Can you stay a while, talk about your semester off?" I hiccupped, and Alexei's hand in my back shoved me toward the stairs. I sprinted up to my room before Nancy could invite me into the study to look at fabric swatches or something.

When I reached my room I shut the door behind me and stood against it, breathing heavily, primed for a major shower and mouth wash.

That was close. And now I owed Alexei the Horrible. Fuck.

A postcard was propped up on my bed pillow. It was a tourist postcard from Fiji, picturing a beautiful dark lady with black hair down to her waist, wearing a grass skirt and bikini top, doing one of those luau-whatever dances at a campfire on white sand with an azure tropical ocean and magenta sunset in the background. A colored pencil drawing was taped on next to her, picturing a short white surfer guy with dirty blond hair and a platinum blond spiked patch at the front. He was standing next to the dancing lady, playing the bagpipes.

Sigh. Bagpipes always make me feel weepy and sexy at the same time, and the one person who knows that about me had written on the other side of the postcard, *Miss me?* The card was signed with a pencil drawing of a pink-veined piece of raw shrimp.

Chapter 5

Perhaps it didn't bode well for my senior year of crap school, I mean high school, to start it with a mild hangover, but there ya go.

Helen was in just as bad shape as me. She had her hand against her forehead when I found her in the cafeteria at lunchtime. "Oh," she groaned. "Headache. Hey, who was the guy you left with last night? He could give a girl serious trapped-in-the-tundra fantasies all night."

The skin on my arms crawled like worms were creeping underneath it. "SHUT UP!" I said. "My stomach is just starting to feel better—don't say things like that. Alexei the Horrible is an annoying protégé of my dad's. I hate him, except I kinda owe him now for helping me skate past the parents last night. But if you ever see him again, don't let on you think he's hot. ICK! His ego is bigger than those Hulk biceps he has."

With this sarcastic grin on her green-lipsticked mouth Helen said, "But you're all about Shrimp, right?" I stuck my tongue out at her. Her likewise response flashed a tongue piercing. Ouch.

All these arty types who are friends with Helen and Shrimp sat down with us at the cafeteria table, a totally new experience for me. If I were Cyd Charisse, private investigator, creating a flow chart detailing the lunchtimes of the past school life of Cyd Charisse, reformed bad girl, it would look like this:

TIME PERIOD	LUNCHTIME ACTIVITY
ELEMENTARY SCHOOL	Alone at end of cafeteria table, wearing black and frowning, eating PB&J sandwich and passing off healthy treats to Gingerbread. Chase cute boy at recess, try to kiss him.
MIDDLE SCHOOL	Repeat elementary school, add in unnecessary training bra.
BOARDING SCHOOL	The "hot weird girl" (to quote evil ex Justin's friends) picking scabs on her arms while waiting in the cafeteria corner for big man on campus Justin, lacrosse team captain, to ditch his popular friends and take her to his dorm room to fool around.
SCHOOL FOR "SPECIAL" KIDS (FREAKS, BLESS 'EM)	The "Goth transfer chick" (to quote soon-to-not-be ex Shrimp's pals) hanging out near the smokers outside, not close enough to get her hair smelling like smoke but close enough to at least look like she belonged somewhere, waiting for Shrimp to find her and take her to KFC.

Helen handed me a vitamin C packet. She said, "Mix this into your water to help with the hangover. Do you want to come over tonight to help me dye the copper hand out of my hair? I am so grounded for life if I don't get it out today, but I was too wasted to do it last night."

This guy sitting next to Helen, with a Ronald McDonald clown-color Mohawk of red hair and black eyeliner smudged around both his eyes, said, "Helen of Troy, you oughta leave the copper hand—it rocks." He turned to me. "So with Shrimp gone, is anyone at this school gonna actually get to know you now?"

I was startled enough by the question, but even more startled by the Crayola assortment of Mohawk and asymmetrical '80s-cut heads of dyed hair that popped up at his question. There must have been seven sets of eyes, more with eyebrow piercings than not, waiting for my answer.

I was all, *I guess so?* This was as close to being in a clique as I have ever been. Don't think that means my skin's about to experience some piercing/tattoo body art makeover situation just cuz that seemed to be the popular form of self-expression at the table. I have a high pain threshold, but it's an emotional one, not a physical one. And the secret fact about me is I am a big ole priss. Still, actual almost-friends in my own peer group. At the rate I'm going I'll be a cheerleader by graduation.

Everyone wanted to know about Shrimp—where was he? I mentioned the postcard from Shrimp in Fiji, but people had heard other rumors. By the time I finished my PB&J sandwich and gave the apple to Helen and kept the pudding for myself, Mission Shrimp had determined that Shrimp was away from school because of any of the following: (1) He was building grass huts for the natives in Papua New Guinea; (2) he had been adopted by a tribe of spiritual fishermen in Tahiti; (3) he was in New Zealand applying for citizenship so he can become the next great Kiwi surfer; or my personal fave, (4) he's on tour in Romania, where he is apparently a huge pop star.

I was almost disappointed to have the mystery solved

soon after lunch when I was waiting outside the guidance counselor's office. I was filling out the paperwork that will allow me to get out of school early for my work-study job this semester (genius plan, CC, genius way to legally ditch school) when who should walk past me on the bench I was sitting on but Shrimp's brother's girlfriend, Delia; couldn't miss her carrot-colored frizz of hair anywhere. She doubled back. I don't know why she looked surprised to see me—I *do* go to this school, really—and anyway what was she doing here?

Much as I am in a major state of Shrimp longing, here was my first live person connection to him and I was mute paralyzed—what if she wasn't happy to see me? Shrimp and I parted on not-great terms, me accusing him of cheating with the Autumn girl and him accusing me of being a spaz *and* crushing on his older brother. Both of Shrimp's accusations were, in fact, true, but when I spent the better part of my New York summer working as a barista goddess in my half-bro Danny's West Village café, The Village Idiots, and telling the clientele the whole Shrimp saga, they had weighed in that I jumped to conclusions about Shrimp and Autumn. From what they heard, Shrimp didn't sound like the type of guy who would cheat.

Of course, if Shrimp hadn't been getting with Autumn *before* I accused him of it, that's not to say he didn't *after*. I HATE that! And I'm not just being a hypocrite considering I did have an almost-fling in NYC with Luis, pronounced *Loo-eese,* whose kisses are almost hotter than his six-pack abs, and with whom I had one physical encounter in which no actual penetration was involved so therefore, doesn't count. I really want to be crazy at just the thought of this

Autumn wench's fingers so much as *touching* Shrimp.

I wonder if I am a stalker or have jealous, potential-homicidal-rage tendencies. That would suck.

But would a stalker get the kind of greeting that Delia heaped upon me? Delia is a dancer and the manager at the Java the Hut store in Ocean Beach, and she performed this ditzy-weird little plié of happiness before taking my hands to lift me from the bench. She wrapped me in a giant hug. "Look who's back," she said. "Cyd Charisse!"

I couldn't even be polite enough for small talk. I had to know: "Where is Shrimp!"

Delia smiled. "He's been in Papua New Guinea with his parents. They just finished up their overseas stint and they've all been doing some traveling in the South Pacific together. He'll be back in a couple weeks. They're coming home, too, supposedly for good. Wallace is inside talking to the guidance counselor about Shrimp's schoolwork and what he'll have to make up when he gets back."

I said, "So are their parents finishing up the Peace Corps thing?"

I heard a chuckle come from down the hall and there was Java, major *sigh,* Java with the mature Shrimp face and added height, the brown hair and brown eyes and surfer bod, Java who still smelled like peppermint tea. I tried not to let out an involuntary moan as he patted both my shoulders. He looked genuinely happy to see me. *Quel* relief.

"Peace Corps!" he said. His laugh sounded amused but a little bitter, too. "Shrimp didn't actually tell you our parents were in the Peace Corps, did he?" I shrugged. Shrimp never had said exactly, now that I thought about it. "Because I hardly think folks with their federal records would be invited into the Peace Corps." I swear Java was about to crack up at the idea.

Delia stuck her left hand out into the air, dangling the wedding finger, which had a shiny little diamond on it. "Guess what! Wallace and I are engaged!"

Holy shit! Delia was going to get a starter marriage of Java pressed against her bosom and wrapping her legs around him, all with the legal authorization of the State of California and the approval of God. Could she be any luckier?

Java said, "Yeah, we're getting married on New Year's Eve. We thought we'd do it at the beach, then we thought, *Ah, that's so tired, let's do this right—big flashy spectacle and all.* So we're having the ceremony and reception at a hotel on Nob Hill. We're on our way now to an appointment at the stationery store to look at invitations, then we're off to register at Tiffany and Crate & Barrel. You'll come to the wedding, right? You'll have a blast. Our wedding planner found us this tight swing band and great caterer and . . ."

And just like that, my formerly unquenchable Java lust/crush was not only quenched, but 99 percent obliterated. Wedding registries at Tiffany and Crate & Barrel? I'm like, *Wallace, DUDE, former SEX GOD, could you be any more bourgeois?* The remaining 1 percent of my crush can remain, out of respect for the sheer gorgeousness that is Java.

Shrimp and I will probably never get married, although hopefully we will live in glorious sin together for many years. We will live in a giant loft overlooking Ocean Beach with a huge bed in the middle with mosquito netting hanging from the ceiling, wrapping the bed into a swirl cocoon that's as cute as it is unnecessary. Our loft will have a telescope at the windows where Shrimp and I will stand naked in the midnight moonlight, looking out over the roaring Pacific and trying to spot shooting stars. There will be an art studio space in one corner for Shrimp, and in the opposite corner will be a giant espresso machine, one of those Eye-talian ones, along with an industrial-size KitchenAid mixer, like Danny has, for me to make coffees and bake treats for whomever wants to come over and hang and do art and be all salon-ness but never *FAB-u-lous*. Shrimp and I will never get bored with each other or buy into the bourgeois institution of marriage.

Sid and Nancy are married, but theirs seems more like a marriage of convenience—she gets his wealthy lifestyle; he gets a beautiful trophy wife. They bicker all the time, but I guess in some ways they love each other— although I *really* hope they're not having sex anymore. The only people I know who really love each other and are friends and life partners and soul mates as much as they are lovers are my brother Danny and his boyfriend, Aaron. And they can't get married in the United States, like all official and legal, even though they're like responsible, recycling, tax-paying citizens. What kind of fucked-up logic is that?

Java and Delia were so excited I didn't want to interrupt them as they yammered on about their wedding of the century, but I really wanted to cross-examine them like in a courtroom drama. When *exactly* is Shrimp coming home? If your parents aren't building bridges or whatever in the Peace Corps, just what *were* they doing south of the equator? Please state for the record, *does* Shrimp miss me, *does* he want me back? *What* is the deal with this Autumn person?

Java and Delia's wedding plans were so fantastically boring I wasn't annoyed that my cell phone was vibrating inside my pocket. I thought, *If it's Nancy—voicemail, anyone else—jackpot.*

And since it was not Nancy, I answered the phone. The caller was Sid-dad's secretary, giving me instructions on where to show up for my work-study job. The plan is I'll spend the semester helping with administrative work at the cafeteria at Sid-dad's company. It's not as good a job as being a barista, but hopefully I will learn about running a food business. But wait a minute—did the secretary actually say the board just decided to close down the cafeteria and now Sid-dad wants me to work at some new restaurant he's invested in—the same one where Alexei the Horrible will be spending his semester off? Was it static on the cell phone, or did I actually hear her say the words, "Everyone here just *loves* Alexei—such a great guy. Your father is so pleased about this project and that you'll be working with Alexei."

So much for my genius plan to get out of school early two days a week. Now I know Ash got not only her innocent baby face from Sid-dad, but also her evil scheming abilities.

Chapter 6

If I thought I was embarrassed to be picked up from school last year by Fernando in the Mercedes sedan, I had a nice surprise coming. Far more embarrassing was having my mother pick me up after school.

Helen and I were sitting at the MUNI stop outside school, waiting for the bus. I was twirling my hair through my fingers, remembering how Shrimp used to love doing that to my hair, and Helen had her sketch pad on her lap, drawing her Ball Hunter comic. Ball Hunter has just discovered that a tourist taking pictures every day at the same spot in front of the Legion of Honor is actually a radical ecoterrorist plotting to destroy the Rodin sculpture outside the museum and replace the courtyard space with a greenhouse. Ball Hunter has alerted the G-men, but they're not taking him seriously. Ball Hunter is going to have to take care of this one himself.

A black Mercedes SUV stopped at the street corner alongside where we were sitting. The passenger's-side window came down. Helen looked at the driver of the car and groaned. "Oh, one of *those* people. Perfect blond driver lady there probably got lost after her Pilates class and needs directions back to The Marina. I HATE those SUV people."

Perfect blond SUV driver lady said, "Hop in, Cyd Charisse. Did you listen to the voice-mail message I left you earlier today? I forgot to tell you that your doctor's appointment is this afternoon, so I just came for you myself."

"Mom!" I said, mortified. I hadn't listened to her message.

Helen's eyes opened wide. "Sorry," she mumbled. "I didn't realize. Call me later." Helen and I may be new insta-friends, but I haven't known her long enough to expose her to my family or its lifestyle, so I guess I couldn't be mad at her for unwittingly dissing my mom. But hey, my mom is the one taking me to the gynecologist to talk about birth control. Helen's mom doesn't even want girls going to her room.

I hopped into the SUV. Nancy drove on, gulping back a vitamin water. She said, "Do you want me to come in with you? Not for the exam, but to talk with the doctor."

"No," I said, almost in a whisper.

One of the prices of our new peace is we are supposed to start family counseling together, so I don't need her in the gyno office with me too. I can take only so much torture. My mother just recently found out, while we were in New York, about what really happened between me and Justin, my boarding school ex, before I got expelled from that school, about how he left me to go to the clinic alone, as if the problem was only mine. And while I'm grateful Nancy forgot to tell me the day of the gyno appointment, because it is probably going to be insufferable and painful having my mind and womb prodded so I'm glad I didn't have time to dread it, Nancy has yet to see through making an appointment for both of us with a shrink type. My personal theory is there's major drama to be mined from *her* teenage years back in Minnesouda and maybe she's not in such a rush to follow through on the counseling part of the Little Meltdown Incident follow-up plan.

"What?" Nancy said. "I can't hear you."

The driver ahead of us whom Nancy had just unsuccessfully tried to cut off gave her the finger from the driver's-side window. I repeated, "NO," to Nancy's question, but louder, then wanted to get off the topic so I said, "Dad is making me work with Alexei. Can I get another work-study job?"

Nancy flipped the bird back to the driver ahead; with her soft pink hand of French-manicured nails and whopping wedding ring rock, the act almost looked pretty. She said, "Don't talk to me about the work-study job—take it up with your father. I'm surprised, though—I thought you'd like working with Alexei. Aren't you all about cute boys?" She giggled—seriously, gross. "Oh, I forgot. Alexei is Public Enemy Number One. God forbid you should think well of a boy at an Ivy League college, one with goals who eats nutritiously and . . ." *Eats nutritiously?* What does that have to do with anything? Like, where do my mother's brain cells come from? "I didn't like you being on a work-study arrangement, anyway. You barely have enough credits to graduate as it is and the classes you do have are not exactly college-preparation level. But take it up with Dad; he always takes your side, anyway. You two voted me off the island on the work-study issue so I'm staying out of it."

Nancy pulled up in front of a medical building off Fillmore Street. She said, "Go on up. I'll park the car and wait for you at Peet's Coffee on Fillmore. The doctor's office has all your information already, and I've talked to the doctor on the phone about your . . . um . . . issues. So, you know, she knows what's going on." Nancy seemed as embarrassed now as I.

I said, "Does Dad know?" It's weird enough that my mom knows about my . . . um . . . issues, but it's also a relief. But if Sid-dad knew too, maybe I wouldn't be his pet anymore. Cupcake daughters don't have abortions when they're barely sixteen years old.

"No," Nancy said. Her tone held an unspoken threat, like she had done me this favor of not telling him—but she still could.

Nancy reached behind her seat and handed me a package. "Here," she said. "Something nice to open while you're waiting in the doctor's office. It's never fun to wait for an appointment with the gynecologist, but it will be fine. Trust me, it's not bad at all, and you'll be amazed how relieved you feel after."

The package was postmarked from Papua New Guinea. I jumped out of the car, ran into the building, and tore open the box. Inside was a painting on the backside piece of a Cheerios box, cut to the size of a 4-by-6 photo. It was a Picasso-style painting, picturing a headless, wet-suited male upper body that was tenderly holding a female head in its arms. When I looked closer and saw the long black hair, the pale skin, and the dark lips, I realized the head was mine.

That picture had to be the best incentive I could ever have to bolt up to the gynecologist's office.

I do appreciate about my mother that she knew that after the whole experience the place I would most want to meet her would be at Peet's, the thinking person's Starbucks. When I got there I ordered a straight double shot in honor of Shrimp, who drinks his espresso straight up and says that lattes and capps are the equivalent of stupid yuppie mixed drinks like Cosmopolitans or Sex on the Beach.

My mom was sitting alone at a table, reading one of her fashion magazines with the pictures of all the emaciated movie stars in the couture clothes. She seemed oblivious that all the males in the coffee shop were staring at her like they wished she'd drop something so they could rush over to pick it up for her. "Well?" she said when I sat down opposite her at the table.

I don't know what kind of progress report she was expecting. She's been to a gynecologist before; she knows what happens. I shrugged.

Nancy said, "What did she talk to you about?" I took the pamphlets from my handbag and spread them out on the table, which seemed to take care of all the guys checking out my mother—maybe it was the picture of genital warts on the cover of one pamphlet, or the big letters H.I.V. on the cover of another. "Good," Nancy said.

She looked sad and like she really wanted more information from me, so I decided to help her out. I said, "The doctor gave me a prescription for birth control, and a long talk about the need to use condoms also. And she said I am okay after my . . . um . . . issues and in great health, though she said I shouldn't eat so much junk food." Which reminded me. I reached into my handbag again to pull out a king-size Nestle Crunch bar that would be excellent dipped in the espresso shots. I didn't tell Nancy the part about how I've been on the pill since the clinic last year, and it was just a new prescription the doctor had given me. Our household operates more peacefully when these types of issues are filtered to Nancy in the form of making her think it was her idea.

Nancy had been the one prying for information, so why

were there tears in her eyes? I said, "What's the matter, Mom? I thought this is what you wanted for me."

"I don't *want* this for you, Cyd Charisse. But I understand the necessity." She paused, sniffed a little, and dabbed her eyes with a Kleenex. "You know, when you were a baby, just a few months old, you had a fit of colic for about two weeks. You screamed and screamed nonstop. I was so young myself, all alone, and I remember feeling helpless and hopeless—honestly I was about to lose my mind from the crying. Nothing could comfort you. And I remember one night just toward the end, when neither of us had slept in days and I was at wits' end, ready to give up, I remember thinking: *If we can just make it through this, we'll be okay.* If we can just make it through *this*. Now, looking back, that seems like yesterday, yet here we are, a very different *this*. Hang in there with me; your mother's just not ready. I thought I was, but it's harder than I expected."

I totally don't understand what she's not ready for. She's the one who elected to send me off to boarding school three thousand miles from home when I was barely fourteen years old. I'd think she'd have let go a long time ago.

But her tear-stained face was so pretty and pathetic at the same time I had to try to cheer her up. "I'll cook dinner tonight," I offered. Nancy is distraught now that Leila is gone and Sid is downsizing the household staff because the kids are older, so now we just have a cleaning person and a landscaper and a part-time baby-sitter, and of course a Fernando, but no live-in cook or nanny. Leila hooked up with some bald dude at her high school reunion in Quebec over the summer and moved back to Montreal to marry him. It's all very Alice and Sam the Butcher and I am extremely jealous of Leila and her true love and all the nookie she must be getting now. But I won't miss Leila yelling at me with her Celine Dion accent about how I am spoiled and never helped with the dishes, even though I did but it was like why bother because every time I loaded the dishwasher, Leila would take everything back out and rearrange it like the dishes would somehow get cleaner if they were all aligned in rows of uniform sizes. Psycho. Unfortunately our psycho was also the anointed preparer of family meals, and Nancy can't cook and has no desire to learn, which is fine for Nancy, because she doesn't eat, anyway, but the rest of us do and we can only eat take-out or beg Fernando to cook *arroz con pollo* so many nights.

My offer to cook got a grateful smile from my mother.

There is this killer shrimp Creole recipe I am aching to try.

Chapter 7

I have a dirty little secret. My fundamental music of choice is punk, but I won't turn down a good symphony. I don't know a concerto from an opus to a C major or whatever, but one thing I know is I love me some thrashin' violins and cellos getting all funky together, with some bangin' drums thrown in and a maestro standing on the podium getting all sweaty flailing his arms around.

It's a shame I am tone deaf, because I wouldn't mind being some anomaly female conductor. When Shrimp and I used to play Job for a Day, maestro was my number one job choice. Shrimp said he would be the guy standing at the back of the symphony, pounding the giant gong when I pointed my conductor's stick at him at just the right millisecond—timing that means the difference between a world-class maestro and just a good one, according to Sid-dad. Conductor *moi* and gonger Shrimp would be having a secret affair that nobody in the string or wind sections would know about, but all the percussion players would have long copped to us. They're just not as gossipy.

We almost didn't make it to the symphony at all because Nancy threw a hissy fit, whining that my short black skirt with an Irish World Cup team football jersey, black leather motorcycle jacket, and combat boots was not appropriate attire for the symphony. Sid-dad took my side, reminding Nancy would she rather I be dressed like a debutante, or would she rather I be exposed to the music? Nancy gave up but she was still sore when we got to Symphony Hall. She was appeased by our balcony box seats above the orchestra, excellent seats for Nancy to inspect the other box seats to see who she knew that might have gotten seats just a little better than ours, and ideal listening perches for Sid-dad and I to shut our eyes and let the music seep through. The Mozart symphony, all lulling and then fierce, inspired a major neon laser show in my shut eyes for a good fifteen minutes. Then the giant gong banged and my eyes sprung wide open. I could feel a set of eyes staring at me from across the hall, and my eyes went from looking at the orchestra below our seats to the box seats directly opposite us.

SHRIMP!!!!!!!!!!!!!!!!!!!!!!!!!!!!!!!!

I wanted to jump out of my seat and into the lobby for some slo-mo movielike reunion, but Nancy would have lost her mind if I had gotten up before intermission, and anyway, Shrimp didn't stand up like he was going to run out to meet me. He didn't even wave, but a sly smile spread across his face. Instead of shooting up, his formerly spiked hair was longer and falling down from his head, and the formerly platinum blond spikes at his forehead had grown out to their naturally dirty blond color. His face looked fuller, tanner, and redder, like he'd been baking in the sun since his temporary exile from SF fog shroud. I almost fell out of my chair and over the balcony with wanting to throw my arms out for him to run into.

Normally I hate intermissions because they seem like a major waste of time and I just want to gag watching Nancy socialize with all her biddy friends about charity galas and *Yes, let's* do *lunch next week,* but the minutes before intermission came for this symphony felt like an eternity. The lights weren't up and the applause barely started the moment the music ended when I bolted from my chair. Nancy was all, "Cyd Charisse! Where are you go—," but I was gone—forget about slo-mo reunion; I was sprinting. I slowed down right as I approached the turn to the lobby bar area. I didn't want to appear too enthusiastic, but Shrimp had beaten me. He was standing at the bar already, not out of breath.

OMG, how much do I love him? He was wearing a canary yellow polyester leisure suit with a white shirt tucked into the pants and a huge collar tucked over the yellow jacket. He looked like some mack daddy disco pimp, bless his hotness. He was taller and heavier than I remembered, by at least two inches and a month's worth of Shrimp's beloved peanut butter milk shakes with ground-up Oreos and brownies, and that's not just because I wasn't wearing platform boots. He came up to my nose instead of my chin as I stood before him.

Strange that two people who've been as intimate as two people could possibly be couldn't even manage a simple touch at their first meeting after the breakup—no rub on the shoulder, no clasp of hands, no hug, and certainly no kiss. It's like there was this invisible beam between us like in the prison cells on *Star Trek* that would go *bzzz* and repel us if Shrimp or I dared to reach over the awkward invisible energy to touch each other.

"Hey," Shrimp said.

"Hey," I said. "You look taller."

"Yeah, Java's now calling me Jumbo Shrimp."

"So, Jumbo, when did you get back? When are you coming to school again?"

"Got back a few days ago, back to school this Monday. Hit the waves today. Ocean Beach seems tame after riding the waves in the South Pacific. Still better than making up three weeks of schoolwork, though."

In my head I was picturing Nancy having a knee-slappin' hysterical laughing fit at my so much as suggesting that I could miss the first three weeks of school to hang out in Papua New Guinea and surf and build stuff and whatnot. I asked Shrimp, "Was Papua New Guinea awesome?"

"Yeah, except for the dysentery the first week. How was New York?"

There was only so much, too much, to say about that!

Concertgoers had filed out from their seats and were milling around the lobby. The chatter level had picked up considerably, so it was surprising we could distinguish the female voice that screeched, "Shrimp! Why did you run off so fast?" The voice was just that loud.

Shrimp's eyes closed for a minute and I think he let out a small shudder.

A heavyset—not fat, just big-boned—late-middle-aged woman with long hair that was equal parts gray and brown and down to her waist came to Shrimp's side. She was Shrimp's height, wearing jeans and an embroidered Central American blouse, and Teva sandals on bare feet that were in emergency need of a pedicure. She was the type of granola lady that Nancy and her committees would like to see sworn in blood to a dress code before being allowed to enter Symphony Hall.

Shrimp looked like he was about to introduce me when the lady scanned me with her brown eyes and then said, "It's Cyd Charisse, of course!" She wrapped her arms around me in a hug so tight she could have squeezed body parts out of me. "I've seen the artwork!"

Shrimp mumbled, "Mom, Cyd. Cyd, Mom."

A short guy, shorter even than pre-Jumbo Shrimp, stood behind Shrimp's mom. He looked like an exact copy of Shrimp, just smaller, quieter, maybe sadder.

He extended his hand to mine and introduced himself as Shrimp's dad. His mumbling was more indistinguishable than Shrimp's.

Shrimp—*with parents*! This had to be the kinkiest thing ever! Shrimp and Java were like lone cowboy brothers who answered to no one but each other.

I started to say, "Nice to meet you, Mr. and Mrs. . . . ," but his mom bellowed, "Please! We're Iris and Billy."

Shrimp could be a retired Supreme Court judge and he'd still better call Sid and Nancy "Mr." and "Mrs."

Iris jumped in to give me another hug, she was almost bouncing me up and down. When she let go, I told her, "Congratulations on Wallace's engagement. I know he and Delia will be very happy." Jesus H. Christ, I'm starting to sound like Nancy. I need to go smoke some weed or shoplift some Hershey bars, *fast.*

Iris said, "Can you believe that? It just makes me so sad. It's bad enough they feel the need to become part of the system like that, but a fancy hotel on Nob Hill? A caterer? Wedding registries? I told them, 'Goddamn, if you need to do this so bad, Billy and I know a spiritual guru who performs ceremonies. Let him do it. We'll have a potluck in the backyard, Billy can play guitar, and we'll throw some Motown on the stereo when folks are ready to dance. Don't waste money like that!' Do you realize how many Third

World families could be fed for a year at the same cost of their wedding?"

Uh, no, Iris, I didn't realize that. I just thought Java and Delia were kinda boring for choosing the cotillion wedding with ten groomsmen and bridesmaids. But *Motown*? Gimme the expensive swing band any day.

Shrimp was like, "Mom . . . ," but she interrupted again. "Billy and I didn't feel the need to marry! We *know* our commitment to one another."

"MOM!" Shrimp said. I've never heard him yell before. His low voice usually sounds like a deep, sexy whisper. I didn't know a mellow dude like Shrimp was capable of yelling, much less that he was capable of being irritable, like a normal person, the kind of person who lives in my family. "Enough already."

The lights flickered, signaling the end of intermission. Iris said, "Cyd Charisse, I've heard so much about you. I need you to come over, soon, this week, absolutely, we'll throw a party. I can see your aura even through all that black you're wearing. Billy, this girl's aura, can you see it? The yellow! Yellower than Shrimp's leisure suit! Promise you'll come over this week, Cyd Charisse? Our friend from Humboldt County just came down to visit and left a nice little deposit, so you know what *that* means. We'll have a great time, really get to know one another."

I couldn't accept the invitation without Shrimp also extending it so I just smiled a little, polite. Shrimp mumbled, "I'll see you at school."

That didn't seem very encouraging.

Iris and Billy said their good-byes and headed back to their seats with their disco king mack daddy son in tow, me standing there confused and wanting to know what's in Humboldt County; maybe if my mother hadn't sent me off to boarding school for so long I'd know what's in my own state. Then just as he was heading up the stairs toward his balcony section, Shrimp turned around and walked back over to where I was still standing in the lobby, watching him, wanting to hyperventilate with happiness—and confusion. Shrimp stood in front of me, and it was like our live awkward slo-mo moment. What were we supposed to do here? Do we really even know each other anymore? Shrimp leaned his face into mine like he was going to kiss me. I *mucho* wanted those full lips of his but I turned my cheek slightly and offered him my hand instead.

We have a long way to go, despite my urge to tear that canary yellow leisure suit from his body and have my way with him.

His face leaned close to my lips again, then diverted to my ear. Shrimp mumbled, "Next Saturday, eightish, party for the parents. Rooftop."

The feel of his soft lips against my hand, the graze of his chin stubble on my wrist, and his breath whispering into my ear had made my legs all Jell-O and I was swooning as I turned around to return to my seat. My eyes fell on Nancy, whom all the men were checking out, with her perfect blond hair in a French twist and her model figure wearing a form-fitting couture evening dress, standing in a corner with a Perrier in her manicured hand, where she must have been watching Shrimp and me.

Nancy had the lemon-sucking face on again, like, *Oh, no, here we go again.*

Chapter 8

I really am so over the Wallace crush, but walking back onto that roof at Java and Shrimp's house, overlooking Ocean Beach with the smell of serious coffee brewing and the view of Java flipping the veggie burgers on the grill while wearing a Java the Hut apron over his wet suit, well, I couldn't help but think, Mmm, break me off a piece of *that*. Something about the smell of the Ocean Beach salt air and eucalyptus trees seeping through the aroma of Java the Hut coffee beans, something about that particular mixture of scents brought me back instantly to the beginning of summer, when Shrimp and I were still On. The smell sent my hormones into immediate overdrive and almost made me forget how I have decided engaged man Wallace has become slightly a sellout and wouldn't I like to see him naked on a honeymoon, all buff and showering our matrimonial bed with java beans instead of rose petals.

I gave myself a mental slap on the wrist and tried to distract myself from further impure thoughts. My eyes searched the rooftop, where a large group of teen to middle-aged people—hippie/surfer/artist types, very grunge, your basic Ocean Beach crowd—were hanging out for Iris and Billy's welcome-home party. I was scanning for Shrimp, whom my eyes spied lying on a hammock and motioning me from where I was standing at the door. I licked the Java-inspired drool from my lips and walked through the crowd toward Shrimp.

I couldn't help but remember that the last time I had been on this rooftop I was in a moonlit, whispered convo with Java—nothing romantic, just dishing about life and past loves and your basic deep thoughts, I suppose—while Shrimp and Delia were passed out in their sleeping bags next to us. My welcome home from that party had been a sentence to Alcatraz, courtesy of Sid and Nancy. Now I am not only past imprisonment but I'm completely paroled, although I did have to promise to be waiting downstairs to be picked up by Fernando promptly at eleven o'clock this evening. Most amazingly the evening air was warm enough for me not to be layered in wool and tights. That is one thing I loved about New York: the late-night summer hanging out, when it's so hot you could just stand in your birthday suit with a fire hydrant spraying you with *agua* and be perfectly content. Danny and his boyfriend have this great blacktop lounge area on the roof of their brownstone building. I guess it's their one consolation for living on a fifth-floor walk-up apartment. They have plastic beach chairs lying around up there with Jackie Collins and Sidney Sheldon books folded inside and card tables for when their buds come over for mah-jongg games, and a karaoke machine that Aaron uses to sing Kylie Minogue songs. From that rooftop you can see the Empire State Building and all of midtown Manhattan looking like a Lite Brite game. From Shrimp and Java's rooftop you can see the Pacific Ocean and Mount Tamalpais in Marin County if it's not too foggy and if you're willing to brave the Ocean Beach chill.

Hammocks are serious business intimacy-wise, so I was glad Shrimp was sitting up in his by the time I reached him. I could feel the *Fatal Attraction* instinct to machete down all the party people just to get rid of them so I could have some personal hammock time lying next to Shrimp. I sent a mental memo to my future, dictating, *Hammock— Watch This Space.* The desire to lie in the hammock with Shrimp spooning me from behind, maybe nestling his head on my shoulder, running his fingers through my hair and massaging my scalp, just the two of us alone together, breathing in the ocean air and each other, was one that would have to hold out a while longer. My mental memo received an instant reply: *CC, play a little hard to get, why don't you? The boy did break up with you and did kinda break your heart.*

I sat down on the hammock next to Shrimp and crossed my arms over my chest. "Hey," I said.

"Hey," he said back.

What is with the *heys*? He's, like, been inside me. You'd think two soul mates would have more to say, but we were both silent after our greetings. Our non-conversation was broken by the sound of the ocean crashing down from across Great Highway. The sound of the ocean breaking our silence was like chocolate syrup poured into a glass of milk, dispersing into awkward dark clumps while waiting to be stirred.

If Shrimp is my one true love, shouldn't conversation come a little easier?

I saw Helen sitting on a bench on the other side of the roof, talking to some surfer-rat guy and a dreadlocked girl. Helen waved at me and I waved back. I considered ditching Shrimp and our empty air to go talk with Helen. I barely know her, and I think I could fill hours of conversation with her (most of it about Shrimp). No pressure.

My wave prompted Shrimp to speak. "You know Helen?" Not the words for which I was waiting: *Oh, Cyd Charisse, I've missed you so much, I think of you every waking second, I love, need, and want you, baby, I can't live another moment without you.*

"Yeah, she's my new chum." To Shrimp's surprised look, I added, "Why, is that so weird?"

Shrimp shrugged. "That's cool. I just never knew you to have girlfriends before."

"Well, maybe you didn't really know me either."

"Vice versa." His tone wasn't angry or mean, and mine hadn't been either. We were just stating facts.

"How do you know Helen?" I asked. "From your art classes?"

"Kinda," Shrimp said. "But mostly cuz our friend has this mild crush on her."

Oh, someone with a crush on Helen! Delicious! I pointed to the surfer-rat guy Helen was talking to. "That guy?" I said.

Shrimp laughed. "Arran the long boarder? No, I don't think so. He's saving himself for some bimbo *Penthouse* ideal that will never happen past his nocturnal fantasies." Shrimp cocked his head in the direction of the dreadlocked girl talking with Helen and Arran. "Her. Autumn."

THAT WAS AUTUMN! My eyes widened as I tried to get a better look at the she-devil who had been haunting my nightmares since Shrimp broke up with me. Autumn was standing beneath a string of red chili pepper lights and appeared to be a light-skinned black girl, but one with the eye shape and facial bone structure similar to the Vietnamese girls at the *pho* soup shops on Clement Street.

She had one of those warm, infectious smiles wrapped by an impossibly perfect-shape mouth—big full lips and gleaming white teeth—that just made me want to hurl. So much for my assumption that any surfer girl named Autumn had to be a red-haired, hairy-armpitted, folk-singing, sun-kissed California white girl, like, fer sure. And so much for my assumption that the Autumn chick was jonesing for my man.

I laughed a little, and for the first time since being back at Java and Shrimp's house, I relaxed. I uncrossed my arms from over my chest and leaned a little closer to Shrimp. "What's that grin for?" Shrimp asked.

"Maybe I'm just surprised. Last summer when I was grounded and Delia told me about how Autumn was your surfing friend and how she had taken my job at Java the Hut, I was like so sure you and she hooked up while I was banished in Pacific Heights."

"I told you when we broke up that nothing had happened between me and Autumn," Shrimp said. His hand on his lap moved to his knee so his pinkie finger was touching mine, and our knees were *thisclose* to knocking. It would be rude to just randomly make out on a hammock at a party where people are socializing all around you, and where your intended make-out partner's parents are being celebrated, right? Even if there clearly was a need to celebrate something else—that the Autumn chick was not a playa in the Shrimp-CC love duel?

I said, "And if I had realized Autumn was gay I wouldn't have been so, you know, hung up on the idea that you and she had hooked up."

Shrimp said, "Oh, we hooked up. After." My hormonal

overdrive shifted from lust to boiling point on the verge of major temper tantrum. I had to summon every ounce of willpower not to SCREAM at the top of my lungs. My temper was held in check by the view of Iris standing next to Java. I had to avert my eyes so Shrimp's mom wouldn't notice my aura turning to THUNDERCLOUD RAGE RAGE RAGE. "Right before I left for PNG. We just didn't, like, finish the job up. It was sort of a *You're here and I'm here, and we're both kinda bored and curious* hookup. Didn't mean anything, y'know?"

Yeah, I do know. His name was Luis, but what does that have to do with anything?

Why does Shrimp have to be so honest all the time? Why can't he ever lie, just a little, if for no other reason than to prevent me from wanting to pounce on over to Autumn and claw her freakin' eyes out. And I wouldn't mind jabbing my hammock partner into a Shrimp étouffée right now either.

My arms crossed back over my chest and I could feel my mouth turning into a jut so mad that the expression was in danger of being permanently molded to my jaw. I said, "Yeah, as a matter of fact, I do know. There was a guy in NYC who worked for my bio-dad. But it also wasn't an all-the-way situation."

I looked into Shrimp's eyes and thought, *Are we even now? Can we move on?*

Apparently not. Shrimp just let it out: "Are you over that crush on my brother?"

If Shrimp and I are ever going to get back on course, one of us eventually has to give, so as an experiment in aura improvement, I figured why not let it be me? I said,

"That so-called crush is like a tumor, but a benign one, see? Do you get it?"

Shrimp's mouth turned into a slight, gnarly half-smile. "I guess," he said. "I kinda have a crush on your mom."

Payback is a bitch.

Iris plopped down next to our hammock, sitting on a stool made from a tree stump. Her presence saved me from responding to Shrimp's proclamation, which would have required me wading into an area so gross all I could picture was a Goya-type painting of me drowning in a boiling cauldron of icky worm-snake creatures wrapping themselves around my flailing self. EWWWWWWWWWWWWWWWWWW!!!!!!!!!!!!

"Cyd Charisse," Iris said. She took my hand in hers. "I'm so glad you were able to come tonight. A little surprised, too. Shrimp, Wallace, and Delia all had wagers going on whether your mother would let you back into this house." Iris shouted toward Delia, who was pumping the keg. "Dee, you owe Shrimp ten bucks!"

Shrimp patted my knee like he was my grandpa—what was that about?—and hopped off the hammock. "I'll catch up with you later," he said to me. Hmmph, maternal avoidance much?

I watched Shrimp from behind—he really has such a nice ass—small and round and just pert—as he walked away to join his brother. The view of Wallace and Shrimp standing together, identical ocean-wind-whipped hair, laughing the same laugh and smiling the same smile, made me turn to Iris, their creator. She was looking at the brothers too, with that mama lioness look of pride. "Blessings on their mama," were the words floating through my head, and from Iris's big smile back at me, I realized the words had traveled from my brain and out of my mouth. Iris reached over and ran her fingers through the front of my hair, like Nancy does when I let her. That simple Mommy touch helped downgrade my boiling-point temperature.

Iris said, "Do you have some room for me on that hammock?" She stood up from the tree-stump chair and wrapped the caftan edges of her long dress tight around her legs. I moved over to give her room but she said, "Oh, no, let's lie down and look at the stars. Of course, with all the pollution here you can't really see the night sky like you can in the South Pacific, but I'm betting we'll see something worthwhile."

Being fundamentally weird and prissy, I did not want to share the hammock with her, but Iris was also the mother of my manifest destiny so I figured better not offend her by suggesting she might be invading my personal space. Luckily Iris lay down in the direction opposite me so we were toe-to-head instead of head-to-head. I must admit, the gentle sway of our two bodies on the hammock was rather nice in the brisk night ocean air, and hey, those stars up there, the ones you could see through the slight fog haze, were right twinkly.

Iris said, "I'm not really a city person, but I do love San Francisco. The eucalyptus smell out here by the beach, it's almost intoxicating. And it's warm tonight, for San Francisco at least! The last time I was here, when we moved Shrimp into this house with Wallace, I had to wear a down coat to be up here on the boys' roof. And it was July!"

Next time I can corral Shrimp into a round of my Job for a Day game, I want to be a concierge at one of those fancy San Francisco hotels, as I am sure tourists would appreciate my knowledge of The City and its microclimates. I explained to Iris, "That's because it's fall, which in San Fran means the arrival of the summer we were denied with fog and supreme chill during July and August. September and October are the best months in The City, warm and sunny, like practically balmy. Of course, if you live in The Mission or Noe Valley you probably get to see the sun every day, but here in Ocean Beach, and lotsa times over in Pacific Heights, you can go days without seeing sun during the summer." The early fall months, warm and sunny *and* minus the summer tourists so ignorant they thought they could experience the California Summer Beach Boys experience in San Francisco, are my fave months in The City. This fall would be the first in three years that I had been home to enjoy it.

"I understand you spent this past August in New York. How did you like it?" Iris said. "Billy and I went there once a few years ago. We protested a G-7 economic summit. We had traffic backed up all along Park Avenue. Good times."

Mental note: Never invite Iris over to meet Sid-dad.

"New York was weird and interesting and scary-cool, and I would like to go back again, but under different circumstances. If I go back I would want to stay with my brother and his boyfriend instead of my bio-dad, and Shrimp should come cuz he would love all the museums and art galleries and, um, just art *everywhere,* like the graffiti on the subways and the hip-hop spray painting on the sides of random brick buildings and on the huge water tanks that sit on the roofs of the bigger apartment buildings. Shrimp would be digging that city something serious."

Why was I telling Iris all this? These were the words

that should have filled my empty-air conversation with Shrimp. I was dying to tell him about New York—and I still hadn't heard about his faraway adventures.

"You have good taste in men," Iris said.

"I agree." I didn't always have such good taste, but Shrimp changed all that.

Iris announced, "Now, for our special treat." I was thinking, *Chocolate soufflé? Did someone make a chocolate soufflé?* They're really hard to make but so delectable, but Iris's idea of a special treat was way different than my own. I lifted my head from the hammock to see Iris reaching into the pocket of her caftan dress, from which she pulled out a lighter and a big fat blunt.

Iris is so the coolest mom ever.

She lit and took a nice long hit. She didn't let out one cough, and she blew rings with the exhaled smoke. Worship her! Caffeine is my drug of choice, but who was I to turn away the J when Iris passed it my way; special treat *indeed*. The smell of that baby was way too nice to bother debating the wisdom of sharing in the experience with my beautiful, unfaithful true love's mother. Mmmm, nice smell. Nice.

"Humboldt's best," Iris said. So *that* is what she meant by the little deposit left by her friends in Humboldt County.

I took a short drag—it had been a long time for me, like sophomore year, and nobody back at that boarding school ever scored bud this sweet and STRONG—but I still hacked out the exhale.

"Try another—slower, shorter," Iris advised.

I took another hit, breathing in slowly so the smoke could go down deep without being overwhelming. Ahhhhh. Nice Humboldt County, well done.

"Tell me about yourself, Cyd Charisse," Iris said. One more hit and I passed the joint back to Iris. I could feel the rage over the Shrimp-Autumn hookup not exactly going away but dissipating into a mellow feeling of *Well, I don't have to like it, but fair IS fair.* Loo-eese.

I kinda felt like singing but instead I talked in beats, like my words had rhythm and I was some beatnik poet. "I'm thinkin' 'bout a perm name change to CC. I'm trying to take my own identity and give that movie star back hers." Come to think of it, I will only call Java by his real name—Wallace—from now on, to downgrade his sex appeal to me.

"College?" Iris said.

"Pass, yes, I will pass," I said, but my J-inspired attempt at rap came out sounding more like *Pssst, Yoda, pssst.*

"CC, I'm thinking you and Shrimp are going to have a fresh start, move past all that nonsense Shrimp and Wallace told me about involving your parents. Your folks just need to relax. You're a grown woman now, independent."

EXACTLY.

I remembered how Nancy had told me, at the time of my Little Meltdown Incident, how Shrimp had come by the house after I left for New York and apologized to Nancy for us being "young and stupid" before the events leading up to Alcatraz. I wasn't sure if that was a sign of his intention for us to get back together once I returned home or just an unfortunate case of sucking up, but suddenly I had to know, right away.

No amount of weed can mellow out the basic hypergrrl in me.

I got up from the hammock. "Laters, Iris," I said. "I need to talk to your son. Thanks for the Humboldt Special."

"You're welcome, CC," Iris said. "And just for the record, *I* have no problem if you ever want to spend the night, so come back soon. I hear you like to bake, and we've got plenty left over for Billy's favorite brownie recipe."

Honestly, Iris, join AA or something.

I walked over to where Shrimp, Helen, Arran, and Autumn were standing. They were clinking plastic cups filled with beer and saying, *"Kampei!"*

Helen said, "Hey, CC, have you met Autumn and Arran? He spells it funny—A-R-R-A-N—but feel free to just call him Aryan. He's quite the fascist pig."

I ignored Autumn and said to Arran, "My brother's boyfriend is also Aaron, but he spells his the double-A way. Shrimp said you're a long boarder. What's that about?"

Arran said, "Yeah, Shrimp thinks short boards are better and long boarders suck cuz so many short boarders think that even though short boarding wouldn't be around without long boarding and hello, *The Endless Summer,* best movie in the world!"

Long boarding versus short boarding: Who the hell cares? I inspected Autumn while Aryan rambled on. Autumn was even prettier up close; had to hate that. She looked like one of those mixed-race girls for whom every best piece of DNA from a dozen different nationalities had blended together to create Dreadlocked Girl with Unaffected Supermodel Potential. Like, you could see her in some magazine perfume ad wearing your basic New York little black dress with bare feet, walking along a wet brick street of loft buildings and industrial office spaces in

Lower Manhattan, no makeup on, just clear lip gloss to frame those perfect full lips and fake eyelashes to make her Asian eyes even more sexy, with a posse of hot motorcycle dudes trailing after her and a caption at the bottom of the mag page reading: MINIMAL. AVAILABLE IN FINE STORES EVERYWHERE.

The need to indulge in some munchies and settle things once and for all with Shrimp beckoned, along with the nearing-eleven-o'clock Cinderella hour. I said to Shrimp, "Do you and Wallace still keep Hot Pockets in the freezer, cuz I could really go for one right now."

Shrimp leaned in close to me, his mouth grazing my ear, sending my heart racing. He whispered, "Don't tell Iris cuz she'll freak, but Java and I are back on meat. We've got some 7-Eleven burritos in the freezer behind the Absolut bottles. Can I tempt you?"

SHAH!

His hand took mine and I latched on tight, smirked at Autumn, and said g'bye to Aryan and Helen.

I followed Shrimp down the narrow stairwell back into the house, not letting go of his hand. We arrived at the fridge and I stood against it, and just like that his body pressed against mine, and the kiss, the We're Officially Back On kiss, was close to happening, when Wallace came through the door.

"Hey, kids," he chirped. He was wearing Delia's rhinestone tiara on his head. My gaze at him was *so* quick and sweet and innocent, but enough for Shrimp to step back from me. Wallace stepped between us, reaching into the freezer to pull out a frozen Absolut bottle. "Don't do anything I wouldn't do," Wallace teased. I was not thinking about how grabilicious Java's, I mean Wallace's, wet suit–covered butt looked as he walked away—really.

Once Wallace was gone I pulled Shrimp back toward me. The new and improved Jumbo Shrimp had all this—how you say?—*girth* that I was dying to savor, but Shrimp leaned back from me. He said, "I think we should just be friends."

Desperation Girl forgot all about the play-hard-to-get memo, and she moved in for that kiss anyway, full-throttle tongue, one hand massaging the back of his neck, the other straying to the center of his body. His mouth tasted like the old Shrimp, like espresso and Pop Tarts, for the few seconds he let me taste him before pulling back.

"I don't know that I'm ready for the craziness again," he mumbled.

The need to grind against him, through him, with him, taste more of his kisses, threatened to overwhelm me. "But the artwork!" I panted. You don't send a girl drawings from below the equator, pictures illustrating your extreme longing for her, unless you want her, bad.

"I didn't say I didn't want to not get back together," he said. Huh? I hate double—make that triple—negatives.

"Good, because I didn't say that either." Whatever I didn't say at this particular juncture, a little baked and a lot confused, I was just trying to get inside his pants. Big difference.

"Then we're agreed. Let's just be friends for now. I've got enough to deal with having my parents back in the house and all this schoolwork I have to make up, and Java is thinking of opening a store in the East Bay, which means I'll be working a lot of hours, and there's the surfing and time for my art and . . ."

No need to beat this subject to death. "I got it," I snapped.

"Don't be like that," Shrimp said. "There's just too much weirdness right now. Can't you feel it?"

I knew he was right, but part of me couldn't help but feel scorned, too. I mean, aren't guys supposed to be all about grabbing whatever piece of booty becomes available to them, no matter the consequences?

Shrimp opened the freezer and pulled out the 7-Eleven burrito for me, like it was a peace offering, but I said, "No, thank you." I called Fernando to come pick me up early. I knew Fernando would take me to Krispy Kreme and be silent and brooding and not ask why my eyes were bloodshot—because I was stoned or because I was heartbroken?

Chapter 9

The irony of my senior year being all about Shrimp is that the guy I can't seem to get away from is Alexei the Horrible. Guess who was in the car when Fernando came to pick me up?

"Hiya, Princess," Alexei said when I hopped into the backseat of the Mercedes sedan. Just the sight of him was enough to ruin my Humboldt buzz. "I guess you forgot all about how to use MUNI, our city's beloved public transportation system." The sedan smelled like the pine tree air freshener hanging from the rearview mirror mixed with sweat and Alexei's atrocious CK cologne.

"Not really," Fernando said. "I insisted. You seen how many H addicts and crackheads live in this neighborhood? She's not taking MUNI home from Ocean Beach at night on my watch. *Loco*." Since Fernando had stood up for me, I didn't point out that Ocean Beach can look depressing but it's also the home of "Just Friends" Shrimp, whose sole presence could brighten any neighborhood's fundamental depressing vibe. But much as I love to think of Ocean Beach as Cyd Charisse–Shrimp paradise, Fernando did have a point. Land O' Beach Bunnies and chirpy-sunny-happy people Ocean Beach is not, what with being overrun by fog and cold and, yeah, seedy hourly motels, grimy bars, and a small but thriving population of hard-core druggies to go along with its glorious Pacific Ocean surf.

"Alexei," I said, "would it be possible for you to get

your own life going and stop worrying about mine? Why are you in the car, anyway?" I reached into my Sailor Moon backpack for my Discman. The Dead Kennedys couldn't drown out Alexei quickly enough.

Pray for me to make it through a whole semester working with Alexei. My first day on work-study I couldn't even tell him it is actually possible that a punk-Goth chick can be personable and even, dare I say, beloved, to customers, or that I can help with fixing the espresso machine when it's clogged, before he snapped at me, "I am not going to spend my semester off baby-sitting the Little Hellion. I don't know what Sid was thinking, placing you in this environment. I can't imagine you have any useful skills." And I just tore into him. Did he know I was Employee of the Month two consecutive months when I had worked at Java the Hut? Did Alexei know how many customers asked for me personally at Java the Hut and The Village Idiots? Was it not a *fact* that I repeatedly worked double shifts, unasked, at both establishments when flaky employees didn't show up because they thought they were too good for minimum wage? Ask me how full the tip jar was when I was on duty—just ask me, Alexei. Then Sid-dad had popped his bald head into the restaurant, along with a group of fellow investors, right as I was about to explain to Alexei the difference between understanding what makes a *job* and what makes a *career*: something called a *work ethic*. "Everything going okay in here?" Sid-dad asked. He looked so happy to see us, especially against the expressionless army of white men flanking him. "Great!" Alexei and I both said.

Alexei turned around to face me from the front seat of the car. His face was flushed deep red but in that healthy way, the color of his cheeks made sharper by the red bandana on his head, tied at the top of his forehead like some Estonian version of Tupac. I felt an involuntary jerk reaction pass through my body, like this brief *sizzle*. Eek, Alexei is not entirely bad-looking, if you go for that type of chiseled face and wrestler bod and overachiever mentality. Which I don't.

"No need for you to go all Chernobyl on me, Princess. Fernando and I were lifting at the gym when you called to be picked up early. Hey, Fernando, did you know Daddy's beloved Little Hellion has busboys at the restaurant dropping trays of food on customers? She's only been on the job two days and already she's helped the restaurant lose its first celebrity customer. Well done, Princess."

"Hey, Fernando," I pitched in, as I placed the headphones over my ears. "Did you know that it was only one busboy and that I can't be held responsible if said busboy is paying more attention to me picking up a menu from the floor than to the fact that he is clearing the table of the Forty-niners' new first-round draft pick?"

"No, that's not how it . . . ," Alexei started, but I jumped right back in, headphones off. Now I was mad, nearing Chernobyl-meltdown mad.

"Hey, Fernando, did you know further that College Boy has you and Dad believing he's taken the semester off from college to get this great experience assistant managing a hot start-up restaurant allegedly cuz it will look good on his MBA applications one day, but really he's at the restaurant BECAUSE OF A GIRL? Go on, Alexei, tell Fernando all about Kari."

KAR-ee, not Carrie, 'scuse me, is the general manager at the swank new restaurant where Sid-dad sucker-punched me into working as a hostess two afternoons a week for work study. The one and only thing Alexei and I have in common is that we both think and act at the direction of the wrong part of our anatomy, and I *know* he has it bad for Kari, and I *know* gettin' wit' her is the reason for the semester off. Sad, really. See, our young Alexei met Kari at a bar in The Marina over the summer. They got to talking. She was interviewing for the Big Job at this new restaurant. Alexei has some weird older chick fetish and he was trying to get into her skirt. Turns out they both also knew a guy a.k.a. Sid-dad, who would (a) definitely give ear time to Alexei's offhand recommendation that Kari get the general manager job, and (b) would love to bend the rules a little and have Alexei work there for only a semester, to get the experience that will one day help get him into Harvard Business School.

How did I retrieve this 411? Well, let's just say there are advantages to having a posse of busboys panting over you, especially ones who like to gossip about their hated boss, Lord Empress Kari.

"That's not true!" Alexei protested from the front seat. His massive shoulders hunched a little. "Kari has opened and managed three top-rated restaurants in the Bay Area and Napa. She's even been profiled in the *Wall Street Journal*. Working with someone of her skill and experience is an unbelievable opportunity, worth taking a semester off. Great for the resume, and great for the bank account. Not all of us have trust funds to put us through college, Princess."

KAR-ee, who is about my mother's age, is Super Career Gal—she wears horrid lack-of-length power suits with fuck-me heel shoes, and she has raven hair shaped into one of those blunt bob cuts with razor-sharp bangs and the rest falling just below her ears, with big baby blue eyes and cute (for an old person) pursed lips. The interesting thing about Kari's otherwise boring face is that she has a lazy eye on her left side and I have to practice staring at her button nose when she talks instead of looking her in the eyes so I don't get busted staring at that nonmoving baby blue.

And, Kari is anything but lazy. She races around the restaurant with a mouthpiece headphone jutting from her ears down to her lips, barking out orders to the kitchen and reception area with this four star general's tone, as if getting tables 12 and 14 put together and set up for a party of thirteen, STAT, is the battle plan that will ensure Allied victory. In my short time working at the restaurant, I've had to master the art of not staring at her lazy eye and also not falling on the floor in hysterics every time she yells into that headphone mouthpiece (that quite frankly is somewhat phallic and obscene against her Kewpie doll mouth—hence why I'm sure Alexei is enlisted as her lovestruck minion).

Proving I was right about Alexei's intentions with Lord Empress Kari, Alexei had turned back around to face the front of the car so I couldn't see his eyes. Even though Alexei is a Horrible, he also has the most honest face ever; you can always tell if he's lying. When I was in elementary school and Alexei would be in the car when Fernando picked me up, I would ask Alexei if he had an extra Capri Sun punch to share with me and he would snap "NO," but then his face would turn red and his eyes would go all simpering puppylike from his lie, then miraculously he would find an extra juice from his backpack and throw it at me. I almost feel sorry for Alexei now because Kari treats him more like a secretary than an assistant manager. From behind my stacks of menus I've already witnessed her sending him to pick up her ugly power suits from the dry cleaner and bristling at him to confirm her hair appointment already.

"*Dios mio,* ENOUGH!" Fernando exclaimed. Fernando slammed the car brakes hard on Great Highway. We'd reached a red light, true, but the hard slam was definitely intended to jolt us in our seats. Fernando did that Jesus–Hail Mary thing he always does, you know, that the Name of the Father, Son, and Holy Ghost crossing-your-hands-over-your-chest business. "Remind me never to have the both of you in the car at the same time again." Alexei and I shut up at Fernando's brake slam and allowed Fernando to listen to the salsa radio station in peace for the rest of the drive down to Daly City.

I want to ask Sid-dad could I just bail on this job and go back to work at Java the Hut, because even working with Mr. "Just Friends" Shrimp and the Autumn wench would be better than a swankster-hip restaurant for Financial District phoneys, but I feel like I have let Sid-dad down a lot in the past, and this time I am going to see this one through. Also there is the remote possibility that despite the new calm in our home, asking to go back to work at Java the Hut, where all the crazy business leading to Alcatraz started, would be like asking to unleash the gates to Hell.

Fernando's cell phone rang just as we pulled into the parking lot at the Krispy Kreme store in Daly City, the 'burb just below San Fran with all the little houses on the hill that look like Monopoly houses. Fernando said, "I need to take this call. Why don't you two get in line? You know what I want, right?"

I hopped out of the car and said to Fernando through the driver's window, "You want a dozen dulce de leche donuts for you to supposedly share with your grandchildren, but really I know you'll eat half on your own, good man, and if they're out of dulce de leche you want straight-up original glazed."

"You got it," Fernando said with a laugh. He started speaking into his cell phone in Spanish.

While we waited in line Alexei said, "There's a Jamba Juice where I can get a Powerboost near here, right?"

"I bet it's closed," I said. "Anyways, live a little, why don't you?"

"I guess one custard doughnut won't kill me. But really, I prefer Dunkin' Donuts back East."

I've had a recent spiritual conversion from Dunkin' Donuts to Krispy Kreme since Luis in Nueva York told me that Dunkin' Donuts are frozen and then microwaved, while Krispy Kremes are baked fresh every day. I'm not sure if that's just urban legend, but I don't think Luis would lie about something important like that, and I am not willing to take the risk.

"Custard!" I said to Alexei. "Those doughnuts suck. They are the ultimate fake out on the doughnut goodness scale. You're at Krispy KREME. If you're gonna splurge on calories, at least get a cream-filled chocolate glaze."

The best doughnut I ever had was at a family-run diner at a truck stop on I-5 one summer when I was little, before Josh and Ash were born, when Sid-dad tried to take Nancy and me camping at Yosemite and we did not last one hour in those sleeping bags before begging Sid-dad to take us to a motel. That truck-stop doughnut, a simple glazed cinnamon twist, was perfection: homemade, hot, moist, melt-in-your-mouth good, a true wonder I don't expect ever to experience again in my lifetime, so I don't know why I was defending any Krispy Kreme flavor so hard to Alexei. But there were loads of people waiting in line ahead of us at the Krispy Kreme store on this Saturday night, which had to be some testimony in support of the institution.

Alexei sighed. "Do you always have to bust a guy's chops? Can't you just relax a little? I think you owe me a small debt of gratitude for a certain pub incident not too long ago, so I'd like to cash in. Please, just shut up."

I protested, "But I cannot pay that debt back by letting you consume bad doughnuts. That would just make me a schmuck."

Fernando joined us in the line. He said, "How about a truce between the two of you be the settlement of whatever this score is already."

Alexei and I both protested. "But . . ."

Fernando put up the Talk to the Hand gesture. He said, "Cheer up. We're going to stop by the nursing home on the way home. Sugar Pie can't wait until after church tomorrow morning for her doughnut."

Chapter 10

The truth is, I've been kinda doggin' Sugar Pie since I got back from NYC. I've been going to the nursing home my usual ten hours a week for community service, and while I always pop my head in to say hi, I haven't been hanging out with her like I used to do. I haven't been logging extra hours in her room playing gin rummy or begging her to read my tarot cards or listening to her explain about Vicki's many different personalities (and quite complicated love life) on *One Life to Live*. Not that hanging with Sugar Pie isn't more fun and interesting than changing linens and reading Harry Potter books aloud to the old folks more HP-obsessed than my little brother, but there's just something about this time of year that makes me remember the secret Sugar Pie and I share: an abortion in our pasts. Also Sugar Pie's got true love now. She doesn't need me ruining her good time.

Much as I am loving this San Francisco fall, I can't help but remember that this time last year I was pregnant and panicked back at boarding school in New England. I was six weeks along before I finally got up the guts to call Frank real-dad and ask him to wire me the money I needed, since Justin was no help and it's not like I had any friends at that school. I can't help but remember that this time last year I was throwing up between class periods and sweating bullets in my bed at night, wondering what to do, feeling completely alone and desperate. I guess part of me can look back now and say, *Huh, a year has gone by, and look how much better my life is now, look how I've changed and look how many great people I have in my life now.* Another part of me, more buried but that seems to come out most when I see Sugar Pie, who was the first friend I made after coming home to San Francisco, that part of me thinks, *Huh, if things had gone differently, I might be living in some halfway house for teenage mothers now, cradling a small baby and wondering was that baby really smiling at me, the mommy, or was it just gas in its tummy.*

Maybe this hurt will go away when fall passes, when the anniversary of the A-date is gone by. I wonder if this is a pain I will feel every year, if every year I will imagine a photo album of what might have been that baby's life: This is how my baby would have looked trying to blow out the candle on its first birthday cake, or this is the baby waving from the school bus on the first day of elementary school. Maybe the year will come when I don't remember at all, and I don't know if that will be a good or a bad thing.

It doesn't help that Sugar Pie has fallen completely in love with Fernando's criminally adorable one-year-old granddaughter, she of the big black eyes on cinnamon skin and cascade of black ringlets. You can't go into Sugar Pie's room anymore and not find his granddaughter toddling around the space, pulling out dresser drawers or handing you *Pat the Bunny* to read to her again. If not for that clinic visit I could now be a mother to a baby who would be just a few months younger than Fernando's granddaughter.

I really do love babies. I love the way their heads of soft hair smell, I love the way they grab on to your fingers, I love when they laugh when you play peekaboo with them.

I especially love when they start screaming and you can return them to their mommies and then go out for a cappuccino—and if the mommies are like Nancy, they then hand off the crying baby to a nanny, to be returned only when baby is being cute again. But tonight I couldn't—or wouldn't—focus on the baby playing in Sugar Pie's room, playing cute for Sugar Pie, Alexei, Fernando, and her mommy, Fernando's daughter. Instead I chose to sit at the corner of the room, licking the cream from the sides of my Krispy Kreme doughnut and staring out the window into the night sky. I was reminded of last year, alone at night in that boarding school bed, fighting back insane food cravings and mood swings and annoying tears. I didn't realize actual tears were visible on my face until Sugar Pie asked, "Baby, are you alright?" Nothing gets by that woman.

"Allergies," I told her.

The beautiful café au lait skin on her face frowned slightly. "Mmm-hmm," she said.

"I don't know why you live here," I told her, kinda curt but wanting to change the subject. Sugar Pie has already corrected me that she lives in an assisted-living facility, not a nursing home, thank you very much, but whatever it is, it's still an institution that smells like a hospital infirmary situated in an ancient moldy Victorian haunted house, like the smell of Clorox and pee and mantelpieces that haven't been dusted in ages.

When I am an old person I hope that if I live in a home like Sugar Pie's that I will also have a premium satellite TV system. Or maybe Shrimp and I will be back together by then and when we look at each other, all gray hair and hunched bodies and wrinkled skin, we'll think, *Wow, you look as awesome as the day I first knew I loved you,* and not, *Whoa, what the hell happened to you?*

"Maybe I won't be here much longer," Sugar Pie said. For an old person, she looks damn good: Her face has some wrinkles that I like to think of as treasure maps to her past, but her skin has a rich, deep color, glowing now from the true love she waited a lifetime to come to her.

Now I was more depressed. Was Sugar Pie saying maybe she would die soon? No, that wasn't possible. She's in reasonably decent health except for the dialysis treatments she has three days a week because of her bad kidneys, and the only reason she moved into "assisted living" was because she doesn't have her own family to take care of her on the days she has dialysis. But on her nondialysis days she's pretty chipper—at least chipper enough to be carrying on a love connection with Fernando (hookup courtesy of *moi*; I know how to match two true loves), who is at least ten years (cough) her junior. Their May-December romance has lasted through the summer and into fall, and it's officially out of the closet, too—grandchildren jumping on the bed and an official dinner at a fancy restaurant with Sid and Nancy and everythang.

"Something you want to talk about?" Sugar Pie asked me.

"I can't talk to you with all these people around," I whined.

"Isn't somebody just a little self-absorbed?" Sugar Pie said. "If you haven't noticed, everyone else in this room is focused on the baby and the doughnuts and *Fantasy Island* on TV Land. You've got something to say, say it. Your moody-girl self is ruining my good time and all these nice people visiting."

I paused. "The first anniversary of . . . um . . . you know is coming up."

"And?" Sugar Pie said.

"And?" I repeated. "And I don't know. Just bumming me out is all."

Sugar Pie pointed to the TV bolted to the corner wall in her room, where the little guy called Tattoo was announcing, "Da plane, Boss, da plane!" Sugar Pie said, "Maybe what's bumming you out is there's a certain other little guy, one you've got to tell what happened. Because if you're wanting that boy you claim is your true love back in your life, you know that's what you've got to do."

"You're the psychic. Is it gonna go okay if I do?"

"No promises, baby. No promises."

"I'm worried," I whispered. Not about the fact of Shrimp knowing about the A-date so much as that for all the time we were going out before, I never mentioned this kinda important piece of information about what had happened to me soon before meeting him. Well, also: guys are just weird about that stuff.

Sugar Pie said, "It's a hurdle to get over, an important one, but not one that should come between you two in the end. This is when you have to remember that some people have no feet."

I looked down at my platform thong sandals, with toe-ringed, black-nail-polished feet. Say what? Call it my blond moment, but it took me a minute to realize what Sugar Pie was telling me: When life deals you lemons, don't make lemonade—get some perspective. BFD.

Chapter 11

The thing about the new peace is that it's actually harder than the old war. Trying to keep my cool with Nancy, now that she's chasing me with college applications (though I'm on record as not wanting to go) or waking me up in the mornings to ask if I want to go to yoga with her (where the Zen teacher man at her yoga studio has a slight boner under his shorts half the time—very distracting), is much harder than the old system. Before I had no hesitation to just scream, "Get out of my face!" and she had no hesitation to scream back, "AHHH!" and then slam a door in my face, after which we could both ignore each other and go about our days, business as usual. In the new regime we're both bound by an unspoken but implicit code to at least try.

So I can't be held accountable that she chose to push our boundaries on my sleep-in Sunday morning, post–Krispy Kreme sugar high and A-date blues low.

"Wake up, honey!" was all she said, very tender, in my ear. I felt her fingers running through my hair and massaging my scalp. But I was startled awake and I muttered, "Get away from me." I brushed her hand from my head, then banged my pillow back into a comfortable position, keeping my eyes closed so I could fall back asleep without the bright morning light waking me further.

She murmured, in that particular Nancy way of hers that grates most when my inner bitch is aching to be let loose, "Someone woke up on the wrong side of the bed this morning."

My eyes popped open to see her lemon face standing over me. "SOMEONE," I hissed, "HASN'T EVEN WOKEN UP YET. GOD, WHAT IS YOUR ANEURYSM? CAN'T YOU JUST LEAVE ME ALONE?"

She rolled her eyes and did the Nancy Classic: a shoulder shrug combined with an audible sigh that could register on the Richter scale. "Someone named Helen—interesting haircut—is waiting for you downstairs. Get up, Miss Teenage Mood Swings." My eyes fluttered back closed. "NOW!" Her shrill pronouncement was probably heard all the way over in Ocean Beach. This time she kicked the wood frame on my futon bed. So much for Nice Mommy Wakey.

My morning did not improve after I'd brushed my teeth and was heading downstairs still wearing my cowgirl flannel pj's, only to trip on a toy machine gun of Josh's lying on the hallway floor. Now I understood why toy guns supposedly promote violence in children: I was ready to kill Josh. "FUCK!" I screamed at the sharp shooting pain in my foot. Sid-dad emerged from my parents' bedroom, next to where I was standing. He was wearing his red silk smoking jacket, which I do appreciate for its supreme style, even if it was the wrong time of day and I've never seen him light a cigar before his evening martini. "Cupcake," Sid-dad said, and I admit, for a sec my mood started to improve, "I'm not appreciating the profane language on a Sunday morning, and I am especially not appreciating hearing you scream at your mother all the way from your bedroom. Show some goddamn respect. Got it?" I almost protested but my foot hurt like a mofo and I could tell from Sid-dad's face that he

wasn't gonna be hearing it. I nodded and mumbled, "Got it."
And then he slammed his bedroom door in my face!

Dag, what did *I* do?

So I was very on the warpath by the time I made it
downstairs to find Helen sitting in the living room with the
AUTUMN wench. This had to be seriously the worst Sunday
morning ever, like, if I had a Do Over card this would be the
morning I would choose to use it. I'd go back to sleep and
be awoken by the puppy Nancy won't let me get licking my
face, psycho Leila would be back in the kitchen making
blueberry pancakes, and Sid and Nancy and the little monsters would already be at the zoo or something. I would
have the whole house to myself to blast Iggy Pop and the
Beastie Boys and Japanese superpop like Puffy Ami Yumi,
and I would dance around the house wearing just my boy
brief undies and a tank top, like Tom Cruise in *Risky
Business,* but with a much better soundtrack.

"Phat crib you live in," Helen teased, sitting on the living room chair surrounded by gazillion-dollar artwork and
brocade tapestry formations up the wazoo.

"Don't give me shit about it," I spat back. This embarrassing House Beautiful is the reason I've yet to invite
Helen over—which of course begged the question, What
was she doing here, and daring to tote along the Autumn
wench, who was sitting next to Helen sporting that big-
tooth smile, radiating sunshine when all I could feel was
Sunday morning *el niño*?

Helen turned to Autumn. "Our CC is quite the gracious
hostess, too, as you can see. Phat crib and a lady to boot."
Helen kicked her bright Converse All Stars upward from her
sitting position, just for the hell of it. She and Autumn, both

dressed in thrift-store punk threads, did look funny sitting on that plush red sofa imported from France. For the first time I realized how I must appear in this house: total clash effect yet somehow belonging and cozy, too.

"So what's the deal?" I asked.

Helen pronounced, "We've decided to take you on an adventure for the day. Your mom already told us you're not doing anything today, and according to your dad—who has quite the sartorial flair for smoking jackets—you historically never even bother to fake doing homework on Sundays. So your mom said so long as you're home by eight, you can come with."

Hmm, which part to explain to Helen first: that I'd just as soon be in a bad mood all day since I'm already in one now and I don't need some cheerful girly adventure package to help that sitch, or that NO WAY am I hanging with the Autumn wench. She can just take her dreadlocked self outta this house and go off wherever, I don't care, but get outta my space. Also, what is *sartorial*?

To my silence, Helen added, "Your mom also said she got you a new espresso machine for your birthday, so I'm thinking you could start off our adventure of a day by pulling us a couple morning brews." Helen grabbed my hand and led me away from the living room, while Autumn remained seated.

When we reached the kitchen I told Helen, "Thanks for thinking of me, but I am not hanging out with that girl. I don't like her."

"How do you know? You didn't even talk to her at the party last night. She's, like, the coolest." Helen looked over the immaculate kitchen with the state-of-the-art appliances and the glass doors leading to an outdoor deck overlooking

San Francisco Bay. "Wow, this kitchen might be bigger than my whole house."

I pointed my index finger and shook my head at Helen, giving her the Don't Start with Me look. I said, "Autumn's also the girl who fooled around with Shrimp last summer."

"So what? I made out with him once in eighth grade. You oughta know better than anybody, that boy just has something about him. Shrimp is just like a delicacy that every girl should get to sample once in her lifetime, at least on some level. But I think all are agreed that you're the girl who's the permanent fixture in his life."

I'm a sucker; that last line did butter me up a little.

But geez Louise, I had no idea Shrimp was such a slut.

Helen must have sensed a softening of my resolve because she said, "Anyway that business with Shrimp and Autumn last summer, that was one night, and it was nothing! She doesn't even like boys that way, really. So just deal. You are better than that."

Now I was almost officially Parkay. I pulled the Hershey's milk from the Sub-Z fridge to make the Cyd Charisse Special, capps with foamed choc milk, and I turned on the espresso machine to get it primed. I said, "I'm not sure quite what you mean by that."

Helen found the Peet's Coffee in the freezer (as Java the Hut beans are banned in this household until Shrimp has lifted his embargo on me) and she handed the bag over to me. "It means," she said, "I think you are better than being some lame-ass chick who is threatened by other girls and thinks of them as rivals rather than friends. It means, I challenge you to make friends with Autumn."

Ash was sitting at the breakfast-nook table eating a

bowl of Cheerios and dipping a Barbie's head into the milk, then swirling the blond tresses around the bowl. "You said *lame-ass*!" Ash said. "Good one." Ash's eyes appraised Helen, starting from the star-spangled high-top Chucks on Helen's feet to Helen's red-and-blue plaid bell-bottom pants and up to her white T-shirt picturing curvaceous Lynda Carter in her patriotic but impractically skimpy Wonder Woman bathing suit uniform. Ash's appraisal ended at Helen's shaved head of black hair that had grown to about two centimeters. Ash said to Helen, "What are you?"

Helen's eyes squinted as she inspected the Barbie hair twirl. She said, "What do you think I am?"

Ash said, "I don't know, but it looks like there used to be a hand colored on your almost-bald head."

"Yeah, copper hand is hard to dye out, turns out. And I'm a Helen. CC's friend."

"Ha ha!" Ash laughed. She almost choked on her Cheerios.

Helen looked toward me, confused. I explained, "She's never seen an actual friend of mine that wasn't a boyfriend in this house before."

Ash got up from her chair and went over to Helen. It's cute; Ash and Helen both have the same body type—short and stocky, like round teddy bears. What wasn't so cute was that Ash then pinched Helen's pudgy stomach, as if she had to prove to herself that her sister had an actual in-the-flesh friend in the house. Ash promoted her voice to a scream for the benefit of our brother, Josh, playing a video game in the family room next to the kitchen. "JOSH! COME SEE! CYD CHARISSE HAS SOME PRACTICALLY BALD, PIERCED FRIEND HERE WHO'S A GIRL!"

Chapter 12

The sexual politics of the Shrimp crowd turn out to be quite complicated. If I were a private investigator creating a flowchart attempting to illustrate their love connections, my head might possibly explode.

Start with Shrimp and me. Broke up. There's me with the pseudo-crush on Wallace, and then there's Shrimp with the rebound one-night almost-stand with Autumn (as in no penetration—a minor technicality but an important one, as it allows me to at least consider Helen's challenge to become Autumn's friend). Now I've found out that Wallace used to date one of Helen's older sisters before settling down with Delia, who reportedly once had a dalliance with surfer dude Arran a.k.a. Aryan, who has a crush on Autumn—completely ignoring Helen's crush on him, because he's so shallow he doesn't even notice if a girl bigger than size six has it for him—while Autumn has the same kind of crush on Helen that I have on Wallace: totally benign and sweet and understood to have no basis in a reality hookup.

If I learned all that just on the bus over to Haight Street, I shuddered to think of all the sexual histories I would discover should Helen, Autumn, and I actually hang out longer than a day. By the time we hit Amoeba Records, I considered it a miracle the whole Ocean Beach crowd at Java the Hut isn't one mass STD invasion.

One of my favorite noises in the world is the rapid-fire sound of customers browsing CDs at Amoeba Records, a rhythmic sound throughout the huge used record shop that almost sounds like it comes from an automated machine: *clickclickclickclick*. Over this noise Autumn was explaining to me about her new vow of celibacy. She's not dating and she's not looking—she's just trying to have fun her senior year. Next year she'll get back in the game, when hopefully she'll be going to Cal, if she gets accepted, which she surely will because she's this brainiac who could be the poster girl for the dream candidate at the Berkeley Admissions Office: part African-American, part Vietnamese, part Irish and German, and a lesbian. But for now, Autumn says, she can't find a high school girl she's attracted to who will actually admit to being gay, and she's tired of hanging out with the surfer dudes because they're all, except for Shrimp and Wallace, basic sexist pigs who let her surf with them even though behind her back they snicker that chicks aren't strong enough to ride the harsh Ocean Beach current. And the reason they let her surf their waves with them is the remote fantasy that said permission will somehow allow them later access to some girl-girl action. Boys truly are idiots.

Helen was trading in some CDs in another part of the store so I asked Autumn, "But what about Helen? Why don't you date her?"

"She claims not to have decided but I am here to tell you—she's not gay. She might be bi a little, but I'm pretty sure her very few girl-kissing adventures have been mostly for the benefit of making her mother crazy. I mean, have you seen Helen with the Irish soccer guys?" We looked up to see Helen flirting with the sales guy at the trade-in counter, their heads both tipped back in laughter because something about the Patti Smith CD was either hysterical or sexy. Even on Haight Street, where grunge Gen Xers + hippie throwbacks + homeless punk kids + yuppie chic = a street with great stores and a lot of scary attitude, Helen could make friends. Maybe that's just Helen—she's one of those rare people like Shrimp who just knows everybody, talks to everybody, likes everybody: a natural extrovert.

"You can't be completely gay," I said. "What about Shrimp?"

There is something about Autumn, how she looks you straight in the eyes, how she projects this natural warmth, that I couldn't doubt the sincerity of her answer. "Shrimp was this one-time thing. Like, I needed to be sure about my sexual preference, and he was just this very safe person to experiment with. And he was feeling kind of sad and confused and . . ."—her hand touched mine over a Smiths CD import—". . . I really am sorry it happened if it's hurt you so much."

Autumn does make it difficult to dislike her. It's a very annoying trait.

I shrugged off her hand but said, "Don't worry about it." I may, in fact, even have meant it.

Helen popped up next to us. "Guess who's over in the jazz section? Aryan! And guess what section he's flipping through? ACID JAZZ! He needs to be brutalized for that. C'mon." Her wide pink face glowed as she stared into the next room. We lingered at the entrance to the other room long enough to see Aryan finger a Kenny G CD. This was just too much, and we all three started laughing so hard we nearly doubled over. We laughed so hard people around us started laughing too, for no reason other than how hard we were laughing. Not that the situation was *that* funny, but somehow our mutual giggles fed and built off each others', the fact of our laughter becoming funnier than the joke, until all three of us collapsed in hysterics on the hardwood floor.

I had probably met Aryan before Shrimp's party when I was working at Java the Hut, if he's part of that whole crowd, but I didn't remember him—after a while all those beautiful surfer guys, with their amazing bodies, identical vocab, and substandard intelligence (but who cares, see Amazing Bodies, above) kind of meld into one, except for one-of-a-kind Shrimp. Usually if you remember one surfer dude you're really just remembering their collective unit. But now Aryan surely stood out of the crowd. He looked up at all the noise and, seeing us, his sun-kissed face went totally pale and you could almost see his mop of curly blond hair turning into fried frizz.

"Hey, Aryan," Helen called over to him from the floor. "I think I see the Yanni CD you dropped on the floor. It's just to the left of your Vans, like next to the Mannheim Steamroller vinyl LP."

I have no idea what a Mannheim Steamroller is, but just the sound of the name was enough to send Helen, Autumn, and me into a deeper round of laughter. We were now laughing so hard tears streamed from our eyes.

Aryan stomped over to where we were lounging on the floor. His eyes were mad but that didn't stop him from checking out the rear-end view of Autumn's denim miniskirt flailing on the floor from our hysterics. Up close and in daylight, I could see that Helen's nickname for him was just right. He was tall, lean, and perfectly proportioned, blond-haired and blue-eyed, but with a determined jut to his walk, like you could see him in a uniform saying *"Heil!"* but his uniform would be a skateboarding one and his *"Heil!"* would be pledging loyalty to some Left Coast leftie-crazy like Jerry Brown.

"Dude," he said to us, straight-faced and clearly not sharing our humor in the situation. "That's so funny I can't stop laughing." He stomped over to Nirvana, I guess trying to salvage his cool.

"Uh-oh," Helen said. "I better go over there and make it up to him. Should I let him use my trade-in credit?"

Autumn and I both shook our heads. "Just be nice," I told Helen. "You don't need to make it up that much. Don't waste a fifty buck trade-in on a crush."

Autumn nodded in agreement. She said, "Kenny G? C'mon, he had it coming. But I can't just stand by and watch you try to make it up to him, cuz I know he'll take advantage of the situation and pretty soon you'll have agreed to take his latest bimbette to get a fake ID. How 'bout CC and I go to the Goodwill store and then meet you at the crepes place in half an hour?"

Helen said, "Yeah," but she was already on her way over to console Aryan, like she'd practically forgotten us.

The weird thing is, I had no objection to Autumn's plan. Okay, I admit it. I like the Autumn wench. Get over it.

Later, when we were sitting at the crepes place and Autumn and Helen were sharing a crepe with heaping veggies and cheeses while I had opted for a plain Nutella crepe, I interrupted their chatter.

"Tell me about Shrimp?" I asked, feeling like my heart was going to combust for wanting to know about him, to hear about him from friends who'd known him much longer than I.

There was a time when being as wild as I wanna be meant popping E numbers with Justin and not bothering to use a condom when we fooled around, or staying over at Shrimp's and not caring if my parents noticed at all. But asking this question of these girls—and finding out its answer—felt much, much wilder and riskier.

Chapter 13

I was sitting in my room quietly on Sunday night, actually doing homework, when I felt this *presence* behind me. I took off my headphones and spun around from my desk to see my mother standing just inside my door, her eyebrows creased, mouth half open, like she couldn't decide whether or not to say whatever she had to say.

"What?" I asked. Her look indicated I was going to get grief for something I did, or she was going to take another stab at lobbying for us to take a weekend away to look at colleges, or worst of all, shouldn't I consider some decoupage in my room?

Nancy hesitated, and then, as if deciding only at that very moment to go through with what she had to say, replied, "What's the 'status' between you and Shrimp?" She actually used the finger quotes for *status*.

God, what is her problem? Why does she want to know everything about me?

"Our 'status,'" I answered, also using the finger quotes, "is we're 'just friends'"—again with the finger quotes. "Are you happy?" Nancy is the one who, for all her taking me to the gyno and seeming to have come around at least to the idea of Shrimp, is also the person who grounded me last summer so I couldn't see him. Sometimes in the new peace I can appreciate my mom in a new way and I know I can trust her, and sometimes old wounds die hard and I can forgive but never forget. And the Shrimp subject is still the most vulnerable one in our fragile peace.

Nancy snapped, "What does that mean, Am I happy? I think I've made it *quite* clear that I am amenable to the two of you having a relationship again, hopefully one that could be less headstrong, maybe a little slower and more cautious. What do you think, that I actually want you to be unhappy?"

"I don't know. Do you?"

She sighed in frustration. "Are you *trying* to make me crazy? I wanted to do you a favor, reach out to Shrimp, and you just . . ."

"What favor?" Whatever her scheme is, it can only be bad, bad, bad.

"I'm organizing a charity art auction for the children's hospital. I thought I would commission Shrimp to create a piece." Charity galas in Nancy's crowd mean an opportunity for rich people to compete for who can look the most anorexic in outfits and jewelry that cost more than it would take to settle a homeless family in an apartment for a year, all under the guise of being "for the kids."

"He won't do it," I informed her. Shrimp's way too cool for that bullshit scene.

"How do you know?"

"I just know."

"Well, Miss Know It All, then why is he downstairs right now in the study with Dad talking about the supplies he'll need and . . ."

"Nuh-uh!" I threw frickin *Moby Dick* onto my bed and rushed downstairs while Nancy trailed behind me blabbing something about, "When I called I didn't think he'd come over this minute."

And for real, Shrimp was sitting at Sid-dad's antique mahogany desk, his dirty blond hair pulled up into a tight ponytail on top of his head, a hairstyle that made him look like a mini sumo wrestler. He was wearing a Hawaiian shirt buttoned to the top with a proper necktie hanging from the collar, and board shorts. Fashion icon—NOT. So hot—YES.

He looked up at me. "Hey."

Oh, no, not with the *hey*s again.

Sid-dad said, "May I get you a drink, young man?"

"I make the perfect martini," I pointed out. I do. Sid-dad taught me to make them when I was little, and he still pays me a dollar every time I make him one.

Sid-dad patted my shoulder. "That's a good one, Cyd Charisse."

"I'm going by 'CC' now," I corrected him.

Sid-dad nodded seriously. "I'm so sorry, CC. How about I get some Cokes from the fridge? Your mother's culinary skills are expanding and I think she's gone to heat some Trader Joe's vegetarian dumplings in the microwave. Maybe soon she'll graduate to full-fledged stove use." He chuckled as he walked out of the study, but he turned back once, shot a last glance at Shrimp, and I'm fairly sure I heard him mutter under his breath, "Odd duck."

I hadn't seen Shrimp since the Just Friends incident at the party at his house, but I had learned a lot about him in the meantime from Helen and Autumn. I almost felt deceitful, going behind his back to get to know him, but isn't that what girls who are friends are supposed to do—talk about love interests, analyze, dish? If so I am right on track with this chick friendship thing.

I know some interesting things about Shrimp and his

fam now. For instance, I learned that Iris had another family before Billy, Wallace, and Shrimp. She was like some bored housewife in Florida, married to a cop, and she had a ten-year-old daughter. Then she met Billy, who had sold her some weed, and she left her husband and kid to start another life with Billy. Just up and left, and then was asked to never return, apparently. So there is some motherless older sister of Shrimp and Wallace's wandering around somewhere, probably the same age as lisBETH—go figure. But the whole past, I guess, and the fact that Iris and Billy dumped Shrimp on Wallace's doorstep so they could cavort around in Papua New Guinea supposedly teaching English and building bridges or whatever, has left Shrimp with some serious abandonment issues. I am not the first girlfriend he's broken up with before she could break up with him.

I *am* the only one who is his true love and who will stay by his side and in his heart for as long as he'll let me—provided he ever lets me back in.

But yuck, I couldn't forget that crush-on-my-mom comment. I get goose pimples of disgust on my arms just thinking about it. Then again, maybe that's what he gets whenever he thinks of me having a crush on his bro, but maybe his goose pimples are from genuine jealousy and not disgust, because let's be real, Wallace and me are a hookup that actually could happen, though never would.

I stood over Shrimp on the other side of the desk where he was sitting, sketching with charcoal. "Are you doing this to get back at me?" I whispered.

He looked up, his deep blue eyes blazing back into mine. "No," he said. "I'm doing this to get *to* you." His head cocked back down and he returned to his sketching.

Hmph, that was a nice thing to say. I think.

"Also," he added, "my parents are driving me crazy at the house. I came over here almost as soon as your mother called."

Ahhhh, my head is just swirling in confusion about where Shrimp and I are. But then I thought, *Why not just run with this moment and learn a little more about Shrimp?*

I sat down on the leather sofa next to the desk. "I still haven't heard how Papua New Guinea was."

Shrimp didn't look up from his sketching, but he did start talking. "PNG was awesome. It's a really beautiful place, but sad and strange, too. There's a lot of poverty and there's also a problem of corporations doing toxic dumping there because the government is sort of nonexistent. It's, like, as beautiful a place as it is depressing. Fiji had to be my favorite of all the places we visited. I could live and surf in that paradise forever. And the people are so nice, you can't believe it."

"How come your parents decided to come home?"

Shrimp looked up to the door, scanning to see if Sid and Nancy had returned to the room, I suppose. "My dad has a little habit of getting kicked out of various places once his talent for growing and selling weed is discovered. I love the guy, but it's just kinda . . . skeevy, y'know?" This struck me as a strange comment coming from Shrimp, whom I've always perceived as being the most nonjudgmental person ever. Shrimp looked around the meticulous room with the antiques and ceiling-high shelves filled with books. "You always used to complain about your parents, but I think you're so lucky. They're, like, solid, you know?"

I nodded. I actually do know.

"So how was New York?" Shrimp asked. "What was your bio-dad like?"

"Disappointment."

"I kinda figured he would be."

"But my brother, Danny, he's so great. I really want you to meet him. And New York! You HAVE to go . . ."

The little monsters barged into the room, screaming "Shrimp! Shrimp!" They both ran over to him. Ash took up residence on his left knee, while Josh kept a manly distance but he had on the idolize face as he gazed at Shrimp. Sid and Nancy followed behind, carrying drinks and steaming dumplings on a tray.

Clearly the new peace has gone haywire. It will never last.

Chapter 14

Shrimp has taken an artist's residency on the deck outside the kitchen at our house. It's a beautiful deck, perched high on the steep Pacific Heights hill on which our house sits, looking down to San Francisco Bay, Alcatraz, and Tiburon, with a great view of the thick strings of fog that roll through the Golden Gate at dusk. Shrimp's got an easel, paints, brushes, and tarps set up on the deck. He's arranged his working space in the back corner where the view is most choice, but in a position so no one can see what he is painting. Strangely when he is gone, none of us peek under the tarps to see the painting, and we are the family always searching for secret hiding spots to sneak peeks at birthday presents. It's like we have an unspoken pact to respect Shrimp's process, and we all want to be surprised at the end when we see the completed product.

If he's painting some oil pastel of yachts sailing into Sausalito, I will seriously lose all respect for him. My respect for him is already in jeopardy because in the weeks since Nancy first commissioned him to do a painting, Shrimp has become almost a fixture in our house. If Nancy brings him one more lemonade out there I don't know what I'll do. It's really making me sick—worse yet, she thinks Country Time is real lemonade. Shrimp worked so late one night that Sid and Nancy let him spend the night on the couch in the study, and their invitation was all low-key and under the radar, too. No drama, no long discussions first, just "Oh, Shrimp, you're still here and it's so late. You've been working so long and your eyes look very tired, why don't you just crash on the couch." !!!!!!!!!!!!! And Shrimp made no attempt to sneak into my room to fool around, though I spent the night sleepless in my room, nearly getting repetitive stress syndrome in my hand from taking care of the business that I wished Shrimp was taking care of for me.

He's actually serious about this "just friends" business. Even Sid and Nancy have bought into the program, and believe me, they are loving it. They get the benefit of saying "Look how we've taken in Shrimp" with none of the disadvantages of worrying about the Little Hellion getting her groove on.

The upside is the anticipation. I am confident that ultimately Shrimp and I will be together again, and I am treating this "just friends" business as an opportunity to become just that—Shrimp's friend, so dragging out the ultimate reconciliation is like extended mental foreplay that will make it just that much more delicious when it happens.

"Hey, pal," I said to Shrimp. I had come home from the restaurant job to find Shrimp out on the deck, painting. His head was thrashing in time to the opera music wafting down from the open window in Sid and Nancy's bedroom upstairs over the deck. Ash and Josh were playing on the deck quietly alongside him, if you can believe that, Ash with her Barbies and Josh on his Game Boy. Having Shrimp and his mellow vibe permeating our house is like having Paxil dosed through the central heating ducts. "Dad wants to know if you're staying for dinner."

"Who's cooking?" Shrimp asked. The Artist has become enough of a fixture to know that if Nancy is "cooking"—she put frozen tater tots into beef stew last week—it's wise to pass, but if I've come home with entrées from the restaurant, or if Sid-dad is firing up the grill, it's worth staying.

"Dad. Steak."

"Staying!" Shrimp said.

The night before, Iris invited me over to The Shrimps' for dinner. She made tofu lasagna. I don't know if the food was bad or it was just the tension in the house—Iris is trying to take over Wallace and Delia's wedding plans, she's constantly faxing menu ideas over to them at Java the Hut during business hours, or she's chewing out their wedding planner for recommending a reception room at a posh hotel that doesn't have a signed union labor agreement in place with its hotel staff—but I found myself sneaking away from their dinner table to call Sid-dad from my cell phone. I figured Shrimp's family needed a moment of privacy anyway. Iris had looked across the table at Shrimp and said, "Your complexion is awfully rosy." Then she sniffed and declared, "You've been eating meat!" And then Billy, who rarely has anything to say because Iris is always there to say it for him, remembered he had a backbone and mumbled, "So what?" Billy's protest was followed by Shrimp and Wallace, who both snickered, "Yeah, so what?" Yikes! I excused myself from the table, my stomach grumbling hard, and ran to the roof upstairs to call Sid-dad to make him promise to grill steak for dinner the next night. All the carrying on between The Shrimps' over the ethics of eating meat and whose business was it anyway, shouldn't it be about personal choice, had made me crave a New York strip something bad.

I'm not so sure Iris and Billy coming home was such a good thing. Wallace and Shrimp seemed happier before, without them. Like, they've been fine on their own, and it's too late now for Iris and Billy to be going all parental on them. To say nothing of the fact that Iris and Billy are basically guests. Wallace bought and owns their house, Wallace is the one who built a coffee business from nothing with no help from them, Wallace is the one paying the bills. I can understand why Wallace isn't taking kindly to Iris going all mother-of-the-groom and trying to dictate how to plan his wedding.

Snooty old Pacific Heights never looked so good, may I just say.

Somehow my house has become a sanctuary. I don't know if it's the new peace or Fernando living here because he's like our family and Leila never was, but this peace is starting to seem sustainable. I am trying to figure out what makes a marriage work when I look at Sid and Nancy. They are the oddest-looking couple—short, old, nebbishy bald guy with tall, young, blond glam wife—yet they work, much better than Iris and Billy; I don't understand why. In the twelve years since Nancy married Sid, I have watched them grow from awkward and polite mates—almost like strangers—to now, I wouldn't say there is great passion between them, but they're content, like they're a team or something. Even when they're bickering—and the peace dividend seems to have resulted in them bickering less (what's that about?)—you know with them that they've got each other's backs.

I really still hope they're not having sex anymore.

The peace is feeling so nice, and having Shrimp around

strange but great, that the A-date anniversary has come and gone and I still haven't told Shrimp. I've told Helen and Autumn, but I didn't know whether he would react as they had—supportive but indifferent too, like it was important that I told them, but what happened was in the past and I had to move on.

Of course Shrimp would take it the same way. I just had to get it over with, tell him so we could move forward, past "just friends" and into true loves—without secrets. Watching Shrimp paint and mock sing the aria coming from Sid and Nancy's bedroom on the second floor over the deck, I knew there would never be a right time, which left only now or never.

I told Ash and Josh, "Mom says it's okay for you guys to watch TV in the family room until she gets home from yoga." They looked up at me, disinterested. Ash said, "No fucking way," and head-banged Barbie into Ken. Josh grinned at me and said, "Nuh-uh." I said, "Go watch TV, and I promise to read to you at bedtime?" Josh said, "Harry Potter?" and I rolled my eyes and said, "Yes," dreading another round of that. But Josh still shook his head at me and pronounced, "Nope." I was left with no choice but to exercise my Big Sister prerogative. "SCRAM!" I yelled, and they were outta there.

I sat down opposite Shrimp. "There's something I have to tell you," I said.

He continued on with his painting. "I'm listening."

How do you start a conversation like this? I didn't know how so I just jumped in, like when Shrimp and I used to go down to Santa Cruz last spring and he would wade slowly into the surf wearing a full-body wet suit but I

106 ✳ Rachel Cohn

would ignore the icy water and just dive right in wearing only a bikini, not even bothering to get my feet wet first, wanting to get over that initial freeze quick. "You probably don't even care about this and all, but, um, there's just something I thought I should tell you. Last year at this time I had an abortion. It was right before I got kicked out of boarding school." Phew—there, I said it. Now we could move on.

Shrimp's hand stopped painting and he didn't look up at me. "Justin?" he mumbled, which REALLY pissed me off.

"Of course Justin!" I spewed, loud. For some reason I have a reputation as a wild child, but the truth is, I have only been with two guys in the biblical sense: Justin and Shrimp. "The same Justin who couldn't be bothered to help and who left me to go to the clinic by myself. What the fuck do you think, by some random stranger?"

Shrimp shrugged, still not meeting my eyes. His silence spoke volumes.

I felt my face turning hot with shame and sadness—but shame and sadness for Shrimp, not for myself, because apparently he was not the cool guy I thought he was, one who could deal with a girl with a past.

Shrimp got up from his chair, placed the tarp over the easel stand, and walked inside the house. Just like that he left, without saying good-bye or *We'll talk about this later.*

If our house has become a sanctuary, suddenly I wanted to be back in Alcatraz, alone in my room, locked up. I raced upstairs but stopped cold when I was passing by Sid and Nancy's bedroom. Sid-dad was slumped at the open bedroom window, with the view out over the deck and back garden. When he looked at me standing at the doorway, I saw his eyes were wet and his face splotchy, and I knew.

"You heard," I said, looking past him to the open window. I should have paid more attention to the decibel level of my voice when Shrimp's head had stopped thrashing in time to the opera music that had been wafting from the bedroom window down to the deck below after the music had been turned off.

Sid-dad nodded.

I thought my worst fear was Shrimp finding out my secret, but now I realized it was my dad finding out. I stood at the doorway, paralyzed, not knowing what to do or say.

"Cupcake," Sid-dad said, and I felt flush with relief, because even if he knew he still loved me to call me by that name, right? "Come in here, please." I went inside the bedroom and he gestured for me to sit on the ottoman by the window.

I assumed he wanted to talk about it, whether to lecture or scream or I don't know what, but instead he burst out crying, which hurt my insides more than that painful procedure ever had. The only times I've seen him cry before, aside from when he gets misty-eyed talking about that Boston Red Sox first base player who let the ground ball slip through his legs and lost the team the World Series, have been when Josh and Ash were born, and when Leonardo DiCaprio drowned in *Titanic.* Sid-dad made no effort to compose himself either as he sputtered, "All I ever wanted was to protect you, for you to have a good life, and now, to know you went through that, let yourself get into that situation." His tears caught up with him in the form of anger. "ARE YOU JUST STUPID TO GET INTO THAT KIND OF TROUBLE?"

"I was," I whispered. Words came furiously from my mouth, like they needed to work double time to make this up to him. "I know. I'm so sorry, Dad. So sorry. It'll never happen again; I'll never not take precautions again. Please don't hate me, please don't be mad at me. It was over a year ago!" I was blubbering uselessly. I could see in his face that I will have to live with this disappointment he sees in me for the rest of my life. I can't change it.

But seeing the emotion on his face, I felt a crossing-over moment too. Since Nancy married him I've basically considered Sid-dad to be my father. He's the only one I've ever known. I've always loved him—what's not to love?—but part of me has held back a little too, distancing him a few degrees in my mind for being my stepfather and adopted father, not my natural father. Since the summer with Frank, I understood, but now I truly got it, indisputably: Sid-dad *is* my father. The best Frank ever felt for me was just wanting to be assured that I was okay. Sid-dad grieves for me, feels for me, hopes for me.

"Of course I don't hate you. Don't be ridiculous. I'm your father—I'll always love you, that never changes. But I'm not so happy with you right now. I know it happened over a year ago, but to find out like this, to know you've gone through this and kept it inside all this time. You've been to the gynecologist since?" he asked. "Been checked out?"

"Yeah," I said, without thinking, "Mom took me after she found out . . ."

The expression on his face turned from anger to something entirely different, something I could only explain as being a look that one married person has for another when one finds out the other has withheld a crucial piece of information about the family.

Alcatraz is an especially wise escape destination right now. I'll just dollnap Gingerbread back from Ash's room and have her join me, for old time's sake.

Chapter 15

Alexei is less a Horrible and maybe just more of a Poor Sucker. His semester off from school is a complete bust. The "assistant manager" at the swank new restaurant in The City has been reduced to sitting next to the Little Hellion, folding napkins and changing lunch menus to dinner menus in the quiet late afternoons after the business lunch crowd rush.

Alexei's upside is I'm fairly sure he's getting some play from Lord Empress Kari. On more than one occasion I have caught him coming out of her office looking disheveled, tucking in his shirt, giving me a typical Alexei glare, indicating I can just keep my mouth shut about whatever is or isn't going on in that office. I can't imagine how a little booty from that horror chick is worth a semester away from his precious college, but who am I to criticize in the love department? I'm not exactly a relationship expert, seeing as how I couldn't even major in "just friends" these days, even if I wanted to.

"Cyd Charisse, you're doing a great job folding those napkins!" Kari chirped at me as she whizzed past the round table where I was sitting with Alexei.

"Thanks!" I said back in my most chipper voice, but Kari didn't hear the sarcasm. She winked her lazy eye at me. "She's a superstar!" Kari sang before stomping to the kitchen to yell at the sous chef for not picking up enough mahi mahi at the early-morning fish market. Even Alexei, sitting next to me, groaned.

The restaurant employs several hostesses across different shifts. I'm the youngest hostess, I work the fewest hours of all on a two-day-a-week schedule, and I work the 2:00 to 5:00 shift, which has to be the restaurant's least busy, least stressful time of the business day. Yet I'm the only hostess whom Kari specifically praises for her napkin-folding skills or for doing such a *fantastic* job seating table 7. Yeah, like pressing creases into a piece of linen or leading a group of people to a table, handing them a menu, and offering a fake smile is so challenging. On the plus side, the sucking up does allow me a certain privilege other hostesses might not get, although none besides me want it: I get to stay extra hours in the kitchen with the sous chefs if I want, chopping veggies, learning how to sauté, watching how soup stock is made.

"Does Kari actually think that all her sucking up to me gets reported back to Dad?" I asked Alexei. "Because I specifically don't talk about this job to him, and if I did, I specifically would not be singing Kari's praises."

If I did talk to Sid-dad about the restaurant, I might tell him that it's Alexei, not Kari, who makes sure the wait-staff shares its tips with the busboys and dishwashers. It's Alexei who wooed the restaurant's new sommelier from a competing restaurant, Alexei who must have grunted through a marathon of miles talking to the wine expert about their shared appreciation of Sonoma chardonnays and the Detroit Red Wings over the treadmills at their mutual gym. Kari may have ultimately been responsible for hiring the wine expert whose great reputation is bringing in a ton of new clientele, but she's not the person who had the "right contacts" to bring the sommelier over in the first place, as she claims.

I am not talking to Sid-dad about the restaurant because my work-study semester is a big fat waste of time, in my opinion. (But if I did, I would be sure to throw in the word *sommelier,* because it does sound impressive. If the SAT had word associations like *Chocolate is to lovemaking as sommelier is to* _____, I would kick ass on that nonsense test.) Hanging out in the kitchen can be fun, but mostly it's just a diversionary tactic to smell yummy ingredients and not think about the Shrimp situation. I don't belong in a place like this. I don't care about fusion cuisine. I could give less of a fuck about an establishment that is considered "hot." I hate changing into a conservative skirt, white blouse, and pumps when I start my shift after school; the uniform is suffocating. I loathe customers who order beet-and-goat cheese salad, pork tenderloin, and apple tartlet, only to barf their meals back up in the ladies' room after, and I know this because volunteering to perform the hourly TP check in the bathroom has resulted in more than a few unpleasant discoveries of spew chunks on toilet seats. What is wrong with people? Customers out at Java the Hut aren't like that. Of course Java the Hut is a completely different crowd in a completely different type of establishment in a completely different nabe—it's like comparing apples to oranges, but maybe I am an Orange in a restaurant of Apples and I can't help but wish to be among my own kind.

Not that JtH is an establishment I will be frequenting anytime soon. In the week since telling Shrimp about the A-date we've barely acknowledged each other at school and the tarp on his unfinished painting on the deck at home has gone untouched. Sid-dad isn't around for me to ask for a job switch, anyway. He left almost right away on a business trip to the East Coast after our talk in his bedroom, when I let it slip about Nancy knowing about my . . . um . . . issues but not telling him.

The peace temperature in our house has experienced a sudden climate change to: burr-ito (to borrow the favored expression of our not-Just Friend right now, Shrimp).

Alexei set down a tray of empty glass candleholders needing fresh candles for us to prepare for the dinnertime tables. He said, "I don't know what Kari thinks, but the sucking up *is* a little extreme. You know what though, kid?" *Kid?* "Fernando was right. You do have a decent work ethic, I'm gonna give you some credit. I thought you would be completely useless and a drain here, but you pull your own weight, for a skinny princess."

"Thank you so much, Alexei. I can't express to you what a relief I feel knowing my work ethic meets your standards." I scrunched up a folded napkin and threw it in his face. He laughed.

"Alexei," I said. "What is the deal with guys and their whole Madonna/whore complex?"

"WHAT?" Alexei said, his face turning that tomato color his Eastern European genes exhibit so well.

"Like, why are guys so into getting a girl to fool around, but once the girl does, then they hold it against her? What is that about? I mean, you have a past—everyone knows the scandal about your first girlfriend in high school being your trig tutor who was way older than you, but do your girlfriends since hold it against you?"

Alexei said, "I don't even know how to respond to all this. Where did this come from?"

"I'd just like some answers is all. And you're the closest heterosexual male that I know who may be able to explain this to me. So?"

Alexei's shrug acknowledged the truth of the question. "Guys are like that. I have no idea why. Any girl a guy dates seriously, he's going to want to think she hasn't been around."

"Are you like that? If, say—hypothetically, of course— you were dating someone like Kari and you found out she had, let's just say some indiscretions in her past, would you then lose interest in her?"

Why am I so stupid? I had a very important question and Alexei was actually a person who might be able to give a reasonable explanation of the Madonna/whore male psychology in his faux intellectual way that might have made sense, but I ruined it by using Kari as an example.

Alexei threw the napkin back at me. "I don't know what you're talking about," he said. He got up from the table to go into the kitchen.

I heard the crash of a tray of water glasses falling to the floor and looked up to see Nancy swishing her bony hips past a busboy, whose mouth was agape at the vision of the tall blonde in the short, soft pink Chanel suit. She didn't turn her back to see the commotion she'd caused; she just continued walking over to my table.

"I thought I would pick you up from work and take you out to dinner," she said. "The baby-sitter can stay late with the kids and make them dinner tonight."

Oh, joy, the mother-daughter combo, with the menfolk

who aren't speaking to them, experiencing a night on the town.

"Nah," I groaned. Nancy would probably want to stay at the restaurant for dinner, just to relish Kari's ass-kissing.

"You can choose the place," Nancy offered.

Well, that was an entirely different matter. "Can we go to Zachary's Pizza in Oakland?" My mouth watered at the thought of tasting the Chicago-style spinach-and-mushroom-stuffed pizza with the wicked stewed tomatoes, oozing with cheese.

I wonder if something is wrong with me. All I ever think about is food or sex.

"No," Nancy replied.

"But you just said . . ."

"I'm not driving across the Bay Bridge at rush hour. It'll take us longer to get there than it will to eat there. And I'm not eating Zachary's pizza. I just fit back into this outfit today. Why don't we stay here? The sushi is good."

You can't just throw a dog a bone like that and take it away, so I wasn't willing to compromise. I hadn't asked for this favor. "No way."

Nancy tried again. "Green's?"

The offer was an interesting power play on her part, as she had suggested only my fave special-occasion restaurant that sits on a dock looking out on the Golden Gate Bridge and Alcatraz, with succulent produce from the Zen Buddhist organic farm in Marin County that's used for an all-vegetarian menu of food that's to die for. Literally. If I were on death row I would want my last meal from Green's, and no one is a bigger carnivore than me. But I still hesitated, so Nancy threw in one more bone, in the form of a set of car keys she tossed me from her handbag. "You can drive," she said.

Oh. My. God. Nancy just wanted my company.

I caught the keys. "I'm there." I've got a learner's permit now, but between school and jobs I haven't had time to practice driving, and Fernando is not exactly volunteering to be the adult in the car when I try to maneuver a large vehicle up the steep streets of Pacific Heights—or scarier still, down the streets. I seem to have issues with how hard to hit the brakes on the downward slopes, and Fernando said there is only so much Excedrin for migraines medication he can take.

After I changed back into my regular clothes I met Nancy at the reception area. As we walked outside where the valet was waiting with her Mercedes SUV, I informed her, "Iris says that SUVs are the cause of oil wars, and that SUVs are a wasteful nation's global disease, polluting the environment. Iris says that driving an SUV is practically being an accessory to terrorism. Iris says . . ."

Nancy cut me off. "Good for Iris," she said, and hopped into the passenger's side.

Chapter 16

I don't think my driving skills are that bad, but Nancy's face was ashen by the time we reached Green's. She ordered a red wine before the hostess could even hand us our menus.

Once I'd checked out the menu I asked Nancy, "So what is the deal with Dad?" I placed Gingerbread on the table, against the fogged-in window.

"You're kidding me with that," Nancy said, avoiding my question and pointing at Gingerbread, who is used to Nancy's abuse so I didn't have to worry about Gingerbread getting in a snit about being pointed at. "I thought you retired Gingerbread."

"Dolls are like old people, Mother. They're not just cute props. They need to be aired out every now and again."

"If you're trying to get me to let you take the car with Sugar Pie as your designated adult passenger, the answer is no."

Damn.

"Are you and Dad fighting?"

"We're fine."

"You don't sound fine," I said. "I heard you yelling at each other from your bedroom before he left for New York. I'm sorry if it's my fault."

"Cyd Charisse . . ." Now I pointed at Nancy, to remind her of my name correction. ". . . Oh, for God's sake, *CC*.

What goes on between Dad and me isn't for you to worry about. He was a little mad and I understand why. . . ."

"Why?"

Exasperated, Nancy said, "This is really a matter between two married people, not for mother and child to discuss."

"I'm not a child," I reminded her.

She took my statement as an excuse to change the topic. "I agree. That's why I thought we should have some time alone tonight to talk about your future. You can't dodge the college talk forever. It's late October already and application deadlines are coming up fast. What are you thinking you want to do? I've left several college brochures in your room, and I've noticed you've tossed them all in the recycling bin. Your academic record may be a little weak, but there are plenty of schools that will accept you, schools I think you might even like. You're not a dumb girl, despite what your rocky transcript might suggest."

"I know, but thanks for the backhanded compliment anyway." Why do adults think every girl who isn't some overachieving nitwit needs to be reassured about her intelligence? Folks, my self-esteem is just fine, thanks. I may not be school smart, and I might do extremely stupid things sometimes, but I know I'm smart. And I'd give me serious Vegas odds to kick the ass of Sarah Scholar at life-skills mortal combat any day.

"I didn't mean it like that and you know it. You're going to have to do something next year after you graduate. What's it going to be?"

Why do I have to DO something? What's wrong with no plan, with no college? I don't intend to be some trust-fund rich girl who lives off Dad's (or in my case, Dads') bank accounts. I plan on making my own way. I just haven't figured out what way yet. But if I wanted to do nothing for a while, what's so wrong with that? It's not like I am applying for citizenship to live in the Nation of Slackeronia.

I don't see me at college, and I don't see the crime in that. I wouldn't mind owning a café or something one day—but later, after I've had time to figure out all that self-discovery bullshit your late teens are supposed to be all about. Anyway, the best future I've ever seriously considered was simply being Shrimp's girlfriend, and that prospect is looking pretty dead right now.

I decided to change the subject back to what I wanted to talk about. "Why was Dad so mad? It's not like you were keeping a secret from him. I asked you not to tell him."

The waiter came for our orders. Nancy said he might as well bring along a whole bottle of wine, because one glass clearly wasn't going to cut it this evening.

Nancy finished her first glass of wine in one long gulp. "If you really must know, the issue is deeper than just me not telling him. He's angry that I kept your confidence when he feels that as your father, it was his right to know. But the reason he suddenly had to leave to close a deal in New York, one that he could have negotiated perfectly well from his office in San Francisco, is the situation brought back the fights we used to have over whether to send you to boarding school. He had thought boarding school was a bad idea from the get-go."

"Why did you do that anyway?" I asked. I took a sip from her second glass of wine. It was a nice cabernet, but frankly a white wine would have been a better match with the meal she had ordered. "Because I hated that place and I never understood what I did so wrong to make you send me there."

"You didn't do anything wrong to be sent there. What would make you say that? Do you really think that? I wanted you to have the best education possible, to meet the right people. I wanted you to have the luxuries I never had."

She looked hurt so I didn't point out, *You wanted me there because having the Little Hellion gone made it easier for you.* The whole situation was very Baroness in *The Sound of Music,* who had wanted to send the Von Trapp children away so she could have Christopher Plummer all to herself and not deal with the messy complications that are teenagers and their hormones and all that.

I love that movie, *The Sound of Music.* Every time the camera pans over Julie Andrews on that mountain singing about those hills being alive, or when the children harmonize the song with crescendos of *ah-ah-ah-ah,* buckets o' tears just stream down my face, out of my control. Maybe that could be my future plan; I'll take a year abroad and become one of those people who go to *The Sound of Music* sing-alongs at movie theaters throughout the world. That would rock as a plan to DO something.

"You and Dad aren't going to separate or anything, right?" I'm not worried, but I kinda am and I do feel bad that my problem got Sid-dad so upset. I poured Nancy a third glass of wine, which she cleared right off.

"Of course not. This is just a bump in the road. Marriage is complicated. It's like being on a ship at sea, rocking back and forth over the long journey. The best you can hope for is to hold steady, smooth sailing, but there will be times when a storm can turn into a crisis. But the storms pass. And then there will be times when the boat . . ."

I moved the wine to the far end of the table, near Gingerbread. Nancy and her nonsense similes didn't need any more help from the *vino*.

"Shrimp is a hypocrite," I told her. She was tipsy—what did I care if I confided in her just a little? She probably wouldn't remember. "He acts like he's all mellow Mister Peace, Love, and Understanding, but that all must be a fake act."

"I noticed he hasn't been by the house to work on his painting. I take it he didn't react well when you told him about Justin."

"Yeah. Want to know the worst part? He actually had the gall to ask if it was Justin's, like he thought it could have been someone else's. He might as well have punched me in the stomach for how much that hurt. Shrimp and Justin are the only guys I have been with, you know—all the way with." A look of relief—and surprise—flooded her face, like she too had thought, because I was caught *in flagrante delicto* with Justin, that I was probably getting that busy with other guys too. Nice to suspect even my own mother thought it possible I had been sleeping around. Wouldn't Nancy be surprised to know that her supposed reformed bad-girl daughter isn't ashamed of her past, but if she had to do it all over again, she might have waited a little longer before doing the deed, but she didn't understand then that once you start with that stuff, there's no turning back? "Why are guys like that? Either you're sacred or you're a slut. There's no winning with them."

"Honey, if you could solve the key to that mystery

about men, you could bottle it, sell it, and become the richest woman in the world. But I will say, not meaning to defend Shrimp's reaction, maybe you just caught him by surprise. Maybe he's had this idealized vision of you and he couldn't deal with having it broken, in that particular moment. He'll be back, and he'll be sorry. It's obvious to anyone how much he cares for you. Be patient, and when he comes around be understanding. But don't you dare apologize to him. That's what they want—for us to apologize for being mere mortal beings, not perfect."

"Are you going to apologize to Dad?"

Nancy sighed. "Well, yes. But in all fairness, I was wrong. About boarding school. And about letting him be a father to you all these years, and yet not letting him in when it mattered most. You made a mistake, but that was in your past and it's nothing you should have to apologize to Shrimp, of all people, about. He had nothing to *do* with it."

Baby tears specked the corners of Nancy's eyelids. I touched her hand across the table. "Maybe I should drive home after dinner."

She yawned. "That would be great."

Chapter 17

I haven't gone so long without a boyfriend, or at least a decent crush, since elementary school. I'm still too mad at Shrimp to ponder how I am going to channel the sexual frustration that is building inside me. Even Alexei is starting to look hot, but we're not talking Loo-eese danger-fling-zone hot. I would have to gag at kissing any lips that might also have . . . done things . . . with/to/on Lord Empress Kari. Blech.

The unexpected bonus of Shrimp being in the dawg-house is that Autumn and Helen turn out to be acceptable in the companion department.

Why did I not have girlfriends before? Because all the girls I knew at boarding school were jerks, or because I didn't know how to be a friend to other girls?

I was worried about H&A spending too much time in the house because you never know when Fernando or Siddad is going to break out with an Asian driver joke, but Autumn doesn't drive anyway and Helen knows more Asian driver jokes than Fernando. Those girls *love* hanging out at my house. It turns out a House Beautiful that has a family room with a huge TV, video games, and tons of movies, a backyard garden with a trampoline, a younger brother who loves roughhousing, and a younger sister who is fascinated watching her Ken doll transformed into Sid Vicious by big sister's friends is not considered a prison by everybody.

I had just woken up on a Saturday morning and was heading downstairs to make a coffee when the front door opened. Helen doesn't bother to knock anymore, she knows the security code to get into the house. She was carrying a take-out tray filled with beverages, and she buzzed past me with Autumn in tow. Helen said, "Ya still got bed head, CC."

I followed them to the kitchen. Fernando was sitting at the kitchen table reading the Spanish-language newspaper. Helen handed him one of the bubble teas with the tapioca balls at the bottom of the cups from her take-out tray. "Here ya go, Ferdie," she said. "The bubble tea store on Clement Street has a D.W.A. drive-up window."

Fernando didn't look up from his newspaper, but he took a sip from the bubble teacup straw. He said, "You mean, the Driving While Asian drive-in window for when you crash your souped-up Honda with the hot-rod racer wheels into the storefront window?" Fernando chuckled. "Asian driver," he said, and Helen finished off his statement in unison with him, "No survivor." Helen and "Ferdie" all but high-fived each other.

I think Helen's mother loves Helen spending time at our house more than Helen does, because then Helen isn't home to abuse her mother about having no fashion sense or to scream at her mother that's she going to ART SCHOOL not to COLLEGE, even if she has to pay for it her goddamn self. Helen has two older sisters—one a first-year law student at Stanford and the other an engineering major at Cal, so Helen's mom must suspect there was a baby switch at the hospital when Helen was born, because Helen is just not conforming to the family's expectations of a nice Chinese girl. Helen smokes and loves beer—and Irish soccer night at the pub. She's really smart but her grades are only so-so. She has a temper—hence "alternative" school. She refuses to work in her family's restaurant. (Helen assures me her mother is relieved on that count.) But Helen has never pretended to be a "nice" Chinese girl. She's just . . . Helen.

Maybe Helen and I were switched-at-birth babies, because she's a natural in my household whereas I am a probable freak of nature here. I could totally groove on living in a cramped flat over a Chinese food restaurant in The Richmond, with a mom who would teach me to make pot stickers and pork buns and tell me brave tales of how she escaped a brutal Communist regime.

"Where's Mrs. Vogue?" Helen asked. "She promised I could look at her old modeling portfolio today. I need to take some photographs for my art school portfolio, and I want to see if I get any ideas looking at some '80s relic flashback."

Mrs. Vogue joined us in the kitchen, holding a grocery list in her hand. She was fully Gucci'd out for her big trip to Safeway. "Good morning, girls!" I think Nancy loves H&A hanging at our house more than they do. She actually likes Helen's nickname for her in tribute to Nancy's favorite pathetic magazine of anorexic bimbos, and Nancy claims I am less pouty and unreasonable when my peers are present. Maybe Nancy oughta worry about getting herself an actual college degree, not me, so then she could stop spouting self-help-books pop psychology, "peers are present" blah blah blah. "I'm on my way to the grocery store. I'm making meat loaf and green bean casserole for dinner! Can you stay for dinner tonight?"

Sid and Nancy have made up since he returned from his business trip, but Nancy is still working extra hard (for someone who hasn't had a job in almost twenty years) to prove to Sid-dad how much she cares for him and how she really can survive without a Leila (she can't). The unfortunate consequence of Nancy's efforts is that our family is being subjected to horrible Midwestern cuisine, the only cuisine in her cooking repertoire, which means dry meat loaf and casseroles made from frozen vegetables and soup mix.

"No, thanks," H&A both said. Like I said, smart girls.

"Fernando," Nancy said. "Sid is at the office until this evening. I'm taking Ashley with me as soon as she finishes getting ready. She needs to be picked up from her birthday party at one, and Josh from his sleepover at two. Here are the addresses."

"*Si,*" Fernando said, taking the slip of paper from Nancy.

Helen handed my mother a bubble tea. "Mrs. Vogue, will you show me your modeling portfolio before you leave?"

Nancy's face brightened. "Yes! Gosh, I haven't looked at that thing in years. Nobody in this household has ever shown an interest, if you get what I'm saying." She looked in my direction. "Come with me."

I'm so gonna get Helen back for this.

Fernando got up from the table. "Tell Sugar Pie 'hi,'" I told him. He didn't acknowledge me as he left the kitchen. Their romance may be out of the closet, but he's a very private person and doesn't like that when he has a few hours to spare, we all assume he'll be at her place. Because he will be.

Autumn sat down in the chair Fernando had vacated.

"Can I use the computer in your family room today to check out some colleges and scholarship programs?" she asked.

"Duh," I said. Autumn lives in a cramped one-bedroom apartment in The Sunset with her dad, who is a poet—that is, broke all the time—and has a crap computer.

"How come you didn't come to the party at Aryan's last night?" Autumn asked.

"Why do you think?" We're at two weeks since I told Shrimp about the A-date: Week one he ignored me at school, and week two he simply didn't show up at school. But I knew he would show up at Aryan's party, so no way was I going.

"He wasn't there," she said.

"Oh." THEN WHERE HAS HE BEEN! "How was the party?"

"Your basic beer, booze, and girls-sticking-out-their-boobs situation."

"So why did you go? It's not like you would meet somebody you'd be interested in with that surfer crowd." Autumn's Shrimpcapade was the experience that made her decide she was gay for sure, but she's not rushing to jump into a relationship. I envy her that—she has that first time/first love to look forward to, but by the time she finds it she'll have really earned it. The waiting may make the payoff better for her.

"To watch over Helen," Autumn said.

"What does that mean?"

It means: Given enough beer, Helen doesn't exercise the best judgment when it comes to doling out, er, certain sexual favors, and not of a reciprocal nature. No wonder she knows tons of guys but has no boyfriends. What does she expect? Maybe I need to have another conversation with Helen about the Madonna/whore boy complex. We chicks don't have to like it, but the fact is it's there, and if Helen wants Aryan for real she better wise up. I am all for sexual liberation, but fooling around when it's not an even exchange is just a raw deal, especially if it's with a guy she really likes, someone she wants to know in more than a casual sense. Has Helen learned nothing from my whole Shrimp debacle?

"NO!" we heard Helen shriek from the living room. Autumn and I hustled to the living room, where Helen was poring over a large black notebook/briefcase type thing with pages of photographs inside. Helen saw us and said, "Your mom is the coolest, CC." Helen held up a black-and-white picture of my mother, about my age, standing on a gritty New York street of graffitied tenement buildings. Nancy was skinnier even than she is now, wearing a short black leather dress and dancer tights with cowboy boots, her blond hair moussed high in front, and eye shadow—dark on one side, light on the other—applied in a rectangular shape from the bridge of her nose across her eyes to the edge of her head, like sunglasses. She looked like a freaking Blondie Debbie Harry new wave goddess.

"Holy shit!" I exclaimed.

Helen pulled out a picture from behind the Debbie Harry photo, a strip of photo-booth shots of my mom laughing and kissing some stubble-faced James Dean-looking stud.

"What's this?" Helen asked.

"Yeah!" I said. "Who's the hot guy?"

Nancy looked uncomfortable and surprised, like she'd

forgotten about the photo-booth shots hidden behind the portfolio shots. But she acknowledged, "Brace yourself, CC. Your mother had a life before you were born. That was my first boyfriend. We ran off to New York together as soon as we'd finished high school. We were barely eighteen years old. I was going to be a dancer; he was going to be a photographer."

"What happened to him?" Autumn asked.

Nancy hesitated a moment before answering. Then: "He died about six months after those pictures were taken. Heroin overdose." For heavy words, her tone was light, but her face had gone pale and her eyes blank.

Talk about a downer on the Nancy past-life discovery. If you had quizzed me yesterday, I would have said Nancy, from her privileged perch lording over Pacific Heights, would have no clue what heroin looked like, she wouldn't even know the diff between a needle user and a pipe user.

I can't imagine how devastated I would be if Shrimp died. I don't know how I could go on. How did she?

Some mental time line calculations fired off in my head. She must have met bio-dad Frank right after her first love died. All my life I've been kind of ashamed that I am the product of my mother's relationship with a married man, not because of the so-called illegitimacy aspect (anyone who cares about that is an idiot), but from feeling that my coming into the world was the cause of pain for a lot of other people. But if it were me and I had just lost Shrimp, I probably wouldn't make the best choices about the next person I jumped into bed with either. I might just want someone to take care of me. Maybe that's what Nancy thought she would get from Frank.

The doorbell rang and we saw Ashley run past us wearing her birthday party velvet frock, white tights on her legs, and Mary Jane patent leather shoes. She shrieked, "I'll get it!" Ash returned to the living room, holding Shrimp's hand.

Nancy had said he would come around, and she was right.

Chapter 18

Ash must have sensed the girl-power-solidarity wave of resentment toward Shrimp coming from me, H&A, and Nancy, because after she saw the expressions on our faces she dropped his hand like he had cooties.

Shrimp's dirty blond hair was loose and curled from the rain outside, and he was wearing khaki cargo pants, flip-flops, and a black T-shirt emblazoned in red with a single word: FEMINIST.

Since when does Shrimp go for the whole Old Navy look?

"Hey," Shrimp said.

One more *hey* from him and I might turn violent.

You'd think a fire was raging in the house for how quickly everyone else got outta there. Nancy hustled Ash outside for her b-day party, while Helen and Autumn suddenly had to take a walk over to Union Street to get some moisturizer.

Without speaking, Shrimp and I both headed toward the kitchen, and then we were out on the outdoor deck again, sitting in the same positions as the last time he'd been in the house, oblivious to the light rain splattering our faces. Fernando had moved Shrimp's painting and materials to the garden shed, but the tarp still covered the painting and we still didn't know what it was.

Moisturizer?

"Where've you been?" I asked him.

"I went up north with Iris and Billy for a week. They had some business up in Eureka, and I needed the fresh air so I went with them. I went camping in the mountains by myself. Needed some time alone."

"What about school?"

"I'm so far behind already, since coming back from PNG. What's it matter? I'm never going to catch up."

"So taking another week off was the answer to that?" Even by my antischool philosophy, his logic was twisted.

"I had stuff to think about."

"What things?"

"What you told me. Having Iris and Billy back home. That I've been eating meat just to aggravate my mother, even though being a vegetarian is a core part of who I am— or who I thought I was. Being back in school when I'm really not feeling it after a few months of getting to do what I wanted to do: surf and art and travel. The fact that the last girl I was with, after you, decided she was gay after we got together."

I hadn't thought about it that way. My head might also need a fresh-air breather if that much was swirling around in it at once, but I would never go outdoor camping for head-clearing R&R. I would go to a spa where beautiful bronzed boys wearing togas would bring me poolside fruity drinks with little tiki umbrellas floating inside.

"And what did you figure out?"

Shrimp may be small but he is all man. He didn't avoid my eyes, flinch, lower his voice, or do any of those shallow-guy maneuvers when they know they're busted. His deep blue eyes looked right into mine, and because he is all heart

I knew he meant what he said. "About most of that stuff, I still don't know. But when it comes to you . . . I acted like a jerk when you told me. I was wrong to ask if it was Justin's. The question just came from my mouth and then I couldn't take it back. Then I got embarrassed on top of being really surprised and uncomfortable with what you'd told me. So I just up and left. I choked—I admit it. I'm not proud of it, but that's what I did."

"Why were you uncomfortable with what I told you?" I needed to know: because it's a reminder that I've been with another guy who's not him? When I know for a fact he's been with more girls than I have guys.

Shrimp mumbled, "I know I wasn't your first, but it's just weird knowing you were pregnant by your ex."

I pointed to the shed at the rear of the backyard garden. "I can go pull a shovel out of there in case you want to dig any deeper."

Shrimp continued his soul-sucking stare into my eyes. "I didn't say it's right, how I feel. It's my issue to get over, not yours."

That's true.

"Do I look different to you?" I asked.

"What do you mean? Since from when you told me about what happened with Justin, or since I first met you?"

"I don't know. Just generally."

He looked completely different from when I first met him. Was that because I had changed, or he had changed? Aside from being bigger, his face was broader, hardened, less pretty-boy handsome and a lot more interesting, especially with the two little zits on his chin. I realized that the first time I had seen Shrimp, at the nursing home with

Sugar Pie soon after being kicked out of boarding school, I had seen him in a shroud of perfection, wanting to escape the memory of Justin. Now I saw him for who he was: just a guy, albeit a beautiful surfer punk guy.

Shrimp said, "Honestly the thing I like about you most, is you never stop looking different to me. I never know what to expect from you. It's aggravating sometimes, but more times just . . . sexy."

Alright, ya got me.

I took Shrimp's hand and we both stood up. We had the huge house to ourselves, which rarely happens, considering how many people either live or work here, but I led him away from the house, down the deck stairs leading to the garden. I opened the tool shed and pulled him inside.

"Your painting is here, whenever you're ready to finish it," I said. I shut the door to the shed. It smelled like rusty tools and oil. The only light in the shed came from a burst of sunlight creeping underneath the shed door. Shrimp pressed me against the shed wall and our lips, already wet from the rain, picked right back up with getting to know each other again. The smell of him, the taste of him—it was like my mouth couldn't get enough of him. His fingers did their familiar dance through my long hair, and he pressed into me at the groin as we kissed, indicating to me the feeling was mutual.

And yet. I've never been a girl who was a tease—if I want it, I'm going to take it—but as good as the kissing felt physically, my brain separated itself out at the same time, remembering him dumping me, and how he reacted about Justin. My brain asked, *Can I trust him not to hurt me again?*

I pulled back from him, breathing hard. My hormones desperately tried telling my brain to back the fuck off, but in an unprecedented underdog victory, my brain prevailed. "Maybe you were right," I whispered. "Maybe we should just be friends for now."

Chapter 19

War has broken out at the house again. Seems like old times!

Frank Commune Day is ruined. In our family we celebrate the sacred day of December 12, the birthday of Frank Sinatra, Sid and Nancy's mutual hero (aside from the real Cyd Charisse, natch). Nancy was raised Lutheran and Sid-dad Jewish, and neither of them cares about religious education or God holidays, so December 12 is all-important at our house.

Our ritual begins at breakfast, when Sid-dad translates the newspaper for us as Frank News. For example: "Kids, Frank Weather today is foggy and overcast till late morning, with the sun expected to burn off the fog around noontime, highs expected to be in the midsixties. In Frank Sports, the Niners have blown another shot at the NFC playoffs; no wild card slots for them this year. Frank Traffic—construction on the 101 means longer than usual delays at the Golden Gate Bridge on the Marin side." Round-the-clock Frank tunes play from every stereo in our house—the good stuff, with Count Basie and Nelson Riddle, not that cheesy "Start spreading da news" crap—and at night we exchange gifts after a huge dinner catered by Sid-dad's fave Italian restaurant in North Beach. The Frank celebration usually ends with Frank movie time in the family room. *Guys and Dolls* and *On the Town* are Josh and Ash's favorites, but if the day has left them too hyper, then we get to watch my fave, *The Manchurian Candidate,* because then they'll be so bored they'll fall right asleep and Nancy will be so creeped out she'll fail to notice that I've eaten the whole tray of cannolis myself.

I was particularly looking forward to this year's Frank Commune Day, because last year I had just come back home after being expelled from boarding school and there was so much tension in the house we barely bothered to celebrate. We ate Frank dinner, and then Nancy and I got into a fight over a certain postexpulsion shoplifting incident, door slams, *I HATE YOU,* the usual yadda yadda yadda. The two celebrations before that I was exiled to New England and didn't get to partake of the December 12th ritual in Pacific Heights.

So this December 12th I was fully ready to par-tay. I woke up that morning eager to get downstairs for breakfast to hear Frank News, as Sid-dad had promised he would branch out into Frank Astrology this year. Nancy stood at the doorway to my room as I was getting dressed. She said, "I'm going to Nordstrom this morning while you all are at school. Do you need me to buy you a heavy winter coat? You'll need one for Minnesota. I've booked us to leave Christmas Eve morning and return a couple days after New Year's. Happy Frank Birthday."

"Happy Frank Birthday to you, too," I said. Some people might celebrate Frank Commune Day by wearing hipster tees picturing fedora-wearing Ol' Blue Eyes, but I chose to celebrate him another way: by dressing like his one true love, Ava Gardner. My Frank tribute ensemble included a tight-waisted, black vintage A-line fifties skirt falling to midcalf length, a blouse with deep décolletage and cinched at the waist, my hair primped in Ava waves, and pedicured, shoeless feet à la *The Barefoot Contessa*. I'd even splurged on a padded Wonder Bra, for Ava cleavage that this Cyd Charisse lacks. As I applied long, thick fake eyelashes to my lids, I reminded Nancy, "But I can't go to Minnesota. Wallace and Delia's wedding is New Year's Eve." I've only told Nancy a thousand times.

"That's too bad," Nancy said. "It's our family vacation, and you know my mother is in very bad health. She's not expected to last the winter. This might be the last year you kids get to see her. Cheer up—your airline ticket is first class, and we'll be staying at a suite of rooms in the best hotel in Minneapolis." Like I could care about first-class plane and hotel accommodations.

"No," I said, voice rising.

"Yes," she said, voice rising higher.

"NO!"

"YES!"

The system of checks and balances on my temper tipped out of my control. "I'M NOT GOING!" I yelled. "YOU CAN'T MAKE ME!"

Aside from no way will I miss Wallace and Delia's wedding, aside from that I am old enough not to have to go somewhere just because my mother has decided for me that I must go, there is the fact that I really, truly hate Nancy's mother. Granny Asshole (as I call her) lives in a gated community in some uptight suburb of Minneapolis, in a house that's situated on a golf course, as if that's not reason enough to hate her. We hardly ever see her. She is not your cute, cuddly Nana either, the Tollhouse cookie-baking, knit-you-some-sweaters kind. She's this stick figure whose diet consists primarily of "soda pop," pâté, and Ritz crackers (Nancy says I get my "miracle metabolism" from her, that's why I can eat anything). Granny Asshole refers to me as "the illegitimate one," Sid-dad as "the Jew," her home health aide is "the colored girl," and she had the gall to call Nancy "porky" when we went to visit after Ash was born and Nancy hadn't yet lost all the pregnancy weight. Spend some time with Granny Asshole and you'll understand why Nancy practically has an eating disorder, or why she ran off with a boy who had a heroin problem as soon as she was of legal age.

I never knew Granny Asshole's husband, my grandfather. He died when I was a baby, probably to get away from her. And I am not going to pretend I am sad about old Granny Asshole kickin' it when I'm not. The last time I saw Granny A was the summer before my fourteenth b-day. She took me aside at the only family reunion we've ever gone to and she explained to me about how superior my church-going cousins in Minnesota were in comparison to my "San Francisco–style family," while I watched as these same charmer cousins lifted twenties from her wallet for beer money without her seeing it. Then she informed me that I had grown up to be a very pretty young lady, but now that I had hips and boobies I better be careful so I didn't turn out like my mother. I honestly do try to find some good in everybody, even in people I dislike. But Granny Asshole, no, I'm sorry, I can't find anything and I am not going to feel bad about it. Some people might just be assholes, and that's just gonna be that.

The equivalent of Nancy getting her Irish up is when she gets her Minnesouda up. Her pale face goes all splotchy red and she spews words in this strange vowel-dragging accent that's just like Granny Asshole's. The diction classes Nancy took when we first moved to San Francisco mostly got rid of that prairie accent, but when she's mad the accent and its accompanying expressions come back fast and furious. "Yew are nooot an adult yet, young laaady, yah? And yew are nooot staying in this hawse alooone while's we're aaawaaay and Fernando is in Neecarahgua for Chreestmas. Yew are goooing to Minnesouda whether yew like it or nooot. Yew are nooot eh-teen yet, missy."

Oh, now I get it. The same woman who took me to the doctor for a birth control prescription back in September is the same woman who's now trying to cock-block me in December. She's worried about what will happen between Shrimp and I, whose "just friends" situation is coming along great. That is, if "just friends" means a guy and a girl who don't have sex but who handhold at lunchtime at school and who share occasional deep French kisses whenever they say good-bye, if "just friends" means two ex-lovers who have taken the time the past several weeks to get to know each other before their inevitable head bangin', boots knockin', bed rattlin', unspoken-but-will-be-fact reunion. Nancy thinks that if Shrimp and I have the hawse to ourselves, it will turn into some unsupervised bang festival.

No matter that I've been going to school every day this year and the grades aren't half bad, no matter that I haven't jumped back into a sexual relationship with Shrimp or anyone else, no matter that I've made friends and developed a life outside of the all-encompassing boy radar, no matter that I've been damn pleasant in this house, too. The fact is: Nancy still doesn't trust me.

"I AM NOT GOING! To Minnesota or to college!" I was so mad I couldn't help but throw that last one in. But merely tossing the word *college* into the ring didn't seem sufficient, so I added, "You can't make me go to see the mother you yourself hate so you can show off how rich and fine you're doing without her in your life, just like you can't make me go to college just cuz you regret that you yourself didn't go. I'm not here for you to live out your dreams through me."

"YOU ARE A SPOILED BRAT!"

"Well, who made me one? You just want me to go away to Minnesota or to college so you can have me gone to a place a spoiled brat doesn't want to be, like you did when you made me go to boarding school!"

I couldn't follow normal protocol and storm away to my bedroom because I was already in it, so I slammed my bedroom door in Nancy's face instead and locked the door.

Chapter 20

The nicest part of "just friends" is I could wait for Shrimp's beat-up, lima bean-colored old Pinto to pull into the school parking lot, and I could go to his driver's-side window and say, "Let's ditch today," with no sexpectations to go along with the ditch day. A "just friend" who is also a soul mate knows without being told and could just acknowledge, "Nice outfit, Ava, but glum face. Fight back home on Frank Day?" as he shifted the car into reverse for us to leave before the school day had even started.

Shrimp's wet suit was in the trunk and his board on top of the car roof, so he drove us out to Ocean Beach. I needed chill time, so he hit the morning waves near his house on Great Highway while I took a long walk on the beach, my bare Ava feet getting seriously burr-ito burrowing through the cold San Francisco beach sand.

I let Nancy call my cell phone three separate times before I bothered to answer it. She didn't scream but sounded tired when she said, "Where are you?"

I couldn't stifle the roar of the ocean behind me so I said, "Where do you think, Sherlock?" I held up the phone to the water crashing on the surf. I put the phone back to my ear and said, "You have to learn to trust me, Mom. I might not be eighteen yet but I will be soon, and if you don't want me to do to you what you did to your mother—run away—you're going to have to let go enough to let me make my own decisions. I'm not missing Wallace and Delia's wedding. They're more like family than your family in Minnesota has ever been, and you know it." I turned off my phone so she could scarf down her usual breakfast roll of Butter Rum LifeSavers and then take a nap while she thought on that.

I realized she might not be smart enough to figure out the right course on her own, though, so I turned the phone back on to call to Sid-dad's office. I could hear "It Happened in Monterey" playing in the background when he got on the phone. He said, "Cupcake, it's Frank's birthday so you get a special dispensation not to get reamed out for starting a fight with your mother and behaving like a child on this very important day. But if you're looking for me to broker a truce, I'll tell you what I just told your mother. The answer is no. I'm tired of being the intermediary. You two work it out yourselves." And *he* hung up on *me*!

Well, I had no solution to this problem because it's Nancy who caused the fight, she should be the one to fix it, so I continued my beach walk. I saw Shrimp in the distant water, surrounded by a small posse of surfers waiting and waiting for the right wave, then paddling furiously once it beckoned. With their bobbing black wet suits against the blue-gray ocean, they looked like a school of dolphins. Ocean Beach is usually cold and foggy, but perhaps in honor of Frank's birthday the day was unusually bright and sunny, which, if you spend a lot of time in Ocean Beach, you particularly appreciate because it happens so rarely. On the rare sunny days, you can see west across the Pacific all the way to the Farallon Islands, or north to the beautiful green hills and mountains of Marin County, and you might think you'll never again see a sight so beautiful and you probably won't, because the dense fog is guaranteed to return to cloud over the beauty.

This was the first time I had Shrimp to myself in the past few weeks and yet I willingly sacrificed him to the sea so I could have time alone. Since getting past the A-date issue, we've been hanging out, but I wouldn't call it dating: a couple Ocean Beach house parties on weekends, some random art adventures like going to the Japanese tea garden in Golden Gate Park and then driving down to Colma, the dead city (literally) where all the graveyards are and where Shrimp likes to go and draw tombstones.

But it was movie night with his family when I realized I could trust him for sure. It wasn't a specific thing he said or did that indicated we were past the Justin fallout, so much as a series of moments. Shrimp chose *Silk Stockings* with the real Cyd Charisse for us to watch, and he melted Nestle Crunch bars over the hot microwaved popcorn just the way I love, without being asked. While the movie played he sat next to me on the couch with his arm around me, massaging my shoulders and neck. Midway through the movie Billy passed me a bowl after taking a hit, but Shrimp took it from his dad and bypassed it over to Iris, knowing I was too content to waste the natural high on Billy's bud. When the movie was over everyone talked about how beautiful and elegant the real Cyd Charisse was, her lovely dance with the pair of silk stockings, and how perfectly matched she was in the movie with Fred Astaire. I said I thought the original, nonmusical version of the movie—*Ninotchka* with Greta Garbo—was superior in my opinion, and everyone looked shocked like I had said something sacrilegious, dissing my namesake. Iris said, "Do you know so much about old movies because you're named for an old movie star?" And I said, "No, I just know as would any reformed social outcast who had spent *mucho* time alone in her room listening to Muzak and watching old flicks." Iris and Billy and Wallace and Delia laughed like I was uproarious, but I didn't see the joke and neither did Shrimp: SOUL MATE.

I wandered along the beach for a good hour before I saw Shrimp emerge from the ocean, walking with that contented-blissful stride he gets after communing with the Pacific. *What would Ava do?* I wondered. In my ear Ava whispered to me from her Forest Lawn perch in the dinosaur-movie-star heavens: *Kid, look here. About that outfit you've got on. Hot stuff! And that boy walking toward you, filling out that wet suit right nice. What's it gonna take to get you two kids back together already?* I tried to explain to Ava about how this "just friends" thing is working out great and the ditch day was just about random chill time with no sexpectations involved, that's just where Shrimp and I are right now, maybe there would be some sharing of a gooey chocolatey drink (Yoo-Hoo, anyone?), but that's it. Ava said, *Why? Haven't you waited long enough? Act Two of True Love can only be drawn out so long.* I tried to explain about how sex changes everything, but Ava snapped something about me being scared and a bore and she had a game of strip poker with Lana Turner, Errol Flynn, and Clark Gable to get back to. Lucky bitch.

Shrimp came to my side, dripping wet, his board at his hip. A strong ocean wind whipped water from his hair onto my Ava cleavage. Did I need more of a sign? Shrimp said, "Were you just talking to someone? I thought I saw your lips moving but I don't see anyone near you or your cell phone in your hand."

I took his free hand, cold and wrinkled from the water. "Never mind. Wanna go back to your place?" I licked his ear, then whispered into it, "To your room?" Not that I wouldn't be agreeable to fooling around on the beach in broad daylight, I guess, but the thought of cold sand on my ass and transient loonies cheering us on from behind the beach dunes was less than hot.

"The time isn't right," Shrimp said.

I actually stomped my foot. "It is!" I said. "It is!" Why can't he be your basic horn-dog male, WHY? My mistake, trying to entice him just after he'd scored with his first true love—the ocean—and was too Zen surfed out to care about scoring another form of action *avec moi.*

His lips covered mine for a brief kiss, just long enough to shut me up. Then he said, "Iris and Billy are probably at the house—they wouldn't care, but I would. And the two of us haven't decided one way or another whether we want to get back together. When we do make that decision it shouldn't be like this, when you're upset, when it's about escaping instead of about us. That's just lame. When it happens, if it happens, don't you want it to be special? Isn't this great just now, you and me, the ocean, the sand, the beach almost all to ourselves?"

"What are you?" I asked. "A girl?"

What if we've waited so long that now we can never do it again, because there never will be a right time? What if neither of us ever at the same time feels the right measure of trust and lust that allows us to cross this invisible "just friends" barrier?

We saw Iris in the distance as we headed up toward the highway. She was walking their new dog, Aloha, a mutt she and Billy adopted from the pound. It's weird that two people who still haven't decided where they are going to live permanently now that they're back in the U.S. of A. would adopt a dog before they knew they had a real home for it, but Wallace didn't seem to mind, probably because Aloha kept Iris too occupied to intrude in the last stages of wedding planning. The eager dog was walking Iris more than she it, though, and she almost ran past us without noticing us. Her mane of brown-gray hair was pulled back into a ponytail, but the strong wind was spraying pieces across her face so she didn't see us until we were directly in front of her.

"Hi!" she said, startled, when she noticed us standing in front of her. She let Aloha loose from the leash and threw a stick for the dog to fetch. If Nancy had been standing before us (and not recovering from a fight earlier that morning), Shrimp and I would have gotten chewed out for skipping school, but on Iris time, who knows if she even made the connection that she was bumping into us on the beach in the late morning of a school day? "Want to take a walk with me?"

Shrimp said, "I need to go change out of this wet suit, but why don't you two go for a walk, then meet me back at the house in half an hour and I will make you ladies lunch? The Shrimp Blue Plate Special: Velveeta mac and cheese." He looked at his mom. "No bacon chunks," he added, and Iris chuckled.

Iris took my hand and we walked back toward the beach. Iris is easier when her family isn't around; she relaxes and she's more a person and less a pseudomom/wife bossing everyone around. Billy is a complete mystery to me; a fellow of few words who doesn't appear to want anyone to get to know him besides Iris. I will say that when his eyes aren't glazed over from being baked, the primary times his face registers emotion is when his sons are around him. He may not be much of a stick-around dad but he loves Wallace and Shrimp, though it's Iris who rules his world. The key to the mystery that is Billy may be that he's no mystery at all, that after decades of smoking herb like some people smoke cigarettes, there's simply not much there to him anymore.

Iris said, "You seem tense. Everything all right, darlin'?"

"Yeah, just a little spat with my mom. She's trying to make me go see her dying mother at Christmas instead of go to Wallace and Dee's wedding."

"Well, don't you want to see your grandmother before she passes?"

"She's an old bat I've only seen a few times in my life. I haven't seen her enough to care, and from what I have gotten to know of her, I've never liked. She's not a very nice person, and I can't just all of a sudden pretend to care about her just because she's sick—that's so fake. I mean, if I had some terminal disease and she came into town like, 'Oh, my beloved grandchild, the years we've lost, let me pretend to care now that you're about to kick it,' I would just projectile vomit or something. Anyway I think I'm old enough to make this decision about what's more important for myself."

Iris said, "I think you're right. What do you think Shrimp would choose, between moving away with Billy and me or staying here with Wallace and Dee?"

Of course I wanted to say, *Shrimp would choose a Cyd*

Charisse commune where friends are outlawed and sex rules morning, noon, and night and no way will his mother be allowed to take Shrimp away from me now that I've found him again, but I didn't. I said, "Why?"

"Well, it's a choice he's going to have to make eventually. And I'm curious what the girl who knows him best thinks he'll choose." It would be easy to think of Iris as just some crazy hippie throwback who cares more about shoving her political opinions down everyone's throats than she cares about the welfare of her own kids, but what elevates Iris from annoying to special is how deeply she cares, when she cares. I could feel in the tense clench of her hand that she was more than worried about whom Shrimp would choose; whether worried that he would reject her or worried that he wouldn't let her go, I don't know.

Nancy ringing my cell phone again allowed me to pry my hand loose from Iris's death grip. Nancy didn't bother saying hello or letting me speak, she just jumped right in: "I'll offer you a trade, a one-time-only, non-negotiable offer. Alexei stays in Fernando's apartment while we're all gone so there's at least one adult on the premises, and you agree to choose two colleges and fill out those applications during the Christmas break. Alexei will be there if you need help with the college applications. Under these terms, you can stay home in San Francisco and go to the wedding, if that's what you choose. Deal?"

"Deal," I said.

Nancy added, "And don't you ever raise your voice at me or lock your door in my face again like you did this morning. We're finished with that. If you want to be treated like an adult, act like one." This time she clicked me off.

Chapter 21

The Chairman of the Board's birthday was certainly not being celebrated at Java the Hut late that afternoon, as witnessed by the obscene level of crank in the coffeehouse.

Helen sat in a corner of the café, violently drawing in her sketch pad. When I glanced at the work, her Ball Hunter comic hero guy appeared to be getting chased by an army of golf-cart-riding Wonder Woman look-alikes, all shaking their fists at him, sunlight beaming off their gold bracelets. "Poor Ball Hunter man," I said to Helen. "What did he do?"

She crouched over her notebook so I couldn't look at it, and she glared at me. "I'm trying to work in private," she snapped. "And I looked for you at school today because I needed your help with something, but now it's too late. What, you're too cool to show up at school now?"

Um, okay, Helen. Need some Midol?

I walked over to where Autumn was bent over, lifting a tray of dirty glasses to take into the kitchen to be washed. When she stood up I saw that she'd cut off her dreads, and was left with a head full of short chunks of hair in search of direction. Autumn has that gorgeous rainbow-coalition face so she can pretty much pull off any hairstyle, but the new look was a complete surprise and I let out an involuntary gasp when I first saw it. While Autumn can pull off any hairstyle, that doesn't mean the new 'do was all that flattering.

"Don't say anything about my hair," Autumn hissed. "I didn't get early admission to Cal and I was freaking out and just started cutting, and now I look horrible."

"You don't look horrible at all . . . ," I started to say, but she breezed past me toward the kitchen. She went through the wrong-side door and got slammed in the face by Delia coming through from the other side. Autumn dropped the tray of glasses onto the floor, splashing water and coffee remnants on the ground. She held her nose while tears surrounded her eyes. "Autumn, I'm so sorry!" Delia said. "Are you okay? Do you need an ice pack? How many times does this have to happen to you for you to remember which door is which, anyway?"

I may have accepted Helen's challenge to become Autumn's friend, but I am not blind to Autumn's faults, the worst of which, I'm proud to proclaim, is the one I suspected to be true about her before I'd even met her: She is the worst waitress/barista ever. She always remembers customers' orders wrong, as if it's that hard to distinguish between skim or whole milk or a latte versus a cappuccino. She has no concept that the cleaning towel is there to fulfill its destiny to wipe spilled coffee, sugar granules, and cocoa powder off the counter at regular intervals, and she could easily send Java the Hut to bankruptcy court from all the glasses she's broken and machines she's permanently damaged. Shrimp says Wallace and Delia won't fire her because Autumn needs the job to save for college, but I think they keep her on because she's so pretty that she keeps a steady stream of surfer dudes coming into the shop, regardless of her barista talents (or sexuality).

The surfer most falsely enamored of Autumn, Arran

a.k.a. Aryan, ran over from the computer terminal, where he had been looking at the Victoria's Secret catalog on-line, to help Autumn clean up the mess she'd spilled. Delia couldn't help Autumn anyway, or tend to her wounded nose, because a tourist bus had pulled up outside the store, probably sucked over to Ocean Beach by the rare day of sun, and a sizable stream of customers had flowed to the front counter demanding caffeination.

Delia ran over to me with an apron in her hand. "Please?" she said. "Can you help me out here?"

Despite the many months since I'd worked the counter at Java the Hut, I said, "Sure." Churning out rapid-fire brews is like riding a bike or performing certain sexual favors—a skill that once you've developed, you never lose. The time working at Lord Empress Kari's restaurant must have spoiled me, though, because back behind that counter I couldn't help but notice how poorly organized the station was or that it was a good thing the health inspector hadn't come by today because the cleanliness situation was not the tip-top shape Kari demands and gets. Lord Empress Kari has her restaurant running like a well-oiled machine, and Java the Hut could have used some of her whip cracking to get it moving like a tight-ship business instead of a café that ran out of small bills to give customers change and needed its expiration dates checked on the stale sandwiches.

Maybe I am not an Orange in a land of Apples, after all. Maybe I thought I belonged working at a place like Java the Hut, but after all the time away JtH felt different. It's still a great hangout but, like, maybe I am not all about the grunge mellow factor anymore. Which isn't to say I have any idea what I am about these days, but I was surprised at how different the Java the Hut coffeehouse felt to me now: part of the past, over, *finito*. Also, truth be told, I've had better coffee.

After we'd taken care of the onslaught of customers, Delia tucked behind her ear a strand of her frizzy red hair that had fallen from the bun at the back of her head, and she wiped some sweat from her brow. "Bless you," she said to me, right as Iris burst through the front door of the café. Iris saw Delia at the front counter, then turned around and walked back out of the door, away down the street. "What was that about?" I asked Delia.

Delia's voice went on the down low. "Get this. Billy had some, let's say 'transactions,' he was handling here at the store, and when Wallace and I realized what was going on we asked him not to conduct business here. Billy was okay with it—you know Wallace walks on water to him—but now Iris is pissed because she says how are she and Billy supposed to afford moving out to their own place if we are obstructing him from making a living? Those two, I swear, if we make it through the next few weeks to the wedding, it will be a miracle."

I don't know what happened in the corner of the café, but we heard shouting and looked up to see Helen slam her notebook shut and storm out of the café, leaving Autumn and Aryan standing next to where Helen had been sitting, stunned looks on their faces. "What's her problem?" Aryan said. He, too, walked out of the store, grabbing his surfboard from the surf rack outside the window, and he headed in the direction of the beach, his long board at his hip.

Delia shrugged. "I have no idea what's going on there, but please can you do me one more favor? The wedding planner is meeting me here in half an hour to go over the last-minute details, and Autumn still has a few hours left on her shift and I really need her help, for what that's worth. Please go talk to her and just get her in a mood so she can help me out here. Pretty please, my darling could-be-my-sister-in-law one day?" Delia whimpered like a puppy dog; she was almost as cute as Aloha.

"Just-friends-in-law," I corrected Delia. I took off the apron and handed it back to her. "I'll go talk to her, but don't expect any miracles. I don't know what I'm doing." What am I, Dear Abby now? It was enough of a battle just to like the Autumn wench, now I have to talk to her about whatever is bothering her? This girls-as-friends business should come with a how-to manual.

Autumn sat at the back of the coffeehouse on the beat-up old sofa with the red sheet covering it. She pulled a book from the shelf, but the Dalai Lama's wisdom about the art of happiness must not have interested her because she flipped through random pages without reading a word or noticing that there were customers milling around who might have liked to sit on the sofa. I sat down next to her. "What the fuck?" I said. Was that a bad approach? What would Oprah have said?

Autumn rubbed her swollen nose, then placed her head in her hands. "Grrrrrrr . . . ," she groaned. "Can we just erase this day from the calendar?"

"Erase Frank Day! Never!" I sputtered, horrified. Then again, Frank Day might not be a priority on her agenda. "What happened?" I asked her. I tried to pat her back, but I must have patted too hard because she flinched and said, "Ow!"

Again, needing a how-to manual here.

Autumn said, "Where to begin? There was the Cal rejection letter that arrived today. I still might get in regular admission, but that was my ace in the hole. If I don't get in there, I don't know where I could afford to go that I would want to go. So strike one. Strike two, this girl at my school, we kind of got together and I thought I really liked her, but now she's going around at school acting like it never happened and all of a sudden she's like practically engaged to some guy she met last summer."

"I thought you told me you weren't going to date this year because of that exact problem."

"And you believed that?" Autumn shook her short mess of hair. "How gullible are you anyway? I might as well tell you strike three. Helen wanted to tell you, but then she kept chickening out because of your Madonna/whore man tirade. She's been having this sort of . . . can't call it 'relationship,' let's call it 'thing' . . . with Aryan. You know, he gets her alone and lets her do the deed, but then he doesn't acknowledge her when they're around other people, acts like there's nothing more between them than just being acquaintances. She likes him so much, even though she won't admit it. He's a great-looking guy, yeah, but I think he's a jerk myself. He's no Shrimp, that's for shit sure. Helen knows I don't like him and that I think she's making a fool of herself over him. I mean, you want your friends to be with someone who deserves them, right?" I nodded. Right, yeah, that's how it works! "So then, just now, Aryan asked me out on a date for this weekend, right in front of Helen. End of scene; here we are."

My first order of business was to pull out my cell

phone and send a text message to Helen inviting her to dinner at my house. Frank Day celebration with Helen's false idol, Mrs. Vogue, might cheer her up, and I would use the occasion to get Helen alone in my room to talk about the Aryan situation. While I had Helen there, I could pull out the dictionary and make Helen read aloud the entry for reciprocity (rĕs'ə-prŏs'ĭ-tĕ). I may also force her to tune in to Dr. Phil or Dr. Ruth or just simply Dr. CC until she acknowledges that oral sex is the same as sex and, stop blushing, Helen, don't do it and think it doesn't count, because it does.

Next I told Autumn, "You're going to get into Cal. I know it. But maybe this is the universe sending you a message not to limit your options. There's a big wide world out there, and Berkeley is just across the Bay. Maybe the universe wants you to spread your wings a little and think of this rejection as an opportunity instead of a defeat." From the picture on the cover of the book resting on Autumn's lap, the Dalai Lama appeared to be nodding at me, congratulating my wisdom and empathy. "I will have a talk with Helen about Aryan and set her straight. It's not your fault Aryan asked you out in front of her, but it is your fault if you haven't made it extremely clear to him that you are one hundred percent gay. He probably knows about your Shrimpcapade, so maybe he thinks he's got a shot with you. Don't let him hold out some unrealistic expectation about getting together with you, especially if you know Helen is interested in him. And have you even come out at your school? Because I don't remember you telling me you have, so maybe the girl you like at school is getting mixed messages from you as well as the ones she's giving herself." This time I gently rubbed instead of bang-patted Autumn's back. "And lastly your hair looks great, but if you don't like it, remember it's not Barbie hair—it does grow back." I could feel the need for a nap coming on; this pep-talk business was exhausting. "Now it's time for me to go home. My mother has turned unexpectedly reasonable, and I need to make up with her for a fight this morning."

Autumn smiled her impossibly perfect, big-toothed, full-mouthed grin. She stood up. "You're not so bad at this," she said as she walked back to her station at the front counter.

"At what?" I called out after her.

"You know what!" she called back.

I got up to leave, but from the corner of my eye I saw an arm signaling me in its direction. I walked to the side of the store with the supply closet to find Shrimp standing inside it, a mischievous grin on his face. He raised both his eyebrows at me playfully—he looked like a surfer Marx Brother—and he gestured for me to join him inside that same supply closet where we used to make out during breaks when we both worked at Java the Hut.

I didn't go inside. I said, "We still haven't had that official talk, pal."

Shrimp's mouth turned down into a sad clown face. A little nookie doesn't always come without strings, buddy. I left Java the Hut to catch the bus to take me home.

Next year on Frank Day I am not going as Ava Gardner. I will be a saint.

Chapter 22

Bay Area drivers, beware: CC is on the loose, officially licensed by the Golden State to operate a motor vehicle. If I had realized earlier the freedom a driver's license bought me, I would have jumped on the to-hell-with-the-environment-let's-drive-everywhere bandwagon the day I turned sixteen. After I passed the test Sid-dad wanted to give me a new car, but I said, "No, thank you, may I just use the car Leila left behind, a tiny, ancient, electric blue Geo Metro that looks like it could be Betty Boop's car?" Nancy said, "We were going to donate that car to charity since your dad still refuses to hire another housekeeper. You don't want that car—take the Lexus." I said, "Please, it's embarrassing enough being in this family without that badge of motor monstrosity distinction. Pass those Betty Boop car keys on over and I am the happiest girl in The City."

A Betty Boop car that's practically a relic qualifies as a legacy car, in my opinion. If I am going to be a proper California girl—or, more importantly, the past and future girlfriend of a certain Cali boy surfer-artist—a legacy car is a serious step in my identity evolution. Shrimp drives his brother's old car, this Pinto from the seventies that used to be their uncle's car. The Pinto is painted the color of a lima bean and has furry dice hanging from the rearview mirror, and Wallace gets tears in his eyes sometimes when he looks at that car, remembering how he loved fixing it up and then passing it on to his younger bro when too many girlfriends complained about it breaking down on the freeway. Shrimp's Pinto legacy car looks like a vehicle that some sixty-year-old woman who smokes Winstons and goes to the grocery store with curlers in her hair would drive completely without irony, yet the Pinto so clearly belongs with Shrimp, like a mangy dog at the pound that just jumps in your arms and that you know is meant to go home with you. Although psycho Leila was close to last on my list of idols and the memory of her frightening Celine Dion accent alone was almost enough to make me fear the karma that might not yet have dissipated from her Geo Metro legacy car, the fact is Leila made extremely good pancakes. I would like to one day make good pancakes, so taking over Leila's car is not necessarily a legacy meaning I want to be like Leila so much as an expression of my desire to accumulate cooking karma during my driving time. Hey, it makes sense to me.

I celebrated taking over Betty Boop legacy car by picking up passengers for girlz night out. Since H&A haven't been speaking to each other in the week since their meltdown incident on Frank Day, I decided not to let them know that they were both included in girlz night out with Sugar Pie. Helen was trapped in the backseat with no leg room, so it's not like she could really physically protest when I pulled up in front of Autumn's place in The Sunset. Autumn herself appeared to hesitate when she glimpsed Helen through the car window from where she was standing on the sidewalk, waiting for the pickup. I stopped the car, hopped out of the driver's seat, lifted the lever for Autumn to get into the backseat alongside trapped Helen, sitting behind Sugar

Pie, and said loud enough for both H&A to hear, "Holding grudges like you two have been doing since the Aryan incident is a prime reason why I have not made friends with chicks in the past, so could you please just be like dudes— buck up and get over it?"

Autumn's chopped dreaded hair was pulled back in a turban so her big eye roll was very apparent, but she did step into the backseat. Then she smushed herself against the side window, as far away as possible from Helen, who then smushed herself against the opposite side, and each of their faces wore identical pouts. Being at opposite ends of the backseat of a Geo Metro, though, meant there were like two centimeters that came between their bodies, so really all the sulking and separating their bodies away from each other was a big waste of time.

I got back into the car and Sugar Pie went to work with the next part of my plan. If there's one thing I have learned in my seventeen years on Planet Earth it's that chocolate is the great equalizer, and after Sugar Pie had passed back the plastic pumpkin filled with chocolate treats, it only took two mini Butterfingers apiece to get H&A to both mutter "Sorry" and then one Reese's cup to get H&A past the soreness over the Aryan incident and into sugar-high chatter. Phew.

I wanted to go to the dive-through restaurant on Geary that's this great burger joint situated in a train car in this kinda seedy neighborhood, but Sugar Pie wanted fancy and also to check up on her true love's godson, Alexei, so that's how we ended up going to Lord Empress Kari's restaurant for dinner. Since my work-study will be over at the end of the semester, Her Majesty has invited me to continue working at the restaurant after Christmas, and I could even work in the kitchen if I want since that seems to be where I always end up hanging out, but I have come down with a big case of senioritis. I have decided to be a big slacker after the New Year and not have a job at all for my last semester of high school. Yeah, that'll mean more school time, but said plan should also allow for more Shrimp time.

Maybe Sugar Pie is now on my parents' payroll, too, because as soon as we were all seated at a table at the restaurant she said, "So how are those college plans coming along?" I didn't have to bother with the Don't Start with Me look, because H&A both jumped in with their plans. Autumn wants to do a double major in psychology and women's studies when she goes to college, and Helen just wants to get the hell out of her mother's house—she doesn't care where she ends up, as long as the place has an art program and is as geographically far from Clement Street in San Fran as she can possibly go. Maybe it was the oyster appetizers, because Sugar Pie's next wave of interrogation involved this question: "Where are you girls standing on the issue of true love these days?"

Autumn said, "I'm outta that game. Love is for suckers."

I'm almost inclined to agree. My half-bro Danny had called me just this morning and told me that not only is his business, The Village Idiots, closing and he's like practically in bankruptcy, but Danny and his true love, Aaron—the true-love couple you can always count on, no matter how bleak the state of love is looking—are on the outs. The thought of Danny and Aaron not being together is just too horrible to think about, though, so I won't, because I know Danny and Aaron will work things out. They always do.

Helen agreed with Autumn. "Yeah, fooling around is one thing, but true love is a lie. Not that fooling around doesn't count." Helen looked in my direction, acknowledging our Frank Night conversation on said topic, and I looked in Autumn's direction so she would know: case covered. Helen added, "Anyway I have no faith in true love. Think about Tim Armstrong and Brody Dalle. I mean, if ever there were two people who seemed so obviously true-love destined to be together, but D-I-V-O-R-C-E . . ."

Autumn said, "Who the hell are you talking about?"

Helen said, "Dude, the Mohawked guy from Rancid who used to be married to the singer chick from The Distillers."

Sugar Pie said, "Brody's a good singer, but she'll never match Tim Armstrong for musicianship."

We all spun our heads in Sugar Pie's direction like, *Huh?* Sugar Pie said, "My next-door neighbor, his grandson listens to that punk rock music and he makes me CD burns to listen to on my Discman while I'm on the chair at dialysis." Sometimes it's beyond comprehension how much cooler Sugar Pie is than 99.9 percent of the population. "So, listen, I have a lot of time on the dialysis chair to think about these things, so here's today's old lady wisdom: True loves may come and go in your lives, but your best friends, those are the people who will be with you throughout your lives, the ones who will stay with you."

Helen, Autumn, and I kinda squirmed at the table, and focused intently on eating our appetizers. I think that we three are bound in some unspoken but implicit agreement to never—EVER—get into some sisterhood covenant where we like vow to be friends for eternity and bridesmaids and godmothers, and we'll never be friends who like "do lunch" and have girly spa weekends where we catch up on one another's lives. H&A and I are just gonna . . . *be*. Simple friends, no complications, and end of this school year we'll figure out then how/if we'll stay in touch once we go in our different directions. Shrimp and I will probably be so back in love and lust by that time that I'll barely notice that H&A are away at college.

None of us had to worry about further gushy sentiments, because the rock-hard body of Alexei stood at our table, holding a complimentary bottle of overpriced sparkling water in a pretty cobalt blue bottle. "Ladies," he said, "compliments of the house." He had a napkin over the bottom part of his arm, all formal and shit as he poured the water into our glasses. Sugar Pie could not help but beam at her true love's godson, like, *My Fernando is partially responsible for how that boy sure did turn out right!*

On the down low, the thing about Alexei is, he wears suits really well. Honestly, he does. He must go to a professional tailor to get his suits altered so that they cling to his body just right. Alexei is like the boy next door who pulled your bra strap when you were kids and now you look at him and go, *Good God, man, how did you get to be so hot?*

Alexei focused his attention on me. "Nice you brought your friends to class this place up. But listen, Princess. Next week, when I'm staying at your house for Christmas, please save the Little Hellion antics."

Alas, while I may acknowledge the hotness that is Alexei, that doesn't mean he's not still a Horrible in personality.

Chapter 23

I served my time faithfully, but while the end of the school semester meant liberation from the work-study job at the restaurant, liberation from Alexei the Horrible was not to be mine.

I believe it's a constitutional right that the day after Christmas should be about sleeping late, lazing around the house all day without bothering to change out of your pajamas, and eating the leftover box of See's Christmas candy. The nonday is supposed to be capped off by watching *It's a Wonderful Life,* then bawling when George Bailey's war hero little brother toasts his big brother as "the biggest man in town," even though it's really his wonderful wife, Donna Reed, who saves the day. In Alexei World, the day after Christmas meant an 8 A.M. wake-up bugle (seriously), an egg-white breakfast followed by a run up the Lyon Street stairs, followed by an afternoon of ambushing the little princess with college brochures. Clearly he pegged me as the wrong kind of princess, though, because his brochures were from the likes of the University of Miami, USC, Hofstra, and Boston University. I did give half a glance to the Chico State, Loyola, and UC-Santa Cruz apps, but finding no brochures for schools I would actually consider or who would consider me (the University of Hawaii, NYU, Hampshire College, or any Semester at Sea boat), I gave up. My punishment was the nighttime video of a speech by

Alexei's hero, Noam Chomsky, that Alexei popped in for us to watch.

Us included a surprise leftover in the house. Since Nancy had cut the deal for me to stay home in San Francisco, I had offered to share baby-sitting chores with Josh's regular sitter so Sid and Nancy didn't have to cancel their trip when Josh came down with the chicken pox a week before Christmas. Josh was better by the time they left with Ash for Minnesota, but not well enough to travel and be abused by Granny A, so he had stayed home with me and Alexei, who was staying at Fernando's apartment on the side of the house while Fernando visited family in Nicaragua. The sitter took care of Josh during the days, and I had him at night.

The meds couldn't knock Josh out, but Noam Chomsky sure had. What does a ten-year-old boy care about a documentary on linguistics mixed with politics (or something), with no dash of special effects thrown in? Josh is a boy so hyper that when he was a baby he used to grip the safety bar on his stroller as he jumped around in the seat so he could watch all the action passing by, until his little body would get so exhausted he would plunge face forward onto the safety bar, dead asleep. Now Josh had exchanged the stroller safety bar for a sister's lap to pillow his head. We were on the L-shaped couch in the family room, Alexei facing the television, and Josh and I on the side part of the couch, Josh with a smile on his pretty face of fading pockmarks, probably dreaming of boy wizards. I looked up at Alexei and asked him, "Are my parents paying you extra to bore us to this extreme, Alexei?"

Shrimp has been so busy in the days leading up to

Wallace's wedding that I've hardly seen him, so I'm almost grateful that Josh got sick and had to stay home—he's great company. Sometimes I love Josh so much I want to gobble him whole; at the same time I'm tempted to make him a nice little Ritalin Kool-Aid when he gets too loud and physical, climbing all over me and never letting me win at *Super Mario,* which he plays with full-body grunts and many curse words learned from Ash. But Josh is also a snuggle bear who asks me, "Are you going away again?" when I put him to sleep, and hugs me extra hard when I tell him I'm not going away that soon but I'll always be his best girl. At least in my mind I will be, but the competition is getting fierce. He's a princely-looking blond boy with the longest, dreamiest eyelashes you ever saw, and despite his proclamation that girls are yucky (except me, of course), he's got babes-in-training from his school calling him every night and he's been invited to more parties his fifth-grade year than I have in the whole of my life. Perhaps it was his fate to get chicken pox and be stuck recovering at home with me, because I have gotten much opportunity to give the bedridden boy many talks about using his power for the good, and I hope when he is a high-school-age popularity boy that he will be the guy who is nice to everyone, from the jock crowd down the ladder to the outcast tier, where his big sister traditionally resided until this last school year. Josh's future girlfriends may feel free to thank me for molding his boyfriend potential from an early age.

Alexei lifted Josh from my lap to carry him upstairs to his real bed. When Alexei came back down, he hit PLAY on the CD player without checking to see what was in the stereo, so we were treated to Ol' Blue Eyes singing classic love songs. With the dim track lighting in the family room, the kid crocked asleep upstairs, and an open bottle of sparkling apple cider on the table, you'd almost think we had some romantic ambience happening. Except it was Alexei in the room, not Shrimp, and suddenly the Doritos I'd been munching caught up with me and a fart exited my body, causing the usually stone-faced Alexei to break out laughing.

If I was going to be humiliated like that, why shouldn't Alexei be also? I asked Alexei, "So did Kari dump you, or are you still going to make a fool of yourself over Mrs. Robinson from three thousands miles away when you go back to school?" College Boy is anxious to return back East to Fancy University now that his semester off is over, but he has been close-lipped (so to speak) about the status of his and Kari's relationship.

In response to my question, Alexei grabbed the remotes on the table. He turned the stereo off with one and turned the television and Noam Chomsky back on with the other. Then he jumped onto the couch next to me and made fanning gestures with his hands. His atrocious CK cologne was a pleasant distraction, in this instance.

Alexei was just looking at me, and we were both sort of laughing and smiling and shoving each other, as two people who mostly despise each other but who don't find the other entirely vile are naturally inclined to do, when all of a sudden the mood changed; a spark ignited. Somehow our mouths drew nearer to each other's by some inexplicable gravitational pull that was as exciting as it was repulsive, and was not purely based on lack o' Shrimp sexual frustration. A mantra played in the back of my mind, reminding me that Shrimp and I were: just friends, just friends, just friends. Didn't that make side orders admissible in the court of platonic aggravation? Yet right as Alexei's lips were about to touch mine, we both pulled back at the same exact second. Alexei said, "You have Doritos breath." I responded, "You have Listerine Strip breath, which is worse." Alexei looked as relieved as I felt that our strange little moment had not materialized into an actual kiss.

Maybe that Noam Chomsky guy would say I experienced a moment of clarity, because what I realized was this: not that Alexei and I weren't into each other that way, but that maybe I am capable of having a platonic friend who's a guy. Just not Shrimp.

I said to Alexei, "So if you'll turn that damn Noam Chomsky video off and put the music back on—I'll trade you Sinatra for classic Aerosmith—I might listen if you want to tell me what's so great about going off to some dumb college, and, like, what you plan on doing with your life once you're finished there."

Alexei poured us fresh glasses of sparkling cider and said, "Make yourself comfortable, Princess. It's gonna be a long night."

"Good, because since you've got me trapped, you might as well tell me all about what happened with Kari, too."

Chapter 24

With Josh's getting sick and getting left behind in San Francisco, the holiday season, and Sid and Nancy taking off with Ash for Minnesota to see dying Granny A, in all that chaos we forgot a very important date that falls the week between Christmas and New Year's: Josh's birthday. The whole situation, in my opinion, was very *Home Alone* meets *Sixteen Candles,* and I was *Clueless* on how to solve it. Josh's friends were all gone on Christmas vacation with their families, so it's not like I could invite them over for an impromptu party, and I was not about to pull a Nancy and take him to tourist trap Bubba Gump Shrimp Co. at Pier 39 for a birthday celebration. There was nothing left to do in this crisis except turn to the one person who could figure it out for me: Sugar Pie. And man, did she come through big time.

If you need to stock a last-minute party with guests who can't leave The City for the holidays, and who might love Harry Potter more than Josh, what better venue than a nursing home—excuse me, assisted living facility? I love old people. Who else would have the time and heart to decorate their party room for an HP-themed party, with an endless supply of fruit punch, Jell-O, and Boston Baked Beans subbing for Bertie Bott's Every Flavor Beans, on just a few hours' notice?

During the car ride over, Josh couldn't figure out why I

was wearing a McGonagall black tower hat, or why Alexei had bulked up his clothing so he'd look even closer to Hagrid size, until we led him into the party room, where an assortment of old-timers were milling around with Sugar Pie, Shrimp, and Helen and Autumn.

Not having the best collective vision, the party group didn't notice the guest of honor's arrival until about a minute after he'd knocked over a bowl of M&Ms in his sprint to retrieve the hastily created Nimbus2000 broomstick in the corner, but the smile on Josh's face when the group finally got around to saying "SURPRISE" in unison was big. His would not be a party with a piñata, and no one in that crowd was up for a game of Twister, but a party full of HP peeps, along with many treats and grown-up dancing to a collection of popular tunes (if you're 70-plus), could more than substitute.

Hmm, future career idea to DO something: create party-planning business organizing last-minute celebrations for forgotten birthdays.

Helen, who made for an interesting almost-bald-headed Hermione with square black geek glassless glass frames on her eyes, grabbed Josh's hand for the first dance under the paper lantern hanging from the ceiling. I doubt Josh knew who Benny Goodman was, but he had no trouble pulling off a postmodern robot dance with Helen to the WWII swing beat. Alexei took Cho Chang—that is, Autumn—off for a dance, while the tiniest Dumbledore ever, Shrimp, took my hand. I've always suspected there is some magic brew between Dumbledore and McGonagall, and our slow dance to the fast number, holding each other tight, my head on his shoulder, soulful silence between us, only proved that.

Shrimp and I danced through several songs, oblivious to the dance partner changes happening around us, until You-Know-Who—Sugar Pie—cut into our dance. Shrimp took her hand, thinking she was exchanging Alexei for him as her dance partner, but she shot him her best Voldemort death glance and took my hand instead. The two dudes left partnerless by Sugar Pie's cut-in, Shrimp and Alexei, exchanged awkward looks but did not move forward to dance with each other. They gave each other the soul brother handshake followed by the obligatory shoulder butt, then they both hot trotted their separate ways.

Sugar Pie said, "That was an awful slow, tight dance you and Shrimp just had to 'Mack the Knife.' Since you didn't notice, I'll inform you for future dances: It's an uptempo number. So is it safe to say you two are back together?"

"We're not there yet, my friend, not quite there."

"When do you think you will be?"

"Did you bring your tarot cards down for the party? Cuz I would like to figure out the same thing. It's just so . . . *nice* . . . between us, so it's like neither of us wants to ruin that. We are disgraces to our teenage libidos. I guess we are supposed to have some Official Talk if we ever decide to officially get back together, but we've both either been too busy or we're just dodging the topic entirely. Sugar Pie, is true love a fallacy?"

The song ended and Sugar Pie and I took seats next to the Hogwarts-decorated dining hall table heaped with cake and candy and—someone was really forward-thinking— bottles of Tums. Sugar Pie took a sip from her Dixie cup of grape Kool-Aid and answered my question. "Maybe you ought to stop worrying so much about some idea called true love, and think harder about the simple, plain reality of what love you have in you to give, and receive in turn. Love that's about the person—the real person, that lost soul boy whose future plans are vaguer than yours, the one too scared to admit how much he needs you because maybe he's afraid of losing you again—and not about some romanticized notion of who you thought that person was. Think about whether you have gotten to know this person well enough this time around to have earned the right to call it love."

"Do you love Fernando?"

"Yes, I think so."

"Is it true love?"

"It's better—it's real, which makes it harder, too, sometimes. Fights and handicaps and him taking off to Nicaragua for Christmas and not inviting this old lady along and all."

Ouch. I asked her, "Are you mad?" Sugar Pie nodded. "Are you going to break up with him?" She shook her head no. I wanted to know, "You're not dying, right? Because you said maybe you weren't planning on living here forever."

Sugar Pie laughed. "Not that my doctor has told me, baby. I may be getting on in years, but this lady isn't planning on going anywhere. Not just yet."

Josh arrived with a THUD on my lap, and banged his head against my chest. The sugar, dancing, and an engaged audience of people who knew the Hogwarts universe better than he had temporarily spent him. He whispered in my ear, "Your other family isn't taking you away, are they?" I looked down at his worried face and suspected this was the question he'd wanted to ask me since I got back from New York months ago, but maybe it was his special day and Sid and Nancy being gone that had allowed him to finally voice it.

I flicked his head, our usual custom. "No, silly," I told him.

For a love child who spent the better part of her life dreaming about her other family, I've barely given them a second thought since returning to San Francisco, except for Danny, of course, who is going to be the cause of my future carpal tunnel syndrome from all the cell phone text messaging I do with him to keep in touch. I did get a Christmas present from bio-dad Frank: a blue Tiffany box containing a chain necklace with a diamond heart-shaped pendant attached, like I am a girl who wears horridly precious trinkets like that. The card inside read, FOR A SWEET SIXTEEN OF A GIRL. Trust me, there is nothing about me that Frank finds sweet. I think the word he used to describe me was *spunky*. (Insert puking sound here.) Last year I might have been thrilled to get such a present from him, even such a sucky one, but this year—and by the way, Frank-dude, I'm seventeen, not sixteen—the necklace only confirmed how little he knew me. I set the Tiffany box aside to donate to charity.

Autumn and Shrimp approached our seats, carrying the birthday cake I'd made Josh, as everyone in the room sang "Happy Birthday." If anyone had told me last summer that my lifetime would witness an Autumn-Shrimp b-day duo celebrating my brother, at my request, I would have either collapsed in hysterics on the spot or possibly gone postal. To quote a great lady, Sugar Pie: "Life is funny, baby, and that's no joke."

After Josh had cut the cake, Autumn came over to sit with me while Helen snapped photos of the party and got the digits for at least three senior gentlemen, her latest flirt pals. She's promised me she's past Aryan, over it, done, *finito,* but natural Helen flirting, no matter the age of her conquest, could never be off-limits. Autumn said, "This cake is delicious. You made this whole thing by yourself?"

"Guess so," I said. "Not a big deal."

"I think a banana cake with chocolate ganache filling and the best buttercream frosting I've ever had in my life is a big deal. Thank your brother in New York for passing on the recipe, from my taste buds. So in all those colleges Alexei told me he's been going through with you, did you find any with a cake-baking major?"

All the college brochures and discussions have only confirmed for me what I already knew: College is not a place for me. I *hate* school, simple as that. I tolerate it because I have to, but when I'm there all I think about is when the school day will end, the weekend come, vacation start, my life begin again. I would rather study European history by going to Europe, or Far Eastern religions by traveling to China and India. I'd prefer to learn the great works of literature by watching Shakespeare in the park, and understand geometry and algebra by jumping off a triangular precipice and determining the distance to the bottom by whether the resulting injury requires an Ace bandage or a trip to the hospital for X rays. Making it through my senior year of high school—the actual school part, not the hanging with friends part—feels like I am a runner standing at my mark for the big race, waiting for the starting gun to signal graduation so I can sprint off to my future and some place that is not not not school.

"Nah," I said. "What about you? Did you finish your apps over the break?"

Autumn said, "Yeah. And I might even have snuck in a few dark-horse contenders."

"Where?"

Autumn's index finger and thumb did the zip lip gesture around her mouth. "I'm not jinxing it."

Chapter 25

The only wedding I've ever been to was Sid and Nancy's, when I was five. They got married at City Hall, and the ceremony was brief, anticlimactic, and itchy—Nancy made me wear this horrible pink frilly dress that caused a rash to break out on my chest and back. I didn't know what to expect for Wallace and Delia's wedding, but I knew they were planning a double-dose party: a joint wedding and New Year's Eve celebration packed into one long, festive night. I assumed the night would suck—any event that requires that much planning, money, and drama is destined to be a letdown—but I was still eager to see how it turned out. Bonus: Since Sid and Nancy were out of town, I could stay out as late as I wanted because Alexei had agreed to stay in the guest room next to Josh's room for the night, in exchange for my code of silence regarding certain sexual indiscretions he'd admitted occurred between himself and his former boss, Lord Empress Kari. Well, he also agreed because in addition to being a quasi-Horrible, he's basically a good guy. I've decided to look past the Kari thing anyway, because Alexei claims his older woman thing is not about age so much as that he's attracted to really smart women, who, according to Alexei, just tend to be older. Whatever, College Boy.

I did the unthinkable and raided Mrs. Vogue's closet for the occasion. Normally I wouldn't be caught dead wearing any pieces from her fashion mag wardrobe, but the wedding was a black tie/evening gown occasion, and Mrs. Vogue did have a small selection of passable dresses to go along with her puke princess ball gowns. Nancy had told me not to wear black or white to a wedding, so as not to appear somber or to compete with the bride's dress, so I chose a slinky gold lamé, spaghetti strap number that dipped low at the breasts and was cut high on the legs— especially high on me, because my legs and torso are longer than Nancy's, so the dress fell only a few inches below my butt. I tried adding a pair of Mrs. Vogue's Blahnik Choo or whatever-they-are shoes, but I kept wobbling on the spiked heels. How does Nancy walk in those fuckers and make it look so effortless? I traded the couture shoes for a pair of flat gold-sequined slippers with red patch flowers that I bought at the dollar store next to Helen's family's restaurant on Clement Street. I twisted my long black hair at the back of my head and placed two red chopsticks from the same dollar store in my hair to hold the twist, applied the dark Goth Chanel Vamp lipstick to my mouth, and I was ready to go.

"No," Alexei stated when I came downstairs, where he was waiting to give me a lift to the hotel on Nob Hill because I promised paranoid Nancy I would not drive on New Year's Eve, which she considers to be like Halloween for drunk drivers. "Go back upstairs and change. You're not wearing that." Alexei would not look like a Horrible in a tux, I suspected, admiring his buff bod decked out in sweats for his big New Year's Eve boys' night watching movies and playing video games with Josh. I so need to find for him an older woman who is not Lord Empress Kari.

I shoved Alexei's rock-hard chest. "Shut up," I said, walking out the front door toward the car. Alexei remained standing at the doorway, as if he expected that I would, in fact, return to my mother's room to choose another outfit.

Standing outside, goose pimples forming on my bare arms from the night fog and chilly Bay breeze, I said, "Seriously, Alexei, drive me or don't, but I am freaking freezing out here, and if you don't get out here now and put the heater on in that car, I am calling a cab."

Alexei, defeated, grabbed his keys from the hallway table, but then walked to the coat closet, rifled through it and pulled something out. When he came outside, he placed a long black pashmina wrap around my shoulders. "Modesty," he said as he opened the car door for me. "Learn about it."

In my eagerness to go to this wedding, I arrived way too early at the hotel, so I milled around alone for a while. I read a trashy celebrity tabloid in the gift shop, but that felt like bad karma so I left. Then I walked around the lobby fountain until I decided to kill the remaining time by taking a stroll around the little park across the street from the hotel. From the street at the top of Nob Hill, I could see the Bay Bridge and the Transamerica Pyramid, but what I particularly noticed was a familiar figure standing under a palm tree in the park, smoking a cigarette.

Wallace must have been nervous, because he is not a cigarette smoker. But how beautiful did he look in his tuxedo, his long brown hair falling in waves from his head, the front strands tucked behind his ears, and his big beautiful eyes staring off into space. If I were an artist I would have mummified him on the spot, to perfect him for eternity. Wallace whistled when he saw me. "Whoa! You sure weren't named Cyd Charisse for nothing!" He smiled, but the hand he held out to me, offering me a smoke, was shaking a little, and not from the cold Bay wind.

"You doin' okay?" I asked him, feeling a blush hot on my cheeks. I shook my head to the cigarette offer.

Wallace said, "I'm good. It's all good. Last-minute jitters, you know. How _you_ doin'? Just think: A couple years from now, this scene could be you and my brother taking the plunge."

I've never thought of myself as being the marrying kind, but Wallace's comment made me realize that (a) Wallace thinks of Shrimp and me as a couple, not "just friends," and (b) I am getting to be old enough where marriage wouldn't necessarily have to be this vague idea; it's something I could actually do if I wanted.

"Hardly," I said. "Marriage is stupid." Marriage to me is something that lonely people or pregnant people do. It's a nice enough institution, I suppose, for the right type of person, but not one with which I plan to bother. True loves don't need an official wedding license to validate their lives together.

"You're not helping," Wallace said with a laugh.

Damn me and my foot-in-mouth disease. "I didn't mean, like, stupid waste-of-time stupid. I meant I'm too young to think about it for myself." That was a lame recovery, but the best I could come up with in the moment. "Delia is a great girl, and I know you two will be very happy."

Wallace let out a little snort. "Happy, yeah. If we can ever get Iris and Billy out of our house. I tell ya, when the parents move back home . . . The slackers have no respect for the time and money it takes to maintain a household.

Parents today—what are ya gonna do?" Wallace stubbed out his cigarette on the ground. "Guess I'd better head back in; it's getting to be show time. See you in a while?"

Wallace leaned over toward my face, like he was going to kiss my cheek good-bye, but instead his lips grazed mine for an electric second. The kiss was romantic but at the same time innocent, as if he was saying *adios* to his single life and I to my crush on him. The fact that Wallace is a perfect ten-point-ohhhhh on the babe scale forgave the fact of his cigarette breath. After he'd pulled back I took a tissue from my purse to rub the slight Chanel Vamp lipstick stain off his mouth. Then I gave him a playful slap on the cheek. He winked at me before taking off back to the hotel across the street.

I found Shrimp lounging around the hotel lobby fountain when I went back inside, giving directions to the ballroom to an arriving guest. If I thought Shrimp looked best in a wet suit, that's because I'd never seen him wearing a tux. "That's some dress," he mumbled when he saw me. It's a good thing I didn't wear Nancy's shoes, otherwise I truly would have towered over him instead of just standing above him by several inches.

"I thought you were planning to wear a powder blue tux with a blue carnation," I said. I flecked a piece of dust from his black jacket, but really I just wanted to cop a feel of him in his tux. I straightened the daisy in his lapel.

Shrimp said, "Delia didn't go for that idea. Go figure. She thought a best man should wear the same style tux as the groom. Women! No imagination, I tell ya." He smiled. He looked and sounded just like his brother: nervous but happy.

I took his arm and we walked to the ballroom, where he left me to join the wedding party, and I took a seat. I've never been a girl who dreams about her wedding day from the time she's able to play Barbie Bride Dress-up Set, Ash's favorite activity, but I was awed at the beauty of the room: ivory and crimson roses everywhere, gold candles glowing, a string quartet playing in the corner, and from the top-floor ballroom a stunning nighttime view of the San Francisco skyline outside the windows, with bright stars made visible in the sky by the cold night wind.

Like Sid and Nancy's wedding, Wallace and Delia's ceremony was brief and anticlimactic, so at first the whole deal seemed like a lot of trouble for such a quick interlude. Delia, who had gone the puke-princess-dress route but did look stunning in her strapless ivory satin gown with beading around the bodice and a train extending a few feet, must have gone to hours of trouble to transform herself into a bride. Her red frizz of hair was straightened and pulled into an elegant updo, and I can't imagine how long she sat in the makeup chair to smooth out all her freckles and get that cover-girl look. I could never sit still that long to be beautified for a ceremony that lasted all of twenty minutes. You couldn't deny the genuine emotion of the ceremony, though. Delia's dad burst into tears when he lifted the wedding veil over her head to give her away, which started a chain reaction of parental tears: Delia's mom started weeping, then Iris and Billy, then Delia's stepmother and her stepfather, and when I looked over at the groomsmen, even Shrimp was wiping a tear from his cheek! In the middle of the ceremony Shrimp stepped to the podium to read a love poem. He looked at me in the audience while he was reading, which made my eye sockets go all wet, and when it came time for Wallace and Delia to say their vows they were both in tears. Waterproof mascara: great invention. I'm not saying all the universal bawling means Wallace and Dee's marriage is destined to last and will be the happiest one ever, but even my cold nonmatrimonial heart warmed from the true love you could feel rising between Wallace and Delia and dispersing through the ballroom like pixie dust.

But true love blahbitty blah blah, let's talk PARTY. A swing band played until midnight, and I mostly stayed at my assigned table, watching people dance. Not knowing many of the two-hundred-something guests, and being skeeved out by all the guys finding Mrs. Vogue's dress to be more stare-worthy on her daughter than I appreciated, I was more than happy to fade into the background for the first hour or so of the reception. Plus, I was dodging my "pal" Shrimp, who seemed caught up in official best man duties anyway, as I was determined we would not get locked into a cliché clock-strikes-midnight New Year's Eve kiss. 12:08 or 1:42, negotiable. The view from my seat offered plenty of entertainment. Delia is a professional dancer, as were most of her friends, so the dance floor could have been a USO party back in WWII from how great these people knew the old moves.

When I returned to my seat from a bathroom interlude, the lady sitting next to me said, "You just missed it, but Shrimp gave a lovely toast to Wallace and Delia. You're Cyd Charisse, right?"

I nodded. "Who are you?" I asked her. She introduced herself as Priscilla, Delia's half-sister from Alaska. Priscilla seemed as desperate for a friend in this room full of strangers as I. She looked like she was in her late thirties and she had curly carrot-colored hair like Delia's. Priscilla told me she'd hadn't decided to come to the wedding until almost the last minute; she was much older than Delia and hadn't been raised in the same house as her sister, and she liked Delia a lot although she didn't know her sister very well and hadn't seen her in a few years, but she was hesitant to come because the only family she knew at the wedding was their dad, and otherwise all the family members came from Dee's mother's side. Priscilla ended up coming to the wedding when her husband back in Anchorage told her that she needed a break from her kids, and he gave her the trip to San Francisco with some girlfriends as a Christmas present. As she spoke I could see that Priscilla thought she'd be getting some peace and quiet with her short adventure away from home, but I suspected on this New Year's Eve she would take rambunctious kids running wild all over her house to not be orphaned in this wedding ballroom. I will probably feel the same as Priscilla if my half-sister lisBETH ever gets married—that is, if I even get invited to lisBETH's wedding. You never know with lisBETH when she's going to go all embarrassed about "Daddy's little indiscretion."

The bubbly I'd been consuming throughout dinner caught up with me after midnight, when the swing band was replaced by a deejay. "C'mon, fellow wallflower," I told Priscilla. I grabbed her hand to lead her to the dance floor as the deejay got the floor pumping with "Dancing Queen" by Abba. I literally had to drag Priscilla from her chair—she really didn't want to go—but once she was on the floor there was no stopping her. There was no stopping CC either, because apparently the deejay had the same five-dollah CD from the remainder bin at Amoeba Records that practically wore out my Discman: *Soul Train—The Dance Years: 1977.* By the end of "Got to Give It Up" by Marvin Gaye, Priscilla and I had both tossed our shoes under the table, and we burned up the dance floor for a good half hour, laughing and bumping and grinding, celebrating. Priscilla taught me how to dance the Hustle during "I'm Your Boogie Man" by K.C. & The Sunshine Band (best song ever) and I showed her it was possible to dance the Macarena to "Don't Leave Me This Way" by Thelma Houston. Priscilla and Delia's semibald carrot-topped father joined us for "Boogie Nights" by Heatwave and showed us his old disco moves from when he was young, but when it came time for the slow disco era song "If I Can't Have You" from the *Saturday Night Fever* soundtrack, he took Priscilla out for a twirl, just the two of them.

Nancy claims I am a punk girl but she is wrong about that. A punk girl cares as much about the politics of the music as she does the sound of it. She knows what's going on in the world, she's fierce, a music snob, and completely dedicated to a punk ideology, fuck all the rest of y'all. I *wish* I could be that girl. Helen is that girl. No, my dirtiest little secret is that I like almost all music, from punk to opera to serious soul, but if you insist on slapping a label on me, you should know that in my heart I am a straight-up disco queen, a good-time girl.

After Priscilla's dance with her dad, she returned to our table for cake and more champagne and we watched Wallace and Delia dazzle the crowd with their *Saturday Night Fever* dance moves. Wallace had passed on the Arthur

Murray ballroom dance lessons in preparation for his wedding and had opted for a disco dancing class at the Ocean Beach senior center, and may I just say, the guy was a regular John Travolta. He and Delia looked amazing on the dance floor, a king and queen in all their glory.

About half past one in the morning, the crowd was thinning out and the music beat simmering down. Priscilla and I shared a last dance to "Strawberry Letter 23," joined by Shrimp, whose official best man duties were finished. His tux jacket was long gone, the tie hanging loose around his neck, and his white shirt unbuttoned halfway down his bare chest. He was sweaty from dancing as well—never looked hotter. We three danced the Bump, Priscilla's specialty, before Priscilla decided to call it a night and return to her hotel room. She hugged me extra hard and whispered in my ear that I'd made an evening she'd been anxious about into a fun one after all. As she left I saw her share a brief conversation and hugs with Wallace and Delia.

"Well," Shrimp said. The disco ball hanging over his head flecked his exposed chest with bursts of light. "Did you save the last dance for me?"

The hotel staff was busy folding away chairs as I took the sweaty hand Shrimp extended to me. The deejay was closing up shop too, and his last song was a slow ballad. "Thanks for looking after Priscilla," Shrimp said. "Delia wanted to spend more time with her, but then Dee got caught up in all that bride business. Delia told me every time she was worried about Priscilla hardly knowing anyone here, she'd see her dancing with you and knew she didn't have to worry about Priscilla after all."

You know how a single song can change everything?

That's how the romantic Aaliyah ballad the deejay was playing affected me. I danced with my head on Shrimp's shoulder, my brain still pondering the pulsating disco anthem by Thelma Houston where she expressed how she was full of love and desire and she couldn't stay alive without her man's love, but my heart tuned to the slow, bittersweet Aaliyah song the deejay had spinning. That song got me thinking about that beautiful angel girl, who died at such a young age, without getting to live what appeared to be a great life ahead of her.

All the champagne had nothing to do with the words I said to Shrimp as the song ended. "I love you," I stated, loud and clear, no mumbling or whispering for this sentiment. "Just friends" was a lie I couldn't live any longer. I didn't care that I hadn't said *I love you* to Shrimp since long before we'd broken up so many months ago, not even knowing then what it was to love Shrimp because when I said those words to him before, I was spouting an ideal I thought I felt that had nothing to do with the actual person. I didn't care if in the present moment, Shrimp—the Shrimp who befriended my parents so he could win a way back into my life, the Shrimp who botched the Justin revelation but who knew it and worked past it, the Shrimp who is forever loyal to parents who act on their best interests, not his—didn't say the words back to me. I just wanted him to know.

"Ditto," Shrimp said.

I guess we did not need the long official conversation about whether we should get back together or not after all.

Chapter 26

We left the hotel together and Shrimp drove us to the original scene of the crime, to Land's End, where he parked his Pinto the first time we got together. That first time, I remember a U2 song was playing on the car radio tuned to the Berkeley campus radio station, and when we did it in the backseat of the car to the sound of Bono's ultrasexy voice, the experience was hot and urgent, infatuated. Shrimp and I had barely met and I was just past the Justin–boarding school thing. It was like neither of us expected our connection to last past a simple, extremely satisfying hookup, and when a relationship developed in the months that followed, we were both surprised—and unprepared.

This time, the experience was . . . careful. The head bangin', boots knockin' reunion I'd been anticipating did not happen. No music played from the radio, and the secluded Land's End spot under the tall trees where Shrimp had parked the Pinto was silent except for the hiss of the Bay wind and the rustle of leaves. Noises I'd never noticed between us before, like the fumbling to open the condom and the squishy-rubbery sound as he placed it on, the creak of the backseat, the awkward grunts, his deep gravel voice asking if I was comfortable, felt especially loud in the car this time around. The feel of our bodies pressed together was sweet, tender, but the earth did not move from our actions, as if we were both too polite to disturb its peace, too cautious to tread deeply in our new territory.

It will get good again. I'm fairly sure. We just had to get past the first time, the second first time.

After, we drove back to his house in Ocean Beach. Iris and Billy and Wallace and Delia had opted to stay at the hotel for the night. Shrimp and I changed clothes—he from his tux into sweats and a T-shirt, and me from Mrs. Vogue's dress into an extra pair of Shrimp's flannel jammies that rode too high on my calves because of my long legs and his short ones. We took Aloha for a quick walk around the block, wearing our pj's and slippers, then returned to Shrimp's bedroom. Shrimp placed a sleep mask over my eyes, not as a prelude to some kinky sex game but so he could unveil, at long last, the painting he'd started at my house that was now standing, covered, opposite his single, unmade bed.

Shrimp is not an *I love you*–spouting type of guy, a main reason why "ditto" gets recycled in his vocab when he has to verbalize the sentiment in return to my words. Shrimp speaks through his art.

"I call this *Blitzkrieg CC,*" Shrimp said as he removed the mask from my eyes. "Look carefully at the face; it's the same one you gave me when I said the wrong thing that day you told me about Justin." Blitzkrieg Cyd Charisse the painting was indeed: my face, with this mad punk snarl that was somehow sexy and inviting at the same time, embedded into the face of the Statue of Liberty. Lady Liberty, the CC version, was not holding her usual torch. She was bent over placing a pair of pink silk stockings on her long, creamy legs, with the Golden Gate Bridge instead of the Brooklyn Bridge behind her, a thick wisp of SF-style fog creeping through its spokes. I'm no art expert, but even I knew the piece was amazing, having nothing to do with me as inspiration and everything to do with the stroke textures and layers of color that dug way deeper than the simple portrait. *Blitzkrieg CC* looked like how he said I looked to him: always different. You could look at this painting a million times and find something new in it every time.

"Wow," was all I could say. Shrimp likes his art to be admired in silence, so I knew not to say more.

We grabbed some down quilts and Aloha followed us upstairs to the roof. Shrimp turned on the space heater, covered up Aloha on the doggie bed, and then Shrimp and I laid down on the hammock next to the pooch. We didn't attempt another round of lovemaking—we were both way too tired—so we curled tight into each other under the blankets and fell asleep almost immediately as dawn rose over the Pacific.

True love, for real, for sure.

Chapter 27

Granny A died on New Year's Day. I think she held out that long so she could get an extra year on her tombstone. I felt sad when Sid-dad called to tell us, but sadder for Nancy than for me. Death generally is a bummer, right, but death specifically when it happens to someone who raised you has to be hard so I felt really bad for my mom. I didn't know what I was supposed to do to grieve for someone I never really knew and didn't particularly like, so I got some pâté and Ritz crackers from Safeway, which Josh and I tried to eat for dinner in Granny A's honor. But the pâté and crackers were seriously gross, so we went over to Shrimp's instead and he made us scrambled eggs and Pop Tarts, which was much better. I didn't have to worry about whether I would seem like a fake grieving granddaughter at the funeral because a blizzard in the Midwest had closed the local airports, meaning Josh and I could not fly to Minnesota for the service, meaning further that I got extra Shrimp time before Sid and Nancy and Ash came back to San Francisco. Thanks, Granny A!

I knew Nancy would be somber about Granny A once she returned home, of course, but I figured she would snap out of it quickly enough when I broke the news to her about the whole didn't fill out any college applications because I was too busy spending the school vacation with my BOYFRIEND thing. Nancy could thank me later for distracting her sadness and turning it into fury.

But proving that hell can indeed freeze over, Nancy did not go ballistic when I dropped the bombs on her. She had been home for a few days but had stayed in her room in bed most of the time. She said she was sick with the flu, but she had a perennially filled box of See's Candy by her bed and a remote control in her hand, flipping between the Home and Garden channel to the classic movie channels to endless episodes of ugly-people makeover shows. I'm sorry, if you are really sick you just want soup and crackers, and your brain can barely focus on *Sesame Street* reruns. On the fourth day that Nancy was home and had failed to wake me up in what would be an unsuccessful attempt to get me to go to yoga with her, I went into her bedroom where she was sitting upright in bed, a tray with cereal and a pot of tea that Sid-dad had made her on her lap. She looked like a fairy princess on the crisp white sheets, wearing a white lace-trim nightgown, with glazed-over baby blue eyes and a white silk scarf holding back her pale blond hair.

"Want to go to yoga?" I asked her. I held up two yoga mats.

Nancy turned her head away from the TV. "I'm just not feeling yoga these days, honey. But thanks." The tone of her voice sounded completely dull and flat. She turned her head back to the TV.

I took the remote from her hand and clicked the TV off and just came out with it: "Shrimp and I are back together and I didn't fill out any college applications because the honest truth is, I just don't want to go."

While her eyes didn't register any reaction, she did sigh her Nancy Classic. Her voice remained at monotone level when she said, "That's nice. Maybe having a boyfriend in The City will keep you from flying the coop. You'll stay home another year with us. Maybe you can take some classes at City College. That would be good, right, Sid?" Sid-dad had come into the room and he sat down on the bed next to her, patted her hand, and placed a kiss on her forehead. "That's right," he said. An actual hint of a smile occurred on Nancy's face, and she placed a quick kiss on Sid-dad's lips in return.

Cough ewwww *cough*!

Since they got back from Minnesota, Sid and Nancy have dropped into a disturbingly low percentile for Bickering Married Couples, and she's touching him all the time now, holding on to his arm, resting her head on his shoulder. And for a supposedly busy-busy-busy CEO, not only did Sid-dad extend his Christmas vacation (which he's never done before—ever) to stay with Nancy for the funeral, but also he's cut back his office schedule so he can be home more while Nancy is "sick." Maybe this is Granny A's revenge to me for not mourning for her more than I do, that her death has turned my household into a mortuary of weirdness.

Nancy asked him, "Could you get me some sugar for the tea?"

Sid-dad got up from the bed. "A packet of Equal coming right up," he said.

"No," she whined. "Real sugar." The shock of Nancy's request made my head want to do one of those 360-degree rapid-spin turns like the psycho possessed child in *The Exorcist*.

After Sid-dad left the room I said, "Okay, something is really wrong with you. What is it? Should I be worried?"

Nancy patted the space where Sid-dad had been sitting and gestured for me to join her on the bed. "No, you shouldn't be worried. I just need some time. Grief takes a long to process."

"I don't understand," I said, trying to put on my sweet voice (even though I don't have one) so I wouldn't sound harsh. "You didn't even like your mother."

"But she was my mother, and I loved her," Nancy whispered, and a flood of tears sprang from her eyes. Dang, if it wasn't for the tray on her lap, I might have curled up next to her and given her a hug or something disgusting like that. When moms are that sad, it's just . . . painful. Nancy added, "There were so many issues left unresolved, so many things I was too proud to tell her, and now I just feel so empty. That's the part the minister never talks about in the funeral sermon, about what can God do to cover up all the emptiness in your heart and soul and every part of your being after you've lost a parent and you're left all alone?"

A silence hovered between us, maybe because Nancy was weirded out that she had confided something so personal to me, and I was weirded out because how was it possible she could feel that empty and alone when she has a husband and three children?

Nancy removed the tray from her bed to the floor, composed herself, and then said, "The sleeping pill has kicked in so I'm going to take a nap. I didn't rest at all last night. Could you please close the door behind you and tell Dad not to bother with the sugar for the tea?"

"Sure," I said. I placed a kiss on her forehead.

Chapter 28

My mother's insomnia has evolved to the point where she's now taking a sleeping pill late at night instead of in the morning, which means she falls asleep just after 2 A.M. and stays asleep at least till Ash and Josh jump on her bed around seven in the morning. Her new sleep schedule is why I can feel my cell phone ringer, set to vibrate, shuddering against my heart where it lies on top of me while I sleep, approximately at 3 A.M. The cell phone vibration is my signal that a certain Pinto legacy car is idling down the street instead of in front of my house (loud carburetor), and it's time for me to get out of bed and sneak out of the house.

So this is not the old Cyd Charisse, sneaking out to do some sneaking around. The new sneaking out routine is all about not bothering my mother's new sleep routine when middle-of-the-night hunger, and quality time with Shrimp, calls. This new routine is all about the letters I-H-O-P.

I could just leave out the front door but that wouldn't be fun, and besides, tapping the security code to open the door can be noisy, and I don't want to risk waking the household. So after Shrimp's vibration signal pounded on my heart, I crawled out of my bedroom window and climbed down the tall tree until I was standing in the backyard, from which I could easily exit the locked gate to the street, except for the little surprise waiting for me at the bottom of the tree this time. Make that big surprise, as in Fernando, sitting in a lawn chair and reading a copy of *Hola* magazine with a little flashlight.

"*Buenas noches,*" Fernando said.

DAMN IT!

"It's not what you think," I told Fernando. "We just go to the twenty-four-hour IHOP on Lombard Street. I just don't want to wake Mom. You know how she's been having a hard time sleeping." My voice gushed with concern, some of it actually genuine.

"If that's the case," Fernando said, "why don't I just come along with you?"

"Why don't you just, then," I stated. That's how confident I am in my relationship with Shrimp since we got back together. I know I can haul Fernando along and Shrimp will be stoked instead of freaked. I'm almost scared by how good things are between Shrimp and me. Easing back into a relationship wasn't that hard after all—it was getting back in that was hard, but once back in, it's been smooth sailing, as Nancy might say, given enough wine. Well, mostly smooth sailing. Nancy is dealing well with Shrimp and I being an official couple again, probably because I'm not going on meltdown this time around if I'm not around Shrimp 24/7. I have other friends now, my own life going, I don't feel like I am going to suffocate if I'm not with Shrimp every second. But now that he and I are back together, it's not like he has an all-access pass to spend the night at my house either, and with the Fightin' Shrimps back at Ocean Beach—Wallace and Delia versus Iris and Billy—his house is not the nicest place to hang these days. Here is the biggest disadvantage of being an almost-adult: you're having safe sex with your boyfriend, you're in a committed relationship, everyone knows you are doing it, but you still have to sneak around to do it, even though you're doing it right! My senior slump this last semester of my high school career has not been about being tired of school (even though I am), as much as sometimes the only time Shrimp and I can be alone together, in privacy, is during the school day.

However, the middle-of-the-night meetings are not about tryst times. They are strictly about the award-winning old-fashioned buttermilk pancakes and hanging out with our friends before senior year ends and we all likely go our separate ways. So even though Fernando got into the Pinto with Shrimp and me, he still looked surprised when we arrived at our usual corner booth, where Helen, her new boyfriend, and Autumn were waiting for us. You know Fernando thought I was lying to him when I said IHOP, and he thought he would be calling my bluff instead of getting a late-night carb feast.

"Yo, Ferdie, right on—gimme five!" Helen said when she saw Fernando. He actually high-fived her back, which made me kind of jealous, as he would never high-five me, the boss's daughter. Helen told her new love, "Move over, Eamon. Make some room for my buddy."

Helen finally moved past the Aryan thing and she's on to a new boy, one who may be a keeper. At least he's sweet, and he believes in relationship as much as reciprocity. Technically he's not a hand-me-down from me, because I never went through with kissing Eamon that night I first met Helen and we hung out at the pub on Clement Street to scope out the Irish soccer guys. She rediscovered him on New Year's Eve at that pub, the same one where no one bothers to ID her. After Eamon got past the initial moment of recognizing Helen and then saying, "Hey, didn't you and your friend give me and my mate the slip a while back?" the two spent the evening slugging back Guinnesses and discussing their mutual contempt for pop punk, Brazilian soccer stars, and the English royal family. Imagine a guy with spiky fire-engine-red hair, green eyes, and crooked teeth, death-pall pale skin; throw in a hot, unintelligible Irish accent along with soccer-dude rock-hard calves and a slight, not entirely unpleasant, postgame B.O., and you can understand why Helen was instantly smitten with Eamon. Boom, Helen is back to firm hetero roots, just like the black roots have finally grown over the once-copper hand on her formerly almost-bald head, now grown out to a most excellent shag. Helen's a babe!

Shrimp sat down next to Autumn, with Fernando on his other side, as the rest of the group has proclaimed that Shrimp and I cannot sit next to each other anymore as apparently we have some PDA issues since we've gotten back together. That's what the bathrooms are there for anyway. I joined Helen and Eamon on their seat.

Autumn handed me a stack of brochures. "I ordered these for you. Have you ever thought about culinary school?" she asked me.

"No," I said. Culinary part—maybe. School part—blech. I handed her a bag of beads that Ash and I picked out for Autumn when we were shopping on Fillmore. Autumn is getting her shorter do un-dreaded and into braids, so Ash and I chose an assortment of crystal beads that we can't wait to see framing Autumn's face. Really, though, I suspect the only reason Autumn is only getting her hair braided is because she's crushing on the IHOP waitress whose sister owns the 'do salon.

Helen asked Fernando, "What's it like to be old?"

All our forks stopped midmouth at Helen's question, not at the rudeness of the question—no pancake is worth waiting on for that—but at the fundamental importance of the question, one that our group had been pondering on a regular basis.

Fernando swallowed his pancake mouthful, let out a little burp, and then said, "I don't know. Ask me when I'm old."

Well, we had plenty of other questions, which is how our IHOP fest turned into an hourlong Fernando interrogation: What does Nicaragua look like? Who were the Sandinistas, anyway? Are grandchildren really so fun and cute, or are they overrated as a species? If you went on *Survivor,* would you win by lying, cheating, and stealing, or strictly on the basis of sex appeal? Just what are your intentions with Sugar Pie?

I tell you, by the end of that meal, I can assure you Fernando will never again worry about me sneaking off to IHOP. He will shove me out the door and beg me not to make him come along.

When we got back home Shrimp and Fernando stepped outside the car and had some words in private. I was still in the car, waiting for my last kiss with my boyfriend, when Shrimp popped back into the car and drove off before I could get out. He stopped and parked the car a few blocks away on Lyon Street, opposite the Presidio.

"What's this?" I asked.

Shrimp leaned into my face. "Fernando and I, we had a man-to-man chat about boundaries. He said so long as you're home in an hour, he'll be cool about it. But only on the condition that you tell your parents that we're having late-night munchie runs at IHOP. He said they won't mind— what they mind is secrecy."

Oooh, *secrecy* as a word coming from my boyfriend's mouth. SO HOT. I pulled Shrimp's face to mine and said a silent prayer thanking Fernando for the extra hour on the DL.

Chapter 29

The good news: DANNY IS MOVING TO SAN FRANCISCO! The bad news: he's a no-good, cheating dawg who left his boyfriend, Aaron, for another man. Danny's new love is a lawyer (I hate him already) who works in The City, and Danny met him at a club where new lawyer man went one night while on a business trip in NYC, and where Danny had gone to shake off the sad news that he and Aaron's business, The Village Idiots, had failed. Danny and Aaron lost the lease on their café and couldn't afford a new space so they closed up shop, and not long after that Danny met new lawyer man, putting a closing notice on Danny's relationship with Aaron.

True love may be a lie.

For a no-good dawg, Danny sure looked chipper when I picked him up at the airport. Danny looked exactly like I remembered him—like me, like Frank-dad, but shorter and sweeter, with an open face that had the gall to be glowing with happiness. At the airport curbside pickup he hopped into my car and kissed my cheek. "It's so great to be in California!" he said. "I just escaped the fourth snow storm this February. I thought if I saw one more snowflake, I would lose it. Ah, California sunshine and CC, too. How lucky am I? This change of scenery is just what I needed. I love it!"

I kissed his cheek back, but then had to say, "Don't look so happy. I am very cross with you."

Danny smiled bigger. The nerve! "Who's looking pretty happy herself?" he teased. Danny lifted a piece of my hair. "Purple?" he asked. Apparently when I proclaimed I would never go for body art as a form of self-expression, I was lying. Shrimp and I were in his rooftop hammock at a rare time when we had the house to ourselves. He was explaining to me about dysentery, which he had in Papua New Guinea, while we were listening to a Prince CD. Then Shrimp and I shared, let's call it a lovely interlude (I told you it would get good again), while the Purple One sang "Erotic City," an interlude so inspired I had no choice but to celebrate it by going to Haight Street to get violet streaks highlighted into my long black hair. Some girls might get tattoos with their boyfriend's name—Johnny Angel or Stud Muffin or whatever—but I prefer a more wash-out-able form of branding to express my love for my man.

"Don't change the subject," I told Danny. "What's his name, anyway?"

Danny said, "Terry."

"That's a girl's name."

Danny did the whistle-snap. "There's nothing girl about Terry, let me tell you. I have never dated a man that beautiful in my life. Wait till you meet him!" The whistle-snap from Danny? Since when did he become a stereotypical Chelsea boy? Danny is the upstanding homosexual who wears wrinkled T-shirts and blue jeans from ten years ago, he has a scraggly mess of black hair and kind brown eyes with dark eyebrows so bushy he practically has a unibrow, and then there's also his avowed love of Pamela Anderson (don't ask me, I have no idea). Danny is the guy that if you didn't already know he was gay you would think he was a fence straddler at best, not a confirmed Friend of Dorothy. I am all for Chelsea boys, I have great appreciation for their beautiful bodies and exceptional fashion sense, and I, too, share their love for *The Golden Girls,* but that's not who Danny is.

"Well, where do you want me to drop you off?" I asked him. "At Terry's house in the Oakland hills, or at the local intervention clinic for bad bad boyfriends who dump their true love just when the going gets tough for some shallow-vain he-man who probably shaves his chest and gets facials more frequently than my mother?"

Danny turned down the car radio and turned his body so he was facing me. "Listen, Ceece, I know this is hard. If you think you're taking it bad, you should know that lisBETH hasn't spoken to me since Aaron and I broke up. She's been too busy helping him find a job and a new apartment, like Aaron is her brother, not me. Dad's freaked out. He's never been comfortable with the gay thing anyway, although he always puts on a PC show about how it's all fine, but at least with Aaron he knew what to expect with me. Aaron is a great person—don't think I am not fully aware of that. We had some great years together, but we'd gotten to be more like friends than mates. Aaron and I were over long before Terry came along. The spark had died. So now I am unemployed and treading in dangerous territory. I don't know what I'm going to do with my life now that The Village Idiots is gone, and I'm so insecure with Terry, I'm sure I'm gonna blow it. I could really use some support. Help me out here, okay, Ceece?"

Faux-wanna-be Chelsea boy or not, he's still my Danny, the half-brother who made my summer in Manhattan worthwhile, the only person clever enough and who would care enough to give me a nickname like Ceece. "Okay," I said.

"So when do I get to meet the famous Shrimp?" Danny asked.

"He's out in the East Bay scouting a new Java the Hut location with his brother this afternoon, but he wants us to get together tomorrow. Maybe we could go get coffee and breakfast together or something."

Danny laughed. "I know your tricks. I am not enabling you to skip school on my account. Let me talk with Terry and maybe all of us can get together this weekend."

"Are you moving in permanently with Terry?"

"No. We're gonna see how it goes—no commitments as of now. I needed to get out of New York for a while, and what better place to escape than the Bay Area? I hardly got any time with you last summer, and it would be great to see Uncle Sid again too. Terry has a huge house with a great kitchen, so I can keep myself occupied just fine while he's working during the day."

Because Danny is a relatively new discovery in my life, I forget that other people besides me, Josh, and Ash have a claim to "Uncle Sid." Sid-dad was a doting godfather to lisBETH and Danny when they were kids, because he and bio-dad Frank were old college roommates and best friends, until Nancy came between them. As I looked at Danny through the corner of my eye, I felt proud to call him brother, and couldn't wait to introduce him to Shrimp and my friends—Helen, Autumn, Sugar Pie—but I can't say I was cool with the thought that Danny planned to hang with "Uncle Sid" during his time in San Francisco.

Weirder than the thought of Danny interacting with

my parents would be Danny interacting with Nancy's mourning period. Mrs. Vogue hadn't been to yoga in a month, and she spends most of her days moping around the house wearing Sid-dad's plush old Ritz-Carlton hotel robe. Neiman-Marcus may possibly go out of business for how long since Nancy has shopped there. While Nancy's cooking skills haven't improved, she has mastered the art of the Duncan Hines mix. We no longer have to sneak sweets into the house because Nancy herself is making them and eating them. I found it hard to imagine how the Danny-Nancy chemistry could mix, especially since they were both at such strange intervals in their own lives.

The good news still was Danny had arrived in San Francisco and planned on staying a while, but the queasy news was having Danny in my Left Coast world may mean the separation gap between the two families can no longer be kept separate. Danny's presence could cause the vortex separating the old friends, and me from my other family and them from me, to close permanently, in a way my short summer Manhattan fling never had.

Chapter 30

True love may be making a comeback.

Helen's eighteenth birthday has passed, but that doesn't mean she's legally sanctioned to bring Eamon upstairs to her room. I feel her pain, so I am doing what I can to help her out. Originally I started hanging out in the kitchen at Helen's mom's Chinese restaurant on Clement Street because my work-study job had ended. Then it turned out I actually missed the restaurant environment, and I was looking for a way to get back at Helen for proclaiming Mrs. Vogue to be the "coolest mom ever." Helen's mom refuses to hire me for a regular shift—she said if her own daughter won't work in her restaurant, neither shall I—but she has been teaching me how to make her most excellent dumplings in exchange for occasional early-evening assistance with vegetable peeling and chopping. Helen's mom would also like me to encourage Helen to get rid of her new copper-spotted tiger-print eyebrows, and she'll throw in noodle lessons if I can convince Helen that proper ladies do not draw action-hero cartoon series about dirty old men with names like Ball Hunter.

The pot stickers Helen's mom makes are so good I have composed a love song to them: "Oh, pot stickers you are so yummy and juicy, so porky and full, love that ginger flava whateva . . ." That's the extent of my song so far, but I am working on a new, international tribute song in celebration of the new delicacy in my repertoire—steamed shrimp dumplings—and inspired by the minor language lessons the kitchen crew at the Chinese restaurant have been giving me: *"Hen hao chi de hsia long bao,* delicious, yummy dumpling, *hsia ren hsia ren hsia ren,* shrimp, shrimp, shrimp."

I was singing my pot sticker song while I stuffed a stack of gyoza wrappers with meat filling when I looked up to see Helen waving at me from the window at the back door of her family's flat, the back door that opens into a hallway leading upstairs to the apartment, or through which the restaurant kitchen can be entered. She must have jumped a dozen backyard fences to get to that back entrance without coming through the front. I saw the spikes of Eamon's fire-red hair behind Helen's head. Got it. I spilled the bowl of vegetable filling onto the floor, causing Helen's mother, who is crazy for cleanliness, to join me pronto under the work table to help clean up the mess. I looked up from underneath the table to see Helen leading Eamon by the hand as they creeped up the back stairs. "Thanks!" she mouthed at me. Ah, *chu lian,* young love.

Helen's sneak reminded me that my restaurant time was over for the day. Shrimp was due to pick me up in his Pinto, as my Betty Boop car does not do Clement Street, because Clement Street does not do parking. We were going to a fancy restaurant in the East Bay to meet Danny and Terry, the first time Shrimp would meet Danny, and I would meet Terry, like a double date. When I got outside, The Richmond fog spread a cold mist over my face while I scanned for Shrimp's car on Clement Street. I was especially excited to see him because he hadn't shown up at school for two days, and I missed seeing him live and in the flesh something bad. Two whole Shrimpless days equaled a veritable drought. I thought: *I am the luckiest girl in the world. I live in the coolest fog city, I have a boss boyfriend, and we're going to meet my new best half-brother and his lover for dinner, all adultlike and fancy. Life is good.*

It would be reasonable to expect some doomsday prospect at this point, just for the sake of irony and all. There I am, standing on my favorite street in San Francisco, life is peachy, I'm in luuuuv, blah blah blah, and then, you know, Shrimp's Pinto bolts down Clement Street and smashes into a fog-covered, double-parked UPS truck. Tragedy ensues; Shrimp is either dead or in a coma, and I spend the rest of my life believing it was my fault for starting to believe in the universe's grand scheme to bestow true love and a good life on me after some really fucked-up years.

The reality wasn't that bad but it wasn't pretty either. When I got into Shrimp's car he didn't kiss me. He announced, "Once we get to Oakland, I can only come inside to meet your brother for a minute. I have to go over to Berkeley to see about a room at some guy's house."

I couldn't go into a tirade about how dare Shrimp bail on the dinner with Danny and Terry, how many times have I sat through dinner the last few months with the Fightin' Shrimps, it's called being a supportive girlfriend and getting to know the important people in your partner's life, because I first had to know, "What do you mean, a room at some guy's house?"

"I'm gonna move over to the East Bay for a while. Now that Dee is pregnant, she wants Iris and Billy out of the bedroom they've been using so she can start the remodel to turn it into a baby room. But Iris and Billy, you know," here Shrimp mumbled low, "they don't, like, have enough cash for a new pad. So they're gonna move into my room for a while, lay low by spending some time up north with their friends up there, and since I am going to help start up Java's new store in the East Bay, I oughta just live over there for a while."

Where should I begin with this bombshell? I said, "How are you going to manage living and working in the East Bay and going to school in The City?" To say nothing of girlfriend time—when did he plan to fit that into this new schedule? What—and who—were his priorities, anyway?

Shrimp played with the dial on the radio station before settling on the news radio station with the traffic report. He is obsessed with hearing the traffic on the :08 every ten minutes. To piss him off I turned down the radio right as the traffic report started.

"Why'd you have to do that?" he griped.

"You haven't answered my question."

We were stuck in inch-along traffic on the freeway entrance toward the Bay Bridge, so it's not like Shrimp could escape my line of questioning. He said, "If you have to know, I'm failing out. I lost my scholarship, and Wallace doesn't want to pay the tuition if I'm failing or just not showing up because I can't catch up no matter what I do. The school was basically gonna kick me out anyway. So I dropped out this week. It was, like, a mutual decision all around."

It certainly was not a mutual decision all around because I'd never been consulted and wasn't I the girl for whom he painted *Blitzkrieg CC,* the one whose cell phone he called at home every night to rap love songs into her ear before she went to sleep? And what about those other so-called important people in his life, the ones called *parents*?

"Iris and Billy signed off on this?" I asked.

"Sure." He shrugged. "They're cool with it. They know I'll get my G.E.D. eventually."

I turned the radio volume back up and changed the station to the pop music station, which was spinning the latest puke-pop princess's saccharine hit. Shrimp gave me a dirty look and changed the station to the alternative music college station playing a morose Radiohead tune. I met his dirty look and changed the radio station back to the pop princess number. Sometimes Shrimp is just too hipper-than-thou. Sometimes I just want to be a geek and listen to bad pop music and not care whether that's pathetic.

"WHAT'S YOUR PROBLEM?" The Artist Formerly Known as Mr. Don't Harsh My Mellow yelled at me. "I hate that shit music. What's the look for? Don't tell me you're mad about me dropping out of school. You hate school. What do you care?"

"I care enough to know I ought to just finish it," I said. I also care enough to know that parents who were "cool with it" were less than cool themselves. I certainly care enough to know that he should have brought all these issues up with me much, much earlier. We'd been sleeping together, talking about our dreams together, assuming we had a future together, for months now, and this was the first I was hearing about all this? Now I felt like all the time we'd spent together since becoming a couple again was a lie, because he had been holding out this crucial piece of him all that time—and I had let him, wanting to bask in the glow of true love.

We settled on the hip-hop radio station and rode in silence the remaining journey to the East Bay. When we reached Piedmont Avenue in Oakland, Shrimp slowed down to look for a parking space as we neared the restaurant. Shrimp said, "I can only come in for a second to meet your brother. Then I'm gonna head over to Berkeley." The car was not quite at a full stop, but I opened my door and hopped out of it. "Don't bother," I said. I slammed the passenger's door behind me. The Pinto came to a complete stop, as if hesitating on how to proceed, then pulled an illegal U-ey and bolted down Piedmont Avenue in the opposite direction.

Danny was waiting for me outside the restaurant. "Terry's getting our table. Where's Shrimp? Parking the car? I can't wait to meet him at last!"

"He's not coming," I murmured. "I don't want to talk about it." I felt stiff in Danny's embrace, wanting to go home, get in bed, and throw the covers over my head.

"Ah," Danny said in my ear as I let go of his hug. "The elusive Shrimp remains elusive."

My hellacious mood didn't help, but it was not the reason I hated Terry. As expected, Terry was a shallow-vain he-man, only worse—he's married to his job instead of his looks. And he's old, like, at least forty, though his fake tan, blond looks, and runner's body gave him the appearance of a much younger man. How could I get to know him, try to like him, if he answered cell phone calls from his office every two minutes? Danny explained to me during our appetizers, while Terry excused himself for a good fifteen minutes to take a call, that Terry is a lawyer, a partner at a big SF law firm, and he was in the middle of closing an important deal. I couldn't imagine Danny's ex, Aaron, even owning a cell phone, much less using it during an awesome meal that a noted Bay Area chef had prepared. I mean, show some respect.

"I'm bored," Danny sighed halfway through his entrée, a fabulous cut steak cooked to perfection. Terry was back outside again on the phone, his salmon untouched on the table.

"Bored with Terry?" I asked, hopeful. That didn't take long.

"You wish!" Danny said. "No, the Terry part, when I get to see him, is great. And I saw you lunge for his phone the last time it rang, and it's a good thing Terry's reflexes are quicker than yours because I know what you were planning on doing to that phone." Danny looked toward the shrub outside the open window behind our table. My brother is truly psychic. "No, I'm living-bored. The 'burbs are killing me. I hate being dependent on a car, but I have to use Terry's car to go out during the day because everything is so far apart, and there's always traffic. And it's so quiet at night at his house up in the hills. I'm a New Yorker. I need energy and noise, subways and cabs, dirt and grime, diversity. I'm actually missing snow and cold—real cold, not this bogus California cold! Every day the weather in the Oakland hills is the same: perfect. Everybody looks the same: perfect. It's boring. Boring, boring, boring."

Maybe my brother, not Shrimp, is my soul mate.

Terry returned to the table, but I caught him checking out the waiter's tight behind as the waiter refilled a wineglass at the next table. In fact, Terry had yet to look me straight in the eyes, because the little time he was in my presence his eyes scanned the room, like he was looking for someone better to mingle with. He must be from L.A. Terry turned to me. "So, kiddo," he said, like he hadn't spent the majority of our dinner away from the table and thereby, in my opinion, forfeited his right to rejoin our conversation. "College in your plans?"

I almost spit out the water I was gulping, because that was when it hit me: Terry was just like bio-dad Frank! These were almost the exact words Frank had asked me last summer, on the one day he'd grudgingly given me some time and we went strolling through Central Park together. Like Frank, Terry was great-looking but with a wandering eye, a deal maker and workaholic, probably incapable of being in a committed relationship—it couldn't be a coincidence that a guy as old and successful as Terry lived in a big house in the hills by himself. Poor Danny and his Oedipal-whatever thingy! Please let this horrid relationship be over soon, I prayed, before Danny's therapy bills grew higher than the debt left over from The Village Idiots' failure.

Before I could answer Terry's question, his cell phone rang. Again. This time my reflexes were quicker, and I grabbed the phone from the table before Terry's hand reached it. I tossed the phone out the window into the shrubs.

Men. Sometimes they just need to be taught a lesson.

Chapter 31

The Sugar Pie–Fernando–Sid-dad hotline must be in full effect because I have been summoned to Sid-dad's study for a Talk. I didn't tell my parents about Shrimp dropping out of school, I haven't mentioned our fight or that Shrimp and I aren't speaking, but my parents can't be completely clueless.

Sid-dad shut the door to his study and started out the Talk with, "So I understand our friend Shrimp is no longer matriculated at school." Our friend Shrimp's painting, *Blitzkrieg CC,* hung behind Sid-dad's desk, purchased for a tidy sum at the hospital charity auction. Nancy sat next to Sid-dad on the leather couch, her hand pressed into his. Those two are getting ridiculous. I have to resist the urge to spontaneously hurl every time they touch each other like that when I'm around. PEOPLE: children are present. Restrain yourselves!

"So?" I said. He's not their kid—what do they care?

Nancy said, "Well, I am just horrified." Good—but I didn't ask your opinion.

Sid-dad said, "But we're not his parents, so we have no say one way or the other in his decision. But we're concerned because we are your parents, and we thought now is a good time to get a sense from you of your intentions."

"I'm not dropping out or failing out!" I said, on the defensive. I was bummed enough about the Shrimp situation. Did we have to have the Do Something talk just now?

Nancy said, "We know that. But we're concerned that you're flailing." I glanced toward Lady Liberty CC in the painting, holding out the silk stockings over her legs, and suddenly I pictured her like a fish just plucked out of the Hudson River and gasping for water, placed on a piece of the tabloid newspaper bound for the morning fish market, headline: FLAILING!

To parents, *flailing* is just another word for *failing*. "What does it take to get through to you people?" I huffed. "I am this close to graduation and I have a perfectly respectable GPA this year. Have some faith in me—how about that? And if you really must know, since you're so nosy, I think Shrimp made a mistake myself. I think he's gonna wake up in a few years and all his friends are going to have moved on, and he's gonna feel left behind and regretting this decision, bad. But I'm only his girlfriend and barely that right now, and I was offered no influence in the decision. So be happy. I would have said not to do it. And Shrimp and I are not even talking now because of how he handled the whole thing."

"Oh," Sid and Nancy both said. It was hard to tell if they looked pleased or surprised—maybe it was somewhere in between.

Sid-dad said, "My secretary has tried reaching him regarding a contact I'd like to give him, but no one seems to be able to track him down." That's the truth. Elusive Shrimp hasn't been by my house, Java the Hut in Ocean Beach, or Sugar Pie's, and he must have been struck with amnesia when it comes to my cell phone digits. I have no idea where he's been since our fight. "I can't condone his decision, but I thought he would be interested in knowing there is a gallery owner here in The City who was at the hospital auction, who is interested in seeing more of Shrimp's work. Could be a tremendous opportunity for the young man."

"Forget about it," I said. This much I know about the elusive Shrimp, for sure: give him an opportunity to turn his art into cash from The Man, not just a charity opportunity accepted to get into my parents' good graces, and Shrimp will disappear faster than you can say *Hang loose.*

Nancy gestured to a stack of brochures on the coffee table. "We're well aware of your feelings about college, and while we don't plan on insisting . . ."

". . . I don't want to go to City College next year, not even part-time—"

Sid-dad interrupted me. "Now whose turn is it to show some faith? We've got your message already: NO COLLEGE. Forgetting that most students your age would be thrilled to have the privilege you take for granted, to go to college without the worry of financing the education or the burden of student loan debt, we nonetheless have heard you loud and clear on this point. You'll be an adult soon; we can't force you to go. And frankly our time is better spent than trying to force this issue. No, these brochures are for culinary school. Your work-study time at the restaurant last fall proved what I suspected: You're a natural candidate for a culinary arts curriculum."

The idea was intriguing, but why did he have to use the word *curriculum*? Talk about a buzz kill. Also, I did not appreciate that my sentence to work with Lord Empress Kari had, in fact, been part of an evil, manipulating scheme to test the waters on my restaurant abilities and culinary inclination. My eyes lingered on the brochures but I didn't reach for them. I couldn't give my parents that much satisfaction.

"There are some excellent schools here in the Bay Area. Your brother Danny and I have been talking about this, and he's recommended a few schools he thinks would be appropriate matches for you," Sid-dad offered, like I was a suspicious cat to whom he was offering his hand to sniff first, before getting in close.

I considered touching a brochure, maybe even lifting one from the table, when we heard loud—I mean LOUD—music playing from the street. I went over to the window and pulled up the shade to see a Pinto in a sea of BMWs and Mercedeses on our street of Victorian and Edwardian houses, shaking from the decibel level of music blasting from its stereo. Those damn tear-inducing Von Trapp children were harmonizing *ah-ah-ah-ah* in full ghetto blaster surround sound. Neighbors peeked from their house windows and some Japanese tourists on the street walked by with their hands over their ears, then snapped photos of the Pinto once they were at a safe enough distance to take their hands from their ears. I don't know why the tourists looked so confused—hadn't they seen *Say Anything*? I'll take Shrimp over John Cusack any day, but Shrimp's knockoff scene had to be inspired by Wallace and Delia's favorite movie, where John Cusack holds the boom box playing the Peter Gabriel song outside the house of his girlfriend.

Oh, the make-up is going to be sooooo good, once we're past the talking (me) and the apologizing (Shrimp).

I looked toward Sid and Nancy, both shaking their heads. "Go," Nancy sighed, waving her hand at me.

"But take a brochure," Sid-dad said, quickly handing me one as I sprinted toward the closed study door. He looked toward the window again, shook his head again, and murmured, "Odd duck."

I grabbed the brochure from his hand and bolted. "I'll be home tomorrow morning," I called out as I got to the front door.

"MIDNIGHT!" Sid and Nancy both yelled.

Chapter 32

Shrimp and I have a secret.

No, I'm not pregnant.

Next September, after I've walked the graduation plank and turned eighteen, I am moving over to the East Bay to live with Shrimp. By then Shrimp will have saved enough money to move out of Some Guy's house in Berkeley, and I will get a job at a restaurant or a coffeehouse on College or Telegraph Avenue. We won't care if we're minimum-wage dirt poor and have to live in some dilapidated shack with crack vials strewn on the ground outside and the cops driving by at all hours, as long as we're together. We'll be making love too often—in privacy, whenever we want, however long we want, buh-bye curfews—to care. When important decisions have to be made, like dropping out of school or taking off to Joshua Tree for some solitude time, we will make those decisions as a team, like Sid and Nancy, Wallace and Delia, Bill and Hillary.

Culinary school was an interesting idea, but I have the rest of my life for that. I'd rather work full-time after finishing high school. Next year is the year that will be all about Shrimp, for real this time. I plan on a full CC makeover to transform myself into an East Bay girl. I will trade in fog for sun, espresso for straight black organic coffee slush, and I will make every best effort to drop the word *hella* every other sentence. In lieu of attending Berkeley, the university, I shall study Berkeley, the food mecca. I will become hella food snob and learn about smelly cheeses, only shop for the best produce at the Berkeley Bowl, and grind fresh pasta instead of making it from a box. Shrimp and I will plaster our living room with Shrimp's art and with record covers—vinyl, not CD—by East Bay icons like Tower of Power and Green Day, and we will have exotic plants, Mount Fuji artwork, and a white noise machine that plays Kitaro to get that Japanese sanctuary love-shack vibe happening.

The person I most want to share this news with, Danny, arrived at my fave Italian café in North Beach looking tired, unshaven, and wearing yesterday's clothes. Not that I expected Danny to spiff up to meet my boyfriend for the belated first time, but I was still surprised at how bad he looked when he walked into the café.

"Terry and I broke up," Danny announced before he'd even sat down. I resisted the urge to jump up from my table and do a little Irish jig that Eamon taught me on a recent IHOP night. "Apparently I was mistaken when I thought our relationship was exclusive."

I am soooooo good, I did not say *I told you so*. I said, "I'm sorry, Danny." Sorry that you're hurting—not sorry that it's over with that loser who was nowhere near good enough for you. "Coffee and chocolate help."

"So does more upbeat music," Danny said. He spoke loud and directed his voice to the barista who was standing near the café's stereo: "Is the Wagner opera so necessary? Ever hear of Puccini or Mozart? You want to encourage customers to relax, not to want to slit their wrists." I guess you can take the New Yorker out of New York, but not New York out of my who-knew-he-could-be-so-moody brother New Yorker.

Shrimp arrived next, also mad moody. All Danny got from Shrimp was "Hey," and this long squint-stare of realization that I had actual blood relatives who looked like me, followed by a slight snarl that only I knew was a snarl; Danny could easily have mistaken it for Shrimp having gas or something. *Or something* being that Shrimp thinks biodad Frank is "bad news" and will need some convincing that Danny is not the same story, though you would think Shrimp would just take my word for it, but boyfriends are weird protective that way.

Shrimp ordered a double-shot espresso and said, "I can't stay long. I couldn't find a parking space so I'm illegally parked in a yellow loading zone, and Iris is expecting me in Ocean Beach to take her downtown to deal with some passport issues."

I would be cross with Shrimp's rudeness except the poor boy is getting slammed from all sides: crashing on the couch at Some Guy's house in Berkeley and having a long commute between the East Bay and Ocean Beach for work, and being the intermediary between Wallace-Delia and Iris-Billy, to say nothing of his girlfriend who would like to toss all his other concerns aside, have exclusive access to his time, and force him to fall instantly in like with her newfound brother. But since I am a patient girlfriend, I could play this scene cool instead of wig out about Shrimp's rudeness, because I knew within a few months, I would have Shrimp all to myself, and now that Terry is out of the picture (hallelujah) Shrimp and Danny will have plenty of time to bond.

Danny has got to be in the All Men Suck frame of mind right now because he said to Shrimp, "Hypothetical situation: You've moved back to Papua New Guinea and Cyd Charisse comes to visit you for a few months to see how your relationship progresses. No pressure, but it's understood it's an exclusive deal, right? I mean, isn't that implicit?" I could see Shrimp's small head realizing that harshing someone's mellow may have been part of bio-dad Frank's DNA lineage.

If Sugar Pie were here she would probably pronounce that it's Mercury retrograde or some astrological disaster time when new beginnings should not be embarked upon. I'd wanted my true love boyfriend and my true love half-brother to meet, but looking at them together at the table now, my mind thought: *abort mission! abort! abort!*

I found a way out when I looked out the café window. I told Shrimp, "Baby, the meter maid is pulling up behind your Pinto. You better go." As I am a fully actualized being, I kissed Shrimp on the lips, which unsnarled his lips just fine. Shrimp said to Danny, "Let's try this again another time, buddy. Later."

"Isn't he great?" I sighed after Shrimp left Danny and me sitting alone at the table again.

"He's exactly as I expected," Danny said. I have no idea what that meant, but I'm going to hold off a little longer on confiding my big news to Danny.

Chapter 33

Since I don't think Sid and Nancy are going to be so keen on my new plan to DO something, as in move in with Shrimp, and I am going to bust if I don't tell someone soon, I have decided I am ready to spill my news to Danny, who can be enlisted to help butter them up. Danny is not only my bridge to my other family back in New York, he shall also, in my grand scheme, become the bridge by whom I eventually break the news to Sid and Nancy.

Spring has sprung and my true love is back in bloom, but not for Danny. Get this: Since his breakup with Terry, Danny has been staying at our house in Pacific Heights. The lease on the apartment in Nueva York where he and Aaron lived is in Danny's name, but Aaron's new place isn't ready yet, and lisBETH still isn't speaking to Danny, and Danny can't be bothered with asking Frank for help, so guess who got him? The "other" family.

At first I wanted to be sick at the thought of Danny meeting Nancy—what could they possibly say to each other? I imagined a puppet show acting out a scene like:

DANNY PUPPET
Ah, so *you're* the other woman who split my family apart?

NANCY PUPPET

Sho 'nuff. My God, I'm getting the creeps by how much you look like the married man who got me in trouble when I was young and stupid, then lied when he said he would always be there for me.

DANNY PUPPET

Well, nice to meet you, I guess.

NANCY PUPPET

Likewise. [puppets butt heads in conciliation]

Sid-dad and Nancy invited Danny out for lunch without me knowing it, on a school day. I'm relieved I wasn't present at the initial meeting and didn't know it was taking place until it was already over. However strange or awkward or just plain *huh* their first meeting was (or maybe it was just me, worrying about how it would go), Danny and Nancy hit it off. Danny, who had spent all his time alone at Terry's house watching music video channels on the satellite TV, said my mother is "full-on bling." She of the full-on bling proclaimed that Danny is "like a kind, happy version of Frank." Soon after the inevitable Danny-Terry breakup happened, as rebound romances with shallow-vain he-men are bound to do, leaving Danny broke and homeless for the time being, "Uncle Sid" and his lovely wife, mother of his illegitimate sister, helped Danny pick up the pieces by offering him their guest room until his apartment in NYC was vacated by Aaron.

Nancy finally has a full-time cook in the house again, and maybe it's the relief of not having to prepare meals, or

Nancy giggling when Danny reminds her, "Butter is not your enemy, Nancy," as he pulls another batch of shortbread cookies from the oven, but she appears to be coming out of her post-Granny A funk. Neiman-Marcus can officially breathe a sigh of relief. There's even color in Nancy's face now, and she's got hips on dem bones from the extra pounds from Danny's baking. She looks great: healthy— and happy. Ash idolizes Danny because the Barbie birthday cake he made for her was a three-tiered masterpiece decorated like a wedding cake. Sid-dad is thrilled to have his godson reinstated in his life, and to finally have someone in the house who will play Fantasy Baseball with him. The exception to all this Danny love is Josh, who HATES Danny. When he was little and didn't like someone, Josh would go over to that person, drop to the floor, and try to bite his/her ankles. Now he just gives Danny the cold shoulder, and cannot be physically removed from his PlayStation whenever Danny is around. Danny doesn't seem to mind—in fact, I would dare say hanging out with my family has helped break him of his postbreakup funk.

We all know where I stand with respect to Danny, even after him wrecking his true love with Aaron. Not only is he my brother, he is also my kindred spirit. And like me, he is a total pyro who likes to burn candles and pour the hot candle wax on hands and arms, then pull it off and smush the wax like Play-Doh. Sid and Nancy don't share this affliction, however, and don't appreciate Ash and Josh being exposed to it, which is how Danny got to be hanging out in my room late one night, door closed, while we burned candles and watched a movie while sitting on my futon.

I said, "There's something I have to tell you." I saw

Danny's concerned face and said, "Gawd, I'm not pregnant, okay?"

Danny, who let out an audible sigh of relief, said, "There's something I have to tell you too."

"You first," we both said at the same time.

I zapped the movie off, some music on, and said, "Shrimp and I are moving in together. Next fall. Will you be there when I tell Sid and Nancy? They'll take it better if you're there to cushion the blow."

Danny: "One, you can't be serious. And two, no way."

Well, well, perhaps Danny is not 100 percent my kindred spirit. I did not expect the You're Just a Kid, You Don't Know What You're Doing reaction from Danny. I answered, "I am hella serious. We're going to get a place in Berkeley or Oakland. We'll have jobs; we're not asking anybody to support us." Danny's face looked less than convinced. Enlisting Danny to my cause had seemed like a no-brainer, but now I needed to defend it to him? I told him, "I spent all this time waiting to get back together with Shrimp. If I can only love him more, even after really not being cool with some of the things he'd done, something must be right about this relationship. Right? Every time something happens that could split us apart, we still end up making it through, stronger and more in love than before. Dude, Shrimp and I are meant to be together. I can't wait too much longer to live with him, share my life with him. Don't give me that look. You have hardly spent any time with Shrimp; you barely know him. You don't know us together, haven't been able to see how real it is."

"If I haven't been able to see how real it is, why do you think that is?"

"Because you won't give Shrimp a chance, you—"

"I would give Shrimp many chances, if he gave me the opportunity. He's not a fellow who likes to make himself known, maybe except to you. I see the artwork every-where—obviously the guy is in love with you—but where is *he*?"

"You don't like Shrimp?" I asked. I wanted so badly for my brother and boyfriend to have a love connection, but the truth was, there was no chemistry between them, not like I'd had with Danny's boyfriend Aaron, that feeling of, *Wow, I'm so glad my sibling has hooked up with you, you're a great person.*

"I like him just fine, what little I've gotten to know him, considering the few times I've met him he's barely mumbled three sentences to me. Shrimp strikes me as just being . . . young. Maybe not ready for the long haul."

"You're wrong," I said. I did not share with him the purple candle wax I was pouring onto my arm.

"I hope I am, Ceece, I really hope so. What do your friends think about this plan?"

"I haven't told them yet, but Sugar Pie, I'm sure she'll think it's great—she's all about the true love. Helen will probably want to move in with Eamon next year, so I know she'll understand. And Autumn, well, she'll probably go to Cal next year so she'll practically be our neighbor, and any-way, I think I deserve a triple-bonus friend score for the fact of even becoming her friend, so I'm sure she'll be sup-portive."

Danny said, "No one deserves bonus scores for the mere act of becoming someone's friend. If that's what you think, you have a lot to learn about how to be a friend."

I couldn't yell at him because the rest of the household was asleep, so I whispered, "Are you quite finished with your CC bashing? Because I think I'm ready for you to leave my room. Why don't you go bake something, spread your perfect-happy-even-after-two-doomed-romances-I-love-everybody self somewhere ELSE?"

Danny didn't look hurt or mad; he just smiled. It really is hard to get under his skin. He must have developed that ability as some post-traumatic reaction from growing up with lisBETH, monster bossy older sister. Danny pulled the purple wax that had hardened on my arm, then placed a finger kiss on the tender spot. "But I haven't told you my news yet."

"What?" I pouted.

"Aaron has moved into his new place. I can go back home. I gotta get around to picking up the pieces and starting my life over sometime—can't live in this California fantasy world forever. Wanna fly back with me, hang out for the Easter holiday weekend? I already talked with your parents. It's fine with them. I could use some company and support easing back into what will be a semi-empty apartment with lots of memories."

New York in spring, just like *Easter Parade* with Fred Astaire and Judy Garland, with mean Danny who wanted my help? Twist my candle-waxed arm, why don't you. "Okay," I said, but still sulking. "Can Shrimp come too?"

"No. Let's see how you survive a weekend alone in a new city without your true love, then you can tell me more about your supposed moving-in-together plans."

Poor, sweet, ignorant Danny. Shrimp and I will prove him wrong.

Chapter 34

I must have repressed-memory syndrome, because I have lived on the East Coast before but I totally forgot what *real* cold felt like. We arrived late on Good Friday night, and an April shower coupled with unusually frigid temperatures had turned the city into a temporary winter wonderland, blanketing the streets in a thin layer of white snow. WOW! Beautiful—and burr-ito like for real. Just thinking about the accessorizing potential—the need for knit mittens, a long, heavy faux fur leopard-print coat (the kind that requires the ritual sacrifice of many teddy bears), maybe a babushka scarf—had me contemplating some thrift-store shopping for Saturday morning, but the cab driver burst my snow bubble during the ride from the airport to Danny's apartment. The many-voweled-name man said, in an accent originating somewhere between Pakistan and Nairobi via Haiti, "New York! Eees crayyy-zeee! Snow today, spring tomorrow!" As he drove us through Central Park, its trees in early bud, looking peaceful and calm as the snow dusted the branches, the driver turned up the news radio station so we could hear the forecast predicting a warm-temperature spring thaw for Saturday.

By the time we reached Danny's building in the Village, after a whirlwind taxi experience in which the driver zigzagged across lanes; ran every yellow light; cut off dozens of taxis, buses, and trucks; and flipped off many pedestrians, I considered popping into the all-night pharmacy at Danny's corner to pick up Fernando's remedy of choice, Excedrin for migraines. But no minor headache could crush my excitement at being back in NYC. Just breathing the cold air and watching the city fly by through the cab window, my heart pounded from the city's energy. The streets teemed with people, cuddled together under umbrellas and wearing snow boots, looking cozy and rarin' for a night that would never end. The bars and restaurants we passed were packed with people, and you could hear music playing from all corners. It was like the cold city had its own pulse and it was hot, hot, hot.

You'd think a person as sensible as Danny would have enough sense not to be excited about returning to an apartment for which you had to climb five long flights of stairs through narrow, dark, and creepy stairways to reach the top of the building, but then again you'd also think that someone with so much supposed sense wouldn't let a gem like Aaron out of his life and out of his apartment to begin with.

Danny's excitement didn't last much past the opening of the five door bolts. When we stepped inside the door, wheezing from the stair climb, I saw that Danny's apartment looked completely different than when I visited last summer: empty. The lease may be in Danny's name, but obviously most of the furniture was Aaron's, because all that was left in the living room was a tattered sofa with a sheet thrown over it, a foldaway chair that looked like it would collapse from the weight of a kitten, and a glass coffee table covered in ring stains—the coasters must have been Aaron's too. Even the drapes were gone, so the view out to the Village scene was bright—and we could see directly into the apartment across the street, where a chunky naked guy was playing guitar and watching TV. Aaron could keep the drapes.

Danny threw his luggage on the floor and walked around the apartment, inspecting. The slump of his body and the high degree of sighing he picked up from Nancy indicated the homecoming was as painful as he'd anticipated. His bedroom was left with only a sleeping bag on the floor, an ancient kids'-room lamp with a base in the shape of a model airplane, and a set of dresser drawers. The spare bedroom that Danny and Aaron used for a study was empty except for a bookshelf with Danny's cookbooks. Danny sighed the Nancy Classic when we got to the kitchen and he opened the fridge. He pulled out a shopping bag that said BARNEY GREENGRASS on it, read the note attached to the bag, his eyes welling up a little, then told me, "Aaron left some bagels and nova for us."

"And this random act of kindness is a cause for sadness because . . . ?"

"Because he went to my favorite restaurant for nova and he got H&H bagels too. He would have had to go all the way to the Upper West Side this morning to pick this stuff up and deliver it here, and just when he's starting a new job over on the East Side."

Didn't I say Aaron was a gem? I knew I was there to be supportive but I couldn't help myself. "Not something I could ever see Terry doing for you. Is Aaron seeing anybody new?"

Danny said, "I have no idea. But Ceece, if you try to play matchmaker you *will* be excommunicated. I wasn't kidding when I said it's over between Aaron and me. That doesn't mean he and I won't always love each other, but we won't be getting back together."

WHY?!?!?! I don't understand how they can still love each other but they're still completely over.

Danny obviously didn't want to talk about it anymore so I said, "Well, I don't like nova—it's too salty for me—so why don't you put that bag away for the morning and order us a proper New York pizza?" That's what I love most about New York, not the arts and culture and diversity and whatever, but the fact that you can order any kind of food—Chinese, Italian, Dominican, Thai, pizza, or whatever—to be delivered to your fifth-floor walk-up any time of the day or night.

Maybe Danny had most been homesick for proper NY bagels and Barney Greengrass nova, but what I most missed about NY was the "grabba slice" that almost–summer fling boy Luis got me hooked on last summer. NY has the best pizza, but it's not just about hot, plump crust or the zesty tomato sauce, it's also about the way it's eaten in New York: Dab the oil off the cheese with a napkin (if you so choose), sprinkle the slice with your spices of choice (I like garlic powder and oregano), fold the slice in half, and then eat it with your hands, starting from the bottom tip (keeping the paper plate underneath the crust side for the oil to run onto, if you have not gone for the previously mentioned napkin-dabbing option).

While we were sitting on the floor eating the pizza, Danny told me our agenda for the weekend: cheap furniture shopping on Saturday morning, followed by a job he had to see about that afternoon, and, biggest bonus, Aaron's note said his band was playing at some dive in the Village on

Saturday night if we wanted to go. WE DID! The downside: Easter Sunday brunch with Frank and lisBETH. "Do we have to?" I asked Danny. There should be some family law where you can pluck just one favorite member of a family and keep them all for yourself and never have to deal with the rest of them. "Yes," he stated, although he didn't look too thrilled by the prospect himself.

Chapter 35

Neither of us slept much that night. Who could, between the excitement of being back in NYC and all the freaking noise? We had to sleep with the living room window open because the chronically banging radiator was too hot. But if I thought the radiator noise was aggravating, it was tame in comparison to the noise coming from the street below: constant honking and brakes screeching, people yelling, and some guy who kept shouting, "Yo, Sal" from outside the bar at the ground floor of Danny's building. The noise, along with the bright night lights followed by early-morning sun streaming through the drapeless apartment windows, meant I didn't get more than four hours of sleep. I slept on the tattered sofa that was too short for my legs so I was crunched into a ball shape all night, and Danny slept through the noise like a contented baby, nestled in his sleeping bag on the floor below the tattered sofa because he got too spooked being in his old bedroom by himself for the first time in years.

I woke earlier than Danny, so I went out for caffeination. The temperature was significantly warmer than that of the night before, but the spring air was still chilly. The streets were wet from the melted snow, which with the brisk cold air made the city feel unusually clean and fresh. I found the closest deli and asked for regular coffee, which I forgot means something different in New York than in the rest of the world—*coffee regular* means coffee with milk instead of straight black coffee—so I had to toss the first cup in the heaping trash can on the street. Then I went into two different cafés for an espresso, one that was too weak and bitter and the other that just plain sucked, both of which also had to be tossed in the trash. Finally I went into a juice bar for a cup of fresh grapefruit juice, because Danny's café and Dean & DeLuca were the only places I remembered where you could get a good coffee in Manhattan, and The Village Idiots was now extinct and I couldn't remember how to get to D&D. Plus, my coffee budget was shot for the whole weekend.

When I got back to the apartment Danny had showered, eaten his bagel and nova, and was ready for us to hit the city. We wandered the streets of the Village, browsing in some used furniture and antique stores. All the furniture was either too ugly or too expensive, though, leaving Danny, who said he couldn't be bothered to go all Martha Stewart with the time, money, or effort required to refurnish the apartment, to settle somewhere in the middle. He opened a credit account at Crate & Barrel, where he bought a basic sleeper sofa that could double for a bed for him until he could afford a new one, a table and some chairs, and a desk. He was all but hyperventilating at the total cost, but I reminded him he had a job interview lined up for later in the day that was a sure thing, and it wouldn't kill him to ask Frank for some help, either. *I* would never ask Frank for help again, but why shouldn't Danny? Frank was just my biological father, and maybe he'd never been Father Knows Best for Danny, but he was still Danny's real dad. If Frank had been willing without a moment's hesitation to help his love child pay for an emergency clinic visit on the QT, he'd probably be more than willing to help his legitimate son if Danny for once asked him for help.

Once Danny stopped looking like he was going to have a heart attack I stepped outside the store to wander around, as completing the transaction was going to take longer than I could spend browsing Crate & Barrel without collapsing from utter boredom. Also I've never paid attention to what furniture costs before, but: Yikes! Shrimp and I will have to get many, many jobs to get our own apartment.

As I walked through the Village streets, I couldn't help but wish Shrimp were here to experience this city with me. The chilly air was so cozy, I could snuggle right into him. The masses of people walking around all looked so different—young to old, black, white, yellow, brown, and red, yuppies to hipsters to freaks to old-timers—that I suspected Shrimp's art could find more inspiration in a block of this city than he ever could in the whole of the East Bay. Shrimp had promised to pick me up at the airport when I got back home, and my first order of business would be to try to sell him on the potential idea of us living in New York together, instead of Oakland or Berkeley. Why not? True love knows no city boundaries, so why shouldn't we keep our options open? Did we have to live in the East Bay? Wasn't it more important that we move in together somewhere than that we stayed near home?

All the thinking about Shrimp and the knowledge that this time next year the two of us would be sharing a love shack made my insides warm. It was probably no coincidence that I found myself stopped at a fence, standing on the sidewalk watching an extremely hot group of sweaty guys wearing long shorts and no shirts playing a game of pickup basketball on the other side of the fence. Saliva was possibly hanging from my mouth down to the pavement for how beautiful these guys were, to say nothing of what amazing hoop players they were: fast, graceful, intense, like an NBA street gang. Them dudes had serious *game*. My eyes homed in on one guy in particular—was I having déjà vu, or was that New York Knicks tall guy with the cinnamon skin and shiny-slick black hair none other than Luis, a.k.a. Loo-EES? When I saw him miss a pass because he was staring back at me, then get slammed by his teammates for losing his focus, I realized, *Yup, that's who.*

Maybe Nueva York is not the city for me to move to after all. The last time I was here I ran into my ex Justin at the Gap on Madison Avenue. What is it about this city and the randomness of running into people from your past, especially the ones who having lustful thoughts about will get you into big, big trouble?

When the guys called a time-out in the game, Luis dribbled the b-ball over my way until he was standing opposite me on the other side of the fence. "Terrorizing the big city again, are you?" he asked, smiling, his eyes appraising me up and down, from my black combat boots with the thick black leggings to my short black skirt to my biker babe black leather jacket.

Small beads of sweat dripped down his face, begging to be licked off. "I'm spending the weekend with my brother," I told him. "What's up with you?"

Luis dribbled the basketball, not needing to look down to see the ball for it to connect with his hand, and my mind had to repeat a mantra in time to the bounce's beat, reminding me: *Shrimp. Boyfriend. Shrimp. Boyfriend.* Luis said, "I went away for a while. Spent time with some cousins down in Virginia, thought I might move down there—fresh air and cheaper cost of living and all that— but I ended up back here. I'm a New Yorker, yo. This is the only place to be where you can feel truly alive, right? So I'm enrolled at Hunter College full-time now, living at my aunt's new house in the boogie-down Bronx, gonna get serious about finishing that business degree already. One of my boys plays ball down here every Saturday, so I came along with today." He had this thick New York accent that sounds ugly until you get used to it, and he was friendly in that genuine New York kind of way that pretends hostility but is in fact gracious, and that you never find in California, where people are all sunny disposition but would prefer not to give you the time of day. "What about you? Did you and that boyfriend of yours ever get back together?"

"YES!" I stated, maybe overkill on the enthusiasm. "We're moving in together next fall. Probably in Berkeley; we'll get a place there." Definitely, Berkeley. Nueva York: bad, bad idea, *loco*ness.

Luis laughed. "Berkeley? No way. You don't belong there."

"How do you know? Have you been?"

"No, but I don't need to. Do you realize there is a bum peeing on the wall next to you, and a crazy lady singing 'Mary Had a Little Lamb' for change behind you, and you haven't even noticed? Does your wardrobe know any color other than black? You're a New Yorker, *niña,* whether you know or not. I didn't spend all that time showing you around for Frank last summer not to know that."

We couldn't talk longer—the game was starting back up and the guys were whistling and teasing Luis to tear himself away from the fence. After Luis and I said our good-byes, I headed across the street to the street corner subway stop where I saw Danny waiting for me at the spot where he'd told me to find him after he left Crate & Barrel.

"I did not just see you and a guy who looked disturbingly like Luis programming each other's numbers into your cell phones, did I?" Danny said.

"You need glasses, old man," I told him as we bopped down the stairs into the skanky-smelly-glorious subway station.

When we got downstairs to the subway platform, as if on autopilot I walked right over to the platform edge to peek into the subway tunnel to see if I could see the distant train lights on the rails indicating a train approaching the station, as Luis had taught me to do last summer. "Check out the New Yorker girl!" Danny said. A train barreled into the station and Danny yanked me back from the edge by the collar on my leather jacket. "But not enough to know not to stand on the platform edge when the train is coming in, idiot!" he shouted over the thundering sound.

We rode the train a few stops to Chelsea, where we walked toward the culinary institution where Danny was going to find out about a potential teaching opportunity. While we were walking down the street I asked Danny, "What is it about the randomness of running into people in Manhattan? I hardly know anybody in the world at all, and yet both the short times I've been in Manhattan, I've run into people I knew."

Danny said, "Aaron and I used to call it OINY—Only in

New York. I have no idea why that happens, but this city is full of those stories. I just ran into a girl I went to college with while I was at Crate & Barrel—she was choosing her wedding registry. Have you ever watched a TV show that takes place in Manhattan and noticed how people are always running into one another, in this city of millions? That's because it happens all the time here. Don't ask me why. New York, man: the world's biggest small town."

We took the elevator up into the culinary institute building in Chelsea, and walked down a long hallway past a series of classrooms with glass windows. In the first window I saw a chocolate-sculpting class putting the final touches on an all-chocolate, lifelike display of white chocolate roses in a dark chocolate vase. Another classroom had a roomful of students wearing chef's whites, standing over a steaming wok, stirring veggies and meats. The last room we passed must have been the Italian cooking class, because the garlicky smell of fresh tomato sauce and the dreamy looks of a dozen middle-aged students hinted that they, like Nancy, may have read *Under the Tuscan Sun* one too many times.

We stopped at an empty kitchen, where Danny led us inside. The haze he'd been in since reentering his ghost town apartment appeared to retreat, and I could see his face coming alive again as he admired the immaculate kitchen full of state-of-the-art industrial equipment. "Why don't you open another café?" I asked him.

"So much work; so much money." He lingered over the huge KitchenAid mixer on the floor, touching his hand along the rim of the bowl so big you could almost jump into it and take a bath. "I don't have it in me right now. I just want an easy teaching job, a regular paycheck without worrying if the balance sheets are in the red or black this month. I can also pick up some cash making some cakes for a friend's bakery. I'll probably have to get a roommate to make my rent if I'm just working part-time, but that's fine. Owning and operating a café is so much work, CC—and I can't go it alone, without an Aaron."

A lady wearing chef's whites and a most excellent white chef hat came into the room and grabbed Danny in a hug. "Looks who's home, finally, back where he belongs! So glad you could make it over during the break in my class!" she said to him.

Danny introduced me to her, saying, "This is my little sister, Cyd. Yeah, I know, 'little' indeed. I brought her along so she can check out the place. She's thinking of enrolling in some courses here."

"No I'm not . . . ," I started to say, surprised, but Danny hustled me from the room because his friend had only a short break to tell him about the job opportunity.

I went outside the empty kitchen and sat on a bench while I waited for my "big," sneaky brother. Along with the many delightful smells coming from the kitchens, I also smelled a plot brewing to distract me from Shrimp.

I whipped out my cell phone and placed a call to Shrimp at Some Guy's house in Berkeley, praying Shrimp and not Some Guy or Some Other Guy at the group house would pick up the phone. I scored. "Hey, beautiful," Shrimp said when he heard my voice. I slid to the other end of the bench, away from the chocolate class, not wanting the heat from the high degree of melt in my heart at hearing Shrimp's gravel voice to affect the class's brilliant chocolate sculptures. "You're not falling in love with New York and forgetting about our plans?" he asked, teasing.

"No way," I answered. Though I acknowledge that the threads the chefs wear, all white and crisp and geometric, are indeed most excellent and accessorizeable and tempting.

"Good. Cuz I'm working on a special piece for you this weekend, to introduce you to a new idea I have about what we should do next year. I'll tell you about it when I pick you up at the airport tomorrow night."

"Tell me now!" Knowing that Shrimp was also thinking about variations on our plans to be East Bay people, I didn't feel so bad about my momentary lapse of considering a pitch for New York.

"Nope. You gotta wait. No words shall be spoken until the art is complete. Gotta run. Some guy here needs the phone." I would so buy Shrimp a cell phone if I didn't know he'd just toss it into the trash, or break it apart and use the parts for an art piece, like he did with the phone Wallace gave him that Shrimp turned into *Cell Phone Interruptus*— smashed cell phone parts glued onto a crucifix with green-sprinkle acid rain falling from the top of the canvas.

Hearing Shrimp's mood brightened my spirits, so I decided not to be mad at Danny's potential manipulation, trying to weasel me to NYC so he could make me fall in love with this amazing city and this place in Chelsea that my eyes and fingers and taste buds were itching to experience.

"So great place, huh?" Danny said when he came out of the kitchen.

"Eh, whatever," I said.

What was not a great place was the "club" where

Aaron's band was playing that night. The "club" was really a narrow pub with a tiny stage at the back, where no one in the place cared about the no-smoking rule and I couldn't imagine them caring about a band playing, either, cuz most of the patrons had their eyes fixed on the Knicks game on the television.

Aaron was sitting at the bar nursing a Guinness when we arrived that night. His long strawberry blond hair was thinning at the top of his head and cut short to just below his ears, falling around his face just enough to partly obstruct a new double chin. When he stood to greet us, I noticed there was a lot more pudge creeping out over his belt buckle than last summer, like he'd been on a diet of beer and complacency since Danny was no longer dragging him out of bed in the mornings to go running in Battery Park. Aaron hugged me but avoided eye contact, then he and Danny had an awkward moment where one tried to kiss the other on the cheek while the other went for a hug, then vice versa, ending with a weak handshake and a pat on each other's arms. They both looked like they knew this first meeting since the breakup, after almost a decade together, was something they had to get through, but they'd both be relieved when it was over.

Aaron's band, My Dead Gay Son, which used to be a motley group of guys he and Danny knew from college who got together to jam at The Village Idiots, with no favored music style, just a melting pot of covers—punk to soul to rock to show tunes—was now a nameless one in search of identity. Aaron said they were thinking of changing their name to Recession Apathy or Hamlet Syndrome, because a majority of the guys had lost their jobs or their wives or lovers in the last year, and none of them knew what they wanted to do with their lives, except play in a band. The band wasn't bad, focused primarily on alt-country type tunes, but rock stars these guys were not.

The last time I'd seen My Dead Gay Son play had been at The Village Idiots last summer, when the jammin' band sounded relaxed and fun. Listening to the dudes play now, tighter from more rehearsal time and with a focused repertoire of songs, was much less fun: They looked and sounded like a sad sack of nice fellows. The experience reminded me of Frank Sinatra Day back in December, when I'd worked the counter at Java the Hut after many months away. I wanted to experience Danny and Aaron as the great couple again, hanging with them at The Village Idiots while My Dead Gay Son warbled through covers just for fun, but everything was different. The past was over, done, *finito*.

There was nothing to do now but look ahead, because you can't force good times to come back, I suppose. Things change. People change. True love maybe can just fade away.

Chapter 36

Easter brunch with Frank and lisBETH demanded no less than a shocking fashion statement from me. I went for the short skirt, sure, but the Goth getup and combat boots would not be adequate for this occasion. I wanted the full "bad girl" look to meet Frank's and lisBETH's impression of me as the wild love child. And what could be more shocking than a "bad girl" wearing a horrendously tasteful, pale pink Chanel suit swiped from her mother's closet, with the couture shoes to go along with, and sheer ivory stockings to complete the look? I'd blown out my hair to WASP straightness, added a headband, and placed a pendant around my neck—the heart-shaped Tiffany necklace Frank had sent me at Christmas, salvaged from the donations pile for the occasion. For makeup, I applied some baby powder to my cheeks to get that society-lady anorexic death glow, and I glossed my lips with a beige matte lipstick. Admiring myself in Danny's full-length bathroom mirror, I considered hanging on to this outfit for Halloween on Castro Street, where I could stroll through the parade introducing myself as Mrs. VonHuffingUptight and hand out museum docent guides to the crowds.

"We're late!" Danny shouted to me from the living room. "C'mon already, CC! I've never known you to be one of those girls who takes an hour to get dressed—what's the problem already?" My look complete, I went to the living room. Danny's face was cross until he caught a glimpse of me in front of him. Then he laughed so hard tears ran down his face and he fell off the sofa. He was still laughing when we got into the cab to take us to Frank's on the East Side.

We asked the driver to let us out a few blocks from Frank's building, because even though we were late we were both dreading this brunch, and also we wanted a little walk so we could admire all the church ladies strolling the avenue in their Easter dresses and fine hats. A guy we passed on the street tried to hand me a sticker. People are always trying to hand you something in Manhattan—advertisements for psychics, band gig flyers, Jesus-freak paraphernalia—so you get used to not reaching out when they try to push paper into your hand. The sticker this guy was trying to hand us said MEAN PEOPLE SUCK, and I sidestepped him to turn it away, but Danny, who was getting tenser as we neared Frank's building, knocked the guy's hand away when the guy tried to shove the sticker in Danny's face. The sticker guy yelled after Danny, "You need this!" Mrs. VonHuffingUptight turned back around and told him, "No, you do, asshole." Mean People Suck sticker-givers are my new most-hated people, after the ubiquitous counter clerks anywhere you go now who have GOOD KARMA! tip jars at their cash registers. Perhaps I am a sucky mean person destined to walk through life without Good Karma! Oh, well. I accept my fate. Could you all go away now, please?

"Well done, Lady Cyd Charisse of New York City," Danny said.

Frank lived in an upscale high-rise condominium building where everything looked and smelled new and fresh. A lot of apartment buildings in New York are old, dank on the inside, and sooty on the outside, but Frank's was a relatively new building, flashy, with a lobby that had a chandelier, big floral displays, and gilded mirrors. The doorman knew Danny but did not remember me, perhaps because of my disguise, and he sent us up without buzzing Frank's apartment.

I was hella nervous as we rode the elevator up into the sky and then walked down the hallway to Frank's apartment. My visit last summer had ended up fine, in this epically disappointing kind of way. We all sort of got along by the end, but I also wouldn't say there was any grand love connection, except between me and Danny. It was like, Well, I met you all and I am glad I did and you are all sort of pains in the asses and you probably think I am too, but I think we can all agree we had some good moments together, and let's just leave it at that. Family, for better or for worse—though I'll take my real San Francisco family over you in a heartbeat. No need to send letters or cards or make regular phone calls or visits, just be well and I'll see you when I see you. Now here we would be, seeing one another again. I can rip on Frank and lisBETH plenty, but the fact of actual face time with them makes it harder for them to be caricatures in my head instead of live and in-the-flesh blood relations.

Frank opened the door. Geesh, he's tall and good-looking in that scary aging movie star way. Sometimes last summer I would sneak long looks at him when he wasn't paying attention, so I could etch his face into my memory. His face looked as I recalled—like mine—but I'd forgotten the sheer physicality of him: his height, his shiny black hair that should have the dignity to be graying or thinning at his advanced age (I bet he dyes it), his orange-tan skin (salon, for sure), how he sucks you in with the salesman's smile and his ease with people. Also he wears very fine, expensive suits. So does Sid-dad, but on him they look frumpy and wrinkled, endearing, but on Frank, full playa.

"Welcome!" he said. He looked genuinely glad to see us, or maybe it was the possible face-lift crinkling his smile. "Come in, Happy Easter." He had Easter baskets with our names on the hallway table for us, with chocolate bunnies and eggs swimming in that fake green grass stuff. Minor point score to Frank for effort.

"How ya doing, kiddo?" he asked me, patting me on the back instead of hugging me (relief). "You're looking well. And, ah, different. This is the first time I've seen you not wearing all black. You look good, kid, you look good." I felt pride and ick, like, *Stop looking at me, you don't know me!* Frank turned to Danny, gave him a stiff hug, and said, "We missed you at church this morning!"

Danny grumbled, "Well, I didn't get the memo about the Vatican embracing my people, so I'm gonna skip on the Catholic services for the time being. But I'm sure you and lisBETH had a lovely mass without me."

Frank looked like, *'Scuze me, sonny boy.* I informed Frank, "I'm not any religion." Mrs. VonHuffingUptight is a natural diplomat.

I liked this moody Danny. If he was going to be the ornery one at the family brunch, that took all the pressure off me. Thanks, Danny!

Danny stepped inside the kitchen for some words with lisBETH in private. This brunch was the first time lisBETH had deigned to see him since Danny left Aaron, and Frank and I both stayed behind so they could have their first reunion in private. I sat down with Frank on the couch, and without realizing it crossed my legs in full Nancy pose. Frank and I didn't have much to say to each other, though, so Frank handed me a piece of the New York newspaper, folded and creased in straphanger style for easy reading on the subway. Frank pointed out a small article in the business section to me. I skimmed the article, which announced that Frank had retired from his job as CEO at the big New York advertising firm.

"Retired?" I asked him. Frank didn't strike me as the retiring type. In fact, he struck me as the type who will be chasing deals as actively as he's chasing skirts until he literally plunges into his grave, expired.

"Canned," Frank said. "'Early retirement' is a genteel way of saying, So what if I built the company up from nothing over the course of the last thirty years, transformed it from a small shop into an industry giant? Who cares about the loyalty and best years of my life I gave that company? The new CEO, my former protégé, and all his chums on the board, that's who doesn't care, lemme tell ya."

Mrs. VonHuffingUptight might have responded, *Well, Frank, DAHling, there is a saying: What goes around comes around.*

"What will you do now?" I asked him.

He smiled. He definitely gets his teeth whitened professionally. "The usual. Consulting. Golf. Tennis. Try to enjoy my life already. Get to know my kids. Got some time if your old man comes out to see you in California?"

Nancy has been pestering me to let her throw a graduation party for me. She wants to make over the garden area at the back of the house, with fantastic flower arrangements and a full-swing catered affair to commemorate the occasion. She said she would be open to inviting Frank to the garden party, if I wanted. But a lavish garden party seems like overkill for celebrating an occasion I'll be glad just to make it through but don't feel the need to observe further. And I'd sooner celebrate graduation alone with Shrimp than be trapped in a Pacific Heights garden party with low-cal hors d'oeuvres and phony expressions of congratulations from Nancy's friends shocked that I even graduated at all. Also the mere thought of My Two Dads sharing a scene, Nancy sobbing in pride between them, gives me the creeps. Danny could stay at our house, but I'm not ready for full integration yet. Garden party—pass.

"If you want," I said, but in this voice that said, *Don't do me any favors, bub.* But my eye caught the Easter basket on the table, and I remembered Frank's warm greeting when Danny and I came in. I knew he really was trying, so I figured I could a little too. "Sure," I amended, sounding nicer. "You could visit sometime."

Frank was clearly searching for something, anything, to say in the long, empty pause that followed between us, and what he came up with was, "So it's getting to be that junior prom time of year. Any special plans? Any fella you're sweet on?"

I touched the heart necklace he'd given me as a "sweet sixteen" Christmas present as I talked. "Well, Frank, as you may recall, I'm seventeen, not sixteen, and graduating, which means senior prom, not junior prom. And I go to an alternative school for freaks. The student council voted to abolish the prom on the basis of proms being a capitalist marketing tool like Valentine's Day, just another form of vicious propaganda intended to separate the haves from the have-nots. But even if there was a prom, Shrimp—that's my serious boyfriend, not just some 'fella'—and I would probably bail on it. Blech, prom. Not our scene."

"Oh," Frank said.

LisBETH and Danny emerged from the kitchen. LisBETH was also dressed in a Chanel suit, although hers was gold. A pink scarf with embroidered Easter bunnies on it held back her long locks of thick, curly, gray-specked black hair. "Don't you look pretty!" she said. The chiquita has no sense of irony. She didn't try to kiss or hug me, so I warmed to her right away. "You look very nice too," I said.

LisBETH had gone to great effort to set the Easter table with fine linens and good china, and she'd laid out a beautiful brunch with an Easter ham, shrimp and avocado salad, eggs, fresh biscuits, and fruit. She must have been up since the crack of dawn to put on this feast for us at her father's apartment. I associate family meals with noise—Ash and Josh banging utensils, arguing with each other, spilling drinks—so I was unaccustomed to a meal that, first off, started with Frank saying grace and then lisBETH leading some Easter prayer, and second, after we were seated, fell into polite silence. To kick start the conversation I asked lisBETH, "Any cute guys come into the picture since I saw you last?"

LisBETH groaned. "My dear, there aren't any single, straight, well-to-do men in my target age bracket left in Manhattan. If it weren't for Aaron's company these last few months . . ." LisBETH shot Danny a mean look. "I am considering adopting a baby, perhaps from Asia or South America. Don't you think that would be fun?"

Ring, ring, lisBETH, time for your wake-up call. You

have a big Wall Street job that requires you to travel all over the world, and you work like at least eighty hours a week. Adopting a baby might sound cute to you, but it won't be cute for baby who wants and needs attention! You're a workaholic, like Frank, and maybe you're not a dawg like him but you're not Superwoman, lady.

"And you," lisBETH said. "College plans?" Seriously, if I get asked that question one more time, I cannot be held accountable for my actions. I *will* lose it.

"Nah," I said.

"Maybe you just need a year off. Go to Europe for a year," she said.

"Nah," I repeated. "I am just not going to college. No joke. And there's plenty to keep me busy and happy in California." Shrimp, Shrimp, Shrimp, I miss you, can't wait to see you tonight at the airport!

Danny said, "I think she should go to culinary school here."

LisBETH snapped, "Oh, so then you could have your little princess sister all to yourself?" There we go, that's the vintage lisBETH we were waiting for. I don't know what's lisBETH's problem—it's not like she's tried to contact me or see me since last summer. She was probably mad because I've gotten Danny all to myself these past few months— even though that's been by her choice.

Danny said, "Or we could all get to know her a little better, if she moved here and pursued the craft for which she has an innate talent."

I speared a piece of shrimp on my fork, dangled it in front of my lips for Danny to see, and ate it.

Frank, obviously wanting to move the conversation in

a new direction, said, "Danny, how is Aaron doing? Have you seen him?"

"He's alright, Pops." I felt Danny's frustration—Danny wanted his father to ask him about his future plans, not his past.

"Well," Frank said. "I'll miss him at Thanksgiving." What the hell did that mean? Frank had no clue the hole he was digging for himself. "I still don't understand why you and Aaron couldn't work it out. So you two needed a break, needed to see other people. But that's over now. Why not give it another go?"

Danny slammed his fork onto his plate. "Is that what you want from me, Daddy, to be like you? Stay in a loveless marriage like you did after your affairs so everyone can be miserable?" Danny got up and left the room. Whoa!

Frank looked at me and lisBETH, as if he wanted to know, *What did I say to deserve that?* Truly Frank lives in the land of the completely clueless and he's never gonna get it unless someone shoves the clues down his throat. I don't know why I wanted to help him, but I did, probably because I don't like to see Danny hurting. I told Frank, "Go talk to him. He'll never ask you for help, but he needs your help. He left his long-term boyfriend for another man, then that didn't work out. He lost his business, practically lost his apartment, and now he's back home starting all over, broke and anxious and alone." Frank hesitated, his Handsome Man eyebrows furrowing as he contemplated my statement, like the obviousness of what I'd told him had never occurred to him. "GO!" I added.

Frank tossed his napkin on the table and followed Danny into the other room.

I reached for a third biscuit. LisBETH makes delicious

biscuits; it's really a shame she never got to do that house-wifey thing.

LisBETH said, "Well, I guess a family holiday wouldn't be complete without at least one fight. You know, you have quite the appetite."

"Thank you. You make great biscuits. Could you pass me some more of that strawberry butter?"

LisBETH watched me eat, probably knowing I was trapped by my hunger and couldn't escape her. Then she excused herself from the table, and I thought she was going to butt in on Frank and Danny's conversation, but instead she returned to the table carrying her briefcase. She opened it and handed me a stack of postcards tucked inside it. There were four tourist postcards, from Cleveland, Beijing, Dallas, and Milan. When I turned them over, I saw each had been addressed to me, dated at different intervals since last summer, and each had a short note from lisBETH.

> *Oct. 18, Cleveland: Did you know the Rock & Roll Hall of Fame is here? We should visit together sometime.*
> *Nov. 30, Beijing: This city makes New York seem like a ghost town.*
> *Jan. 23, Dallas: Do those cheerleaders from this city's basketball team annoy you as much as they do me?*
> *March 2, Milan: Clothes, food, clothes, food: BLISS.*

"Uh, thanks?" I said to lisBETH.

She said, "I've never had a chance to mail these to you. But I do think of you sometimes." She looked at me hopefully, like maybe I had been writing her postcards too but also not getting around to mailing them. I guess I could, if I ever thought of it. In the future, I decided, I will. LisBETH, my new postcard pen pal—signed, sealed, but delivered.

I felt like I owed her a confidence in return since I had no cryptic correspondence to share. "My boyfriend and I are moving in together in the fall," I said. "But don't tell; it's a secret so far."

"You're not getting married or pregnant, are you?" she said, like, *Don't compete in my territory of ambitions!*

"Ew, no way," I said. Hmm, thought brewing. "LisBETH, I have this friend who goes to one of the Ivies around here. He's a business major, straight-A student, straight-up good guy. I think he needs a part-time job next fall. Do you think your firm would look at his resume?"

LisBETH took a business card from her briefcase and handed it to me. "Tell him to give me a call. I'd be glad to at least help him get his foot in the door."

Hee hee: LisBETH, older single woman, intelligent but overbearing NYC career gal, wants to be a mommy, meet Alexei the Not-So-Horrible, overbearing Ivy League stud with the older-chick fetish, living in the tri-state area during the school year, would make great babydaddy. I'm a genius; I don't need college.

Later, after Frank and Danny had returned to the table looking calmer and happier, if tired, we finished the meal in peace. When it came time to leave, Frank gave me a minor hug—the kind where you lean in and pat but don't make full body contact—and said, "I'll be hoping to see more of you in the future."

I said, "Likewise, Frank."

In the cab on the way back to Danny's apartment, Danny slumped his head onto my shoulder. "That was awful!" he said.

I massaged the back of his neck. "Oh, come on, now. It wasn't that bad."

Chapter 37

Here's how I know Shrimp loves me. He picked me up that night in the arrival area inside SFO instead of a curbside pickup. You don't go to that trouble unless it's true love.

I was so happy to see him I lifted him in my arms when he hugged me. I know he's the guy and he's supposed to do that, but he's also on record (T-shirt variety) as being a FEM-INIST, man enough to deal.

"Nice to see you too!" Shrimp said after I let him down and smothered his face and neck in kisses. "New York agrees with you. God, you look awesome." We shared a long, deep airport kiss, the kind that if you're disembarking from an airplane and you're not in love, you want to slap the couple upside their heads for sharing in public.

I said, "New York is like a shot in the arm—makes you feel alive! But all the feeling more alive did was make me miss you more, make me more excited to get home to see you." Repeat above kiss, add in one additional minute and three groans of "Get a room" from passersby. When we pried our lips apart, I asked, "What did you have to tell me?"

Shrimp said, "You have to wait a little longer, till we get to the special place." I assumed he meant our make-out spot, Land's End, but that was very out of the way if he still had to go to Some Guy's house in the East Bay after dropping me home in Pacific Heights.

In fact, the special place turned out to be Outback

Steakhouse in Daly City. "Huh?" I said, when he pulled into the crowded parking lot. What special announcement could a vegetarian have to make at the "Australian" steakhouse that's probably about as Australian as Frank Sinatra was Venezuelan?

Once we were seated at a booth, I ordered Shrimp on the Barbie in honor of guess who, and guess who ordered the Walhalla pasta with no meat. Once the waitress had taken our orders, Shrimp started in. "First announcement is this: Iris and Billy are moving to New Zealand. A friend of theirs has some property down there and invited them to take over the guest house, oversee the property when the friend is gone, and Iris and Billy will have some land to use as well. They're becoming organic farmers."

"Farmers." Indeed. Is there such a thing as organic marijuana? I wonder who is running them out of town: Wallace and Delia or the feds. "That's nice for them," I said. "I hear it's very beautiful there."

"Exactly!" Shrimp said.

My brain connected the dots: Outback Steakhouse . . . Australia . . . close to New Zealand . . . "Exactly!" . . . OH SHIT. I had barely finished computing Shrimp's logic, but he left me no chance to respond. He was going for it.

Shrimp stood up from his side of the booth and got down on bended knee on my side of the booth. He held out his pinkie finger, dangling from it a hand-carved wooden ring, with a setting carved and painted like a kiwi. This isn't happening, I thought. DO NOT CRY! This is Outback Steakhouse in Daly City, for God's sake—and Shrimp is a vegetarian.

Shrimp looked up into my eyes. "I know you're not the

marrying kind, but I'm wondering if you would make an exception for me? I've been working on this ring for you ever since Iris and Billy told me their news. I really want to move to New Zealand with Iris and Billy. The surfing is killer there, and I can do my art, and we could travel all around Australia and Indonesia and Bali. I loved that part of the world I saw last summer, and I want more—but it's no good without you there with me. The East Bay idea was alright, but this one is so much better! We can go backpacking Down Under—Tasmania, Sydney, Perth—then on to the Asian Pacific islands and all over NZ. Surfers are like their own community, they always help each other out, so we'll always have places to crash wherever we go, and we can make cash at odd jobs when we need to. We can stay with Iris and Billy as home base. Their friends who made the offer to them have a killer place—huge, they say. Fuck, I love you so much, it's, like, painful. You are the coolest babe I could ever want to share my life with. What do you say?"

A waitress carrying a large tray of entrées bumped into Shrimp from behind his kneeling position, pushing his face onto my knee, so now he was looking up at me like a puppy.

I had no idea what to say, so I nodded my head in confusion and just plain being overwhelmed by the proposal. Shrimp took my head nodding and the unfortunate tears streaming down my face for a yes. And I didn't have the heart to reeducate him, not when he placed the ring on my left hand, stood up, held his hands out for me to stand up, and this time he lifted me in the air. Our fellow Outback Steakhouse diners applauded, much "oohing" and "ahhing" came from the nearby tables, and two comp bottles of

Foster's, Australian for beer, landed on our table—which the restaurant manager promptly took away when neither Shrimp nor I would tear our lips apart to show ID.

I was grateful now that Shrimp had chosen Outback Steakhouse for his proposal, because no one Sid and Nancy knew would be caught dead here, and my parents would have simultaneous heart attacks when I got around to telling them, so better not to have spies breaking the news to them first.

After the crying and the kissing and the applauding, Shrimp and I sat back down opposite each other in the booth. I took his hand from across the table, admiring my new ring. I said, "I know I want to be with you." In fact, maybe marriage wasn't such a bad idea. If we got married, we'd be locked down. No distractions, like Loo-eese or surfer chicks, could have the potential to pull us apart. And why bother to transform myself into an East Bay girl if I could gallivant across the flip side of the world with my soul mate? Well, it would be far from home, and Sid and Nancy had been supportive so far of my relationship with Shrimp, but this new development would tip them over the edge into hysteria and fights and all-out disapproval again. Alcatraz would no longer be an option this time around, though, because I'm almost eighteen, and after that birthday I can do what or go where I want, with whom I want, so long as I am willing to make my own way. And if I want to marry Shrimp, dedicate my future to him because he's the best future I could ever imagine, well, that's my choice to make, not theirs. Sid and Nancy, or Ash and Josh, Danny, or Sugar Pie and Fernando, Helen and Autumn, my family, the people I care about most, they would just have to live with my decision and the fact that I will not be present to share their lives. They will have to love me just the same, and I will have to get over the hurt of missing them.

But crashing with Iris and Billy as our "home base"? I said, "I'm not so sure about the following your parents, though. Maybe that part's not the best idea."

"But they go to cool places," Shrimp said. So? They're also crazy irresponsible! Iris and Billy do whatever suits them in the moment—like abandoning Iris's daughter from her first marriage so they could be together, or leaving fourteen-year-old Shrimp with Wallace so they could go to Papua New Guinea. Nancy might also be crazy, but at least she's not irresponsible—and she's in for the duration of the game, come hell or high water. (She's also not really crazy, although I will jump into the Grand Canyon before admitting that to her face.) I like Iris and Billy okay—they did, after all, breed Shrimp—but I don't want to attach my destiny to theirs.

I pointed out, "New York is cool. That doesn't mean I'm going to live there because bio-dad Frank does."

"This is different and you know it. And you said yes." Shrimp stood up on his side of the booth and thumped his chest like Tarzan. "SHE SAID YES!" he announced for any of the diners in the packed restaurant who might not have caught the earlier bended-knee proposal scene. He did a little hip-hop dance on his seat before the restaurant manager came back over and asked him to be seated or be asked to leave.

Only I didn't say yes, not just yet. I'm thinking.

Chapter 38

So we're having a wedding and a new baby in the family. Nancy got her garden party after all.

We chose May 15 for the wedding day, the anniversary date of Frank Sinatra's passing from this mortal earth, because Sid-dad said he wanted that date to now be associated with new beginnings for the people in his family. Since he was throwing the wedding, he thought he should have some influence in choosing the date.

I wore the lavender Chinese silk gown that lisBETH gave me last year, that had been her grandmother's (mine too, even though I never knew her) favorite dress, but I couldn't deal with those high-heel horrors called fancy shoes, so I went barefoot with black toenail polish and a wood-carved pinkie toe ring that had a kiwi setting. Shrimp changed his hair for the occasion, so he looked like he did the day I first met him— short mop of dirty blond hair with a patch of platinum blond spikes at the front of his face. He wore an oversized hand-me-down suit and tie from Wallace that made Shrimp look like an earnest Sunday school teacher with punk hair, from the Church of the Stoked. The look of infatuation on Shrimp's face in the back garden at my parents' house that day was the same one he gave me that first day we met at Sugar Pie's room at the home. When I looked back at him, in this haze we've been in ever since Outback Steakhouse, I knew I will never love another person in my life the way I love him.

As Sugar Pie and Fernando said their vows to the judge under a trellis custom-built for the occasion, strung with white roses and vines, I stood at Sugar Pie's side, her maid of honor, and Alexei stood at Fernando's side, the best man. Chairs were set out in the garden for the ceremony, but it was a small affair, strictly family and a few friends. Fernando's daughter and grandchildren were there, Sid and Nancy and the kids, Helen and Autumn, and Shrimp, Wallace, and Delia. Iris and Billy left for New Zealand almost as soon as they received the call to go. Nancy sat next to Dee, patting Dee's growing belly, and discussing morning sickness.

Delia is due in November, and Nancy is due in December. Trust my mother to do something fashionable like get pregnant at her advancing age. Nancy seems happy but reluctant. Sid-dad is ecstatic. He is already interviewing for a new housekeeper and nanny, so in the end Nancy wins again. I don't think their new addition is like some TV show where the writers have run out of plot lines so they throw in a late-in-life baby to rejuvenate the tired old parents. I'm going to go out on a limb here and say that two people who married for convenience—Sid so he could be a dad and protector, Nancy so she could be rich and a protectee—have now, more than ten years after the fact, fallen in love with each other. And baby makes six. It's still disgusting, but maybe not totally.

The apartment at the side of our house has been renovated for wheelchair access for Sugar Pie's dialysis days, and Sugar Pie will move in after the honeymoon at Disney Land with Fernando's grandkids. I think someone should build a senior citizen commune that's also an amusement park, where the wrinkles on the old people's faces are like a map of their lives, and all the rides are custom-designed to accommodate wheelchairs and memory loss and a complicated array of prescription side effects.

After last Christmas, when Fernando didn't take Sugar Pie to Nicaragua to meet his family back there, she asked him, "Are you in this or aren't you?" Fernando said he'd thought it would be too difficult to travel with her because of her dialysis needs, and Sugar Pie said, "Where there's a will, there's a way, and I repeat: Are you in this or aren't you?" So Fernando said, "*Si,* I'm in if you're in." But where Sugar Pie just meant she wanted the next trip to Nicaragua because she heard it was a really cool place, Fernando meant it's time to get legal with this true love. And that is how Sugar Pie came to be a bride for the first time at age seventy-something, and probably the only person I will ever meet who's done a reverse nursing-home swing, moving out of one to start a new life instead of going into one to wait to die. She made a beautiful bride in her white suit and church lady hat, standing with the cane that Ash and Josh decorated with strings of flowers and mini chocolate bars. It was Fernando, the tall, broody man of steel wearing a most excellent Italian black silk suit, who was the weeper during this particular ceremony.

After the ceremony I took Alexei aside to hand him lisBETH's business card. I told him, "Just because you're an insufferable faux intellectual doesn't mean Wall Street wouldn't be lucky to have you. Here, this is my sister's card. She's a managing director at some big investment firm. She needs a college student to help her out part-time next fall. Call her, okay?" Rule #1 of Matchmaking, by Cyd Charisse:

Always go for the sneaky setup, where the two interested parties meet without knowing they're being matched. That's how I got Sugar Pie and Fernando together, and I'd have to say the evidence is weighing in favor of my methods on that one.

Shrimp came to my side and took my hand. I looked toward Sugar Pie and Fernando, holding hands and beaming, and I thought, *Sugar Pie waited a lifetime to have her moment. I'm barely eighteen and I could have mine now if I want. But would mine be as heartfelt, as accepted by my friends and family? Would mine last?* Josh came to my other side and latched on to my other hand. He looked up at me with that beauty-boy face and said, "Shrimp said you guys are taking me to the rickety roller coaster at Santa Cruz after your graduation. You're going to stay here all summer and not go away again like last summer, right?"

I've been thinking about Shrimp's proposal since the Outback Steakhouse, and letting Shrimp think that we're going through with it, but only at this moment, seeing Josh's trusting face, did I realize my answer. Soon I will have to tell Josh that when I assured him I wasn't leaving, I meant it at the time, but things change, people change. I will be going.

But first I have to tell Shrimp.

Later that evening, after the guests had gone home and the party cleaned up, Shrimp and I took a walk through the Presidio to talk about our plans. We wound up at Fort Point, at the old brick military building underneath the Golden Gate Bridge, where the Hitchcock *Vertigo* movie lady with the freaked-out eyebrows jumped into the freezing cold Bay and poor chump Jimmy Stewart had to dive in to rescue her.

We sat down on the ledge at the water, our feet dangling over the Bay. I am not a drag-the-moment-out type of girl, so I just came out with it. I told Shrimp, "If I'm going to be on an island, I want one that's a city at the center of the universe, not one that's its own nation at the bottom of the world. I don't want to be so far from my family. If I wanted to be married, I would want you for my husband and life partner, but no way am I ready to be married yet. Can't we go to New York instead?"

Shrimp answered like from a script, like he'd been practicing what to say when the moment of truth came. "I want to surf, to travel, to paint, without the burden of a steady job or the need to make rent. It's both our freedoms I want." He breathed on my neck like how I love, and while I didn't push him away I pulled back from him so we were looking at each other eye to eye.

"You say it's both our freedoms you want, but really I think its yours you want."

He rubbed the kiwi ring that I'd moved from my toe up to my finger. "If that was true, would I have made you this?" he asked. He brought my finger to his lips.

"Yes," I stated, though I did not stop his finger sucking. He's an artist; that's what he does—speak through his art. But a kiwi ring was about his desire to go to New Zealand and not lose me at the same time, not about his desire to marry me. I don't want to be a wife because Shrimp is hedging his bets. "You have to choose between New Zealand and your girlfriend."

"I can't," he mumbled, letting go of my finger.

I kissed him long and hard so he would know that when I took my mouth from his, there was no bitterness to my words. "You just did, baby."

I could feel the relief in his mouth when he leaned back in to kiss me. We didn't need words to finish this conversation. Hands, bodies, and lips could take care of the rest of our conversation, in private, in the back of that legacy Pinto.

Chapter 39

If my life was a movie, here is where my closing scene voice-over would tell you (in lame-actress voice filled with precocious teen melancholy and über-wisdom) that, *I thought my year was all about Shrimp, but, in fact, it was really all about me.* A quick clip montage would remind moviegoers searching for the last vestiges of popcorn from the bag on the sticky theater floor that, along with falling crazy deep in love (but not crazy koo-koo, like last time), I also became a member of my own family and found out there are chicks my own age who are actually cool and friend-worthy. Well, technically I only made two new friends, and I have to disagree with Danny—I DO deserve a triple bonus score for Autumn, but that doesn't make me like her or Helen any less, or take away from the fact of: girlfriends.

The life-as-movie montages would bleed into that last scene with the all-important soul mate and true love. Insert over that scene a soundtrack song by folky-arty singer with stringy hair who basically sounds like a bored white person, and watch as Shrimp and I have our fade-into-the-sunset good-bye at dusk on the rare sunny day at Ocean Beach, right as the big red sun falls over the horizon on the Pacific. Our good-bye would be bittersweet; not a dry eye in the house as the two lovers take off their separate ways. But then—surprise! Don't leave the theater quite yet, kids, because there I am popping up next to Shrimp on the plane to New Zealand, giving him some snarky comment about not letting him get to see the flip side of the universe without me, and blessings on the screenwriter for throwing the word *antipodean* into the final dialogue before the big screen kiss. True love, fading into the sunset as the plane travels over dusk skies. Roll credits.

In the not-movie starring the not-movie-star Cyd Charisse, we got the Ocean Beach last scene, but on what had to be the most frigid, fog-ridden day of the year—seriously, you could see our bodies cutting through the mist as Shrimp and I walked along the beach. At least in New York when you get that cold, you get snow too. You can do stuff with snow. You can't do anything with fog.

New Zealand was an interesting prospect, and I'm sure the costume changes merited by the new culture alone would have been worth the trip, but in the end I decided to split the difference with my family. I won't be going Down Under, but I will move to New York. I will be Danny's roommate for a while, get a café job, and take some classes at that culinary school where Danny will be teaching, and if I like it, maybe I will apply to the Culinary Institute of America next year.

I'm not going to New York alone, it turns out—my triple bonus score is coming along too. Autumn surprised us all by turning down Cal in favor of a scholarship and *mucho* student loan debt at Columbia, so we're gonna conquer Manhattan together. Helen, who you'd think would be the one most eager to escape to freaktown NYC, is staying home in California. She got rejected by the art schools she wanted—apparently Ball Hunter is "derivative"—but Helen surprised us more than Autumn by deciding to go to UC-Santa Cruz, where she's going to show those fuckhead art school people wrong. She won't admit it, but although Helen said her choice allows her to stay close to her boyfriend, the dirty truth is, I think Helen wasn't ready to be so far from Mommy yet.

Gingerbread is doing a reverse retirement, like Sugar Pie, and has been permanently liberated from Ash's captivity (Ash says she is getting "too old" for dolls anyway—yeah, right), so she's coming along to Nueva York with Autumn and me. Fifth-floor walk-ups are a bitch, though, so Gingerbread's probably just gonna hang out on my bed in Greenwich Village.

I understand now how Danny and Aaron can still love each other, but they're still over, done, *finito*. Why does it hurt more to lose someone you love than someone you despise? Shrimp and I both understand: I love you, you love me, but you're going your way and I'm going mine, and let's not fool ourselves into believing one of us will be waiting around for the other. We will never be that couple who lies and says, "We'll always be friends," because we won't. We'll always be each other's first loves, and I suspect we'll always find our way back into each other's lives, but friends? I doubt it. Maybe later in my life Shrimp will make a great second husband, after I've married for tempestuous passion the first time around but then husband number one leaves me for the teenage baby-sitter when I become a super-successful restaurant mogul who thought she was doing a great job balancing career and family, and maybe she was but she just married a schmuck the first go-round. Shrimp will have gotten all that travel and wanderlust out of his system, and I will be ready for some rest after the city that never sleeps, and we can move to Ocean Beach to raise my kids, with maybe some new ones thrown in if we're feeling very Nancy derivative, back in the place where it all started. I can cook and bake and he can do art and surf at Ocean Beach, and we will be settled and old.

Shrimp and I shared the long, deep Hollywood kiss at Ocean Beach, but we were so cold from the extreme chilly temp that our lips were almost blue and in danger of freezing onto each other's. Maybe the teeth-chattering, bone-shivering cold was a cosmic message from God or Buddha or Allah or whomever for Shrimp and me to let go already. After our Ocean Beach time, Shrimp had to leave right away for the airport for his trip to NZ. I elected not to go to the airport with him. I can't be that girl, crying and regretting and holding on till the very last second. I won't be that girl, because I want to be her. I want the tearful good-bye, the long, clinging kisses, the false promises and the running to the airline counter to buy a ticket to follow Shrimp to the end of the earth, if that's what it takes to be with him.

He'll always be in my heart, but I have taken measures to ensure Shrimp physically remains with me for a lifetime, no matter what part of the universe he's in. On the obscure nonsexy flab that hangs under my arm (placement choice out of respect for prospective future boyfriends), I have a new tattoo, my first, picturing a pink-veined piece of raw shrimp. He got a tattoo of a mini Nestle Crunch bar on the same spot on his arm.

Our final-scene movie kiss was broken by the barking of Aloha, the dog Iris and Billy left orphaned, except, of course, Wallace and Delia have kept Aloha; they wouldn't let the dog be punished because of the grandparents-to-be's fickle ways. Even Aloha was too cold for this scene and wanted to go home. Shrimp's lips parted from mine, but I leaned into him for one more taste of his espresso-flavored mouth. My lips left his, touching his cheeks, his nose, his eyes, to freezer burn the feel of his cold face into my memory. "Burr-ito," Shrimp said.

Memory load complete, Shrimp took my hand as we walked toward Great Highway. I'm not worried. When we cross over the dunes at Great Highway and see Wallace and Delia's car waiting on the street to take Shrimp to the airport, I will let Shrimp's hand go. I will walk away and not be tempted to look back. I know that at the end of the road, there will always be a Shrimp.

About the Author

Rachel Cohn is the best-selling author of the teen novel *Pop Princess* and the middle-grade novel *The Steps*. Her first novel, *Gingerbread*, introduced the characters Cyd Charisse and Shrimp. Rachel was inspired to write a follow-up to *Gingerbread* by all of the reader mail she received asking what happened to Cyd Charisse after Cyd returned home from her summer in New York City—and if Cyd Charisse and Shrimp would get back together. Wanting answers to those questions herself, Rachel wrote *Shrimp* to figure it all out. Visit her Web site at www.rachelcohn.com.

About the Author

Rachel Cohn is the best-selling author of the teen novel *Pop Princess* and the middle-grade novel *The Steps*. Her first novel, *Gingerbread*, introduced the characters Cyd Charisse and Shrimp. Rachel was inspired to write a follow-up to *Gingerbread* by all of the reader mail she received asking what happened to Cyd Charisse after Cyd returned home from her summer in New York City—and if Cyd Charisse and Shrimp would get back together. Wanting answers to those questions herself, Rachel wrote *Shrimp* to figure it all out. Visit her Web site at www.rachelcohn.com.